CHARLES WILLEFORD

HIGH PRIEST OF CALIFORNIA

The Easy Thrills of a Cheap Pick-Up

"I want you to know that last night was the most wonderful thing that ever happened to me. I love you, Russell." She sighed.
"I love you too. Now let's get the hell out of here."

Ruthless used car salesman Russell Haxby becomes obsessed with seducing a married woman in this sardonic tale of hypocrisy, intrigue and lust, set in San Francisco in the early fifties. Classic hard-boiled fiction where every sentence masks innuendo, every detail hides a clue.

Author Charles Willeford, a former Californian with 17 novels to his credit, now lives in Miami, Florida because "the crime rate—the highest in the nation—provides a writer with an exciting environment."

"The prose is clean and tough and flows easily."
—*The New York Times Book Review*

"Absolutely brilliant in every regard."
—Stanley Ellin

"Willeford, writing with quiet authority, has the ability to make his situations, scenes, dialogue, sound absolutely real."
—Elmore Leonard

TURN THIS BOOK OVER FOR SECOND COMPLETE NOVEL

Publishers/Editors:	Andrea Juno and V. Vale
Production Editor:	Catherine Reuther
Managing Editor:	Francisco de Oliveira Mattos
Photographers:	Bobby Neel Adams, Ana Barrado
Typesetting:	Caroline Ewing, Susan Becker, Leslie Pollock
Photo Session Models:	Christine Alicino, Susan Arick, Clara Bellino, Luther Blue, Michael Dingle, Madeleine Gavin, Annette Kerns, Francoise Remy de Cournon, Jeff Sand, Elliott Shannonhouse
Layout:	Mary Sheppard, Deborah Valentine, Ed Wojciechowski
Book Design:	Andrea Juno

Paperback: ISBN 0-940642-11-5
Hardback: ISBN 0-940642-12-3

Library of Congress Card Catalog Number: 87-061283

BOOKSTORE DISTRIBUTION: Subco, PO Box 10233,
  Eugene OR 97440 (503) 343-6324
U.K. DISTRIBUTION: Airlift, 14 Baltic St, London EC1 Y0TB,
  U.K. (01) 251-8608

SUBSCRIPTIONS: $35 for 3 issues ($45 air overseas/$50 for Australia/
  Asia). Write for catalog.

RE/SEARCH PUBLICATIONS, 20 Romolo #B, San Francisco CA 94133
  (415) 362-1465

For permission to reproduce this play, contact Jim Trupin, Jet Literary
Associates Inc, 124 E. 84th St Suite 4-A, NYC NY 10028.

Printed in Hong Kong

All photos: Bobby Neel Adams, except for portrait of Charles Willeford
  by Ana Barrado
Cover photos: Bobby Neel Adams

CHARLES WILLEFORD
HIGH PRIEST OF
CALIFORNIA

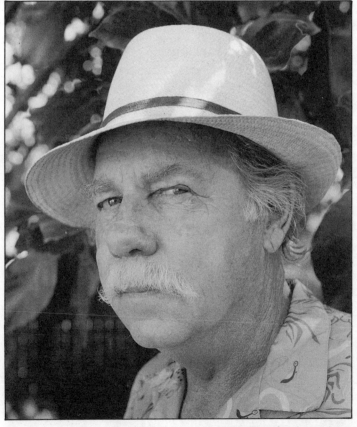

Charles Willeford by Ana Barrado

 RE/SEARCH PUBLICATIONS
20 Romolo #B, San Francisco, CA 94133

Original cover from the 1953 Royal Giant paperback edition of HIGH PRIEST OF CALIFORNIA.

I NTRODUCTION:

**CHARLES WILLEFORD:
NEW HOPE FOR THE LIVING**

by Lou Stathis

Okay, what we got here, book-wise, is one of those stiff little mini-slabs of sugar-loaded gum, the kind that ejaculates a gushy green surprise into your mouth when you clamp down hard on it with your teeth. Guy-wise, we got Charles Willeford; not one of your better known pulp-jungle Tarzans, but definitely a joe who could've modeled for Kurt Vonnegut's Kilgore Trout line of cement overcoats.

Which means, all wack metaphors aside, that Charles Willeford is yet another underrated writer of the pulp-*noir* school, a serious practitioner of his craft forced by external judgment to ride the bumpy rear-end of the literary bus. And a damn crowded little area it is back there, too, packed tight with such shabbily dressed second-class citizens as Jim Thompson, James M. Cain, John D. MacDonald, Cornell Woolrich, Horace McCoy, David Goodis, and dozens of others similarly unfortunate. Packaging is what we're talking about here—how someone *else* decides to dress you to best serve their interests (which ain't always harmonious with your own). And business is what we're talking about, too, the business of exuberantly sleazy, cleavage-cluttered '50s paperbacks.

The reality of the situation was that *no one's* golden prose was immune to this sort of undignifed treatment back in the grunt-and-pant Stone Age of mass-market paperback publishing. Glandular pandering was simply the most commonly utilized sales tool of the era, and *everyone* was smeared with the same lurid brush. (My personal fave bit of salesmanship is a 1956 Berkley edition of *Intimacy* by that notorious titan of titillation, Jean-Paul Sartre, depicting on its cover a flirtatious French floozy whose flimsy peasant blouse barely conceals a monumental pair of *Tits de Triomphe.* Oh, those naughty existentialists!)

Some writers so tarnished were later able to drag themselves from the generic tar pit, hose the slime from their bodies, and with the aid of a little belated "discovery" and grudging mainstream recognition, walk these mean streets with a modicum of self-respect (or, if the poor guys had the misfortune to die first, witness all the retroactive verbal reverence from the spirit realm). The requirements for this sort of resurrection appear to involve at least one of three key factors. First, the existence of memorable film versions of the author's books. (Question: where would James M. Cain be today without the movies of *Double Indemnity, Mildred Pierce,* and *The Postman Always Rings Twice?* Answer: forgotten.) Second, a quixotic editor who's a fan of the writer's work, and somehow manages to convince his/her bosses that uniformly packaged editions of the stuff will sell. (Usually they're wrong, but reissue series like Ballantine's Cornell Woolrich, Avon's Richard Stark, and Black Lizard's Jim Thompson have had an impact far beyond what their unspectacular sales figures would indicate.) And finally, an author who is such a tough and tenacious old bird that he continues to write—and even, my god, get better!—long after any sane sonofabitch would've guzzled a quart of Liquid Drano, or at the very least changed careers. (Elmore Leonard is only the most recent finisher of this endurance marathon, while the just-deceased John D. MacDonald is probably the best known and most successful.)

And now, it looks like Willeford's turn in the rediscovery spotlight. Howcum? Well, now that the validity of the pulp-*noir* tradition in mid-century American fiction is finally coming to be acknowledged, guys like the aforementioned tough-guy crew are getting some payback for their years of scorn-suffering. At the very least, their fictionalized moans of despair and dislocation are being recognized for what they are—encapsulizations of the times as trenchantly authentic as the more self-consciously constructed, critically praised dark fictions of the period (Mailer, Jones, O'Hara), and, needless to say, a fuck of a lot more fun to read, however roughly-hewn. But Willeford probably would've remained in the manual-typewriter graveyard, his books scattered too sparingly to maintain any collective impact, were it not for his leap onto Resurrection Route #3—publication in promotion—friendly rapid succession of three chillingly matter-of-fact, slyly intense, and giddily hyper-real crime novels that serially detail the life of a rather unappealing Miami homicide cop named Hoke Moseley.

These coldly glittering, Leonard-esque entertainments—*Miami Blues,* which the author wanted to call *Kiss Your Ass Goodbye* (1984), *New Hope for the Dead* (1985), and *Sideswipe* (1987)—aren't so much displays of new tricks the old guy's learned in his later years (he's two notches short of seventy), as they are mastermixes of everything he's been doing for the last thirty-five, freezing down his accumulated knowledge into one merciless, nipple-hardening ice cube. These are *scary* motherfucking books, lulling you with blandly innocent faces and then sneaking up behind you with exacto knives to open your spine like a puffed-up fish belly. Nasty.

Consider, for example, a Willeford staple: the asshole protagonist, formerly just another ingredient in the hash and now a blue-plate special tour-de-force that distinguishes his work. This carefully delineated spectrum of scoundrels began with the relatively benign unpleasantness of *High Priest's* Russell Haxby (mere sociopathic manipulation), and *Cockfighter's* Frank Mansfield (only a stubborn, pathological solipsist). In the Hoke Moseley books, Willeford's taken off the kid gloves and brought out the *real* charmers, like psycho-with-a-heart Freddy Frenger of *Miami Blues,* and *Sideswipe's* Troy Louden—a Guinness-worthy piece of sickness—who cheerfully tells us that he's "What the shrinks call a criminal psychopath. What that means is, I know the difference between right and wrong and all that, but I don't give a shit." Thanks for clearing that up for us, Troy.

These creepy characters, all of 'em, are the quintessential villains/products of our time—smiling, kids-next-door who reflexively mimic TV-transmitted behavioral normals while they blithely commit acts of astonishing brutality, without once perceiving a contradiction or experiencing a conflict, moral or otherwise. Forget Stephen King's *IT*-things, guys, *these* are the monsters we have to fear most, because like Jim Thompson's Deputy Sheriff Lou Ford, they are the killers inside us.

Though Willeford's doppelganger demonology might put him on common ground with psyche-surgeons like Thompson and Cain (ditto his doom-shadowed world-view with fatalists like Woolrich and McCoy), it's his complete lack of sentimentality and melodrama that sets him apart from the pack of so-called "tough-guy" writers—romantic, moralistic, soft-boiled wimps to a man. Seething with forbidden sex and pustulent with stomped-down desire, their overwrought prose could barely keep the howling mastiffs of toxic emotion at bay.

Their protagonists were mostly losers, humanity's rejects, tossed around in the backwash of American post-Depression ascendancy, unable to make the adjustment to the freedoms and responsibilities of prosperity. They were the bugs living under the Statue of Liberty's skirts. And while these macho specimens—characters and writers alike—were working up a musky sweat defending their manhood against the ravages of their own weaknesses, Willeford sat coolly by in the backyard, playing hardball with a whiplash bat and a deadly pair of baby blues, Clint Eastwood to their Eli Wallachs. His guys might've been rejects, but they'd made a point of assimilating themselves into the American fabric, cloaked with the leisure suits of normalcy. And Willeford's prose is as flat-toned and evenly cadenced—as emotionally *neutral*—as the blank visages of his feigned-human socio/psychopaths. The narratives are not dramatized, hyped up, played out, or affected as one would a literary gesture—they're just plain *told,* the careful accretion of detail adding up to an incontrovertible truth of insight. It's a flat, sunlit terrain, as American as the Bob's Big Boy 'round the next bend; the same terrifyingly banal landscape you find in the works of Philip K. Dick and David Lynch.

Just where the hell did this guy Willeford *come* from, anyway? And—maybe I shouldn't ask—how does he come by such bloody easy familiarity with the sick mind? No big deal, the man himself insists. Just a typical American life, really. Born on January 2, 1919, in Little Rock, Arkansas, Charles Ray Willeford III was orphaned before he knew the difference, and a drifter before he knew what the word meant. He spent most of his rootless adolescence in boarding schools and some with his grandmother, who took him in when he was eight. But he hit the road in his early teens when it became clear that the old girl couldn't really support the two of them (not an uncommon Depression reality). This time as a fifteen-year-old hobo is recounted in the first volume of his autobiography (yet to find a publisher), while Volume II, *Something About a Soldier (1986)* picks up with his sweet-sixteen enlistment in the Army Air Corps and subsequent stationing in the Philippines. What with the Depression, then the war, then the promise of a hefty retirement pension, and the masses of free time military life allowed, Willeford's retreat into the service became a twenty-year career. Finding the Air Corps too boring, Willeford re-upped into the cavalry, and spent WWII as a tank commander with the 10th Armored Division in Europe, coming home with a fistful of medals (Silver Star, Bronze Star, a couple of Purple Hearts, and the Luxembourg Croix de Guerre), and shrapnel wounds in his face and ass.

Willeford is as laconic about his wartime experience as he is in detailing his characters' murderous eccentricities. "The abnormal becomes normal in combat," he offers by way of explanation. "You do lots of things without thinking—if you thought at all about getting hit, you wouldn't be able to function. I just walked around over there and didn't think about it—I felt I had a kind of charmed life, even after I was wounded. You become something of a Schopenhauer fatalist; if it's your time to get hit there's nothing you can do about it, so that's that. I was actually enjoying what I was doing. I was a professional soldier, so I was getting to put into practice stuff I had been learning for years. And like most everybody else at the time, I bought the whole bill of goods—we were fighting a "good" war against an enemy who was evil, making the world safe for democracy, fighting by the rules of war. Now I know better; there are no such things as "good" wars. Nothing ever changes because of them, 'cept some people make money and lots of good young kids are killed for nothing. It's always for nothing."

Willeford, at least, got some novelistic raw material out of the experience. "A good half of the men you deal with in the Army are psychopaths. There's a pretty hefty overlap between the military population and the prison population, so I knew plenty of guys like Junior in *Miami Blues* and Troy in *Sideswipe*. Like, some of these other

Tankers I knew used to swap bottles of liquor with infantrymen in exchange for prisoners, and then just shoot 'em for fun. I used to say, 'Goddamn it, will you stop shooting those prisoners!' And they would just shrug and say, 'Hell, they'd shoot *us* if they caught us!' Which was true, they used to shoot any Tankers they captured. So that sort of behavior became normal to them, and I used to wonder, 'What's gonna happen to these guys when they go back into civilian life? How are they gonna act?' You can't just turn it off and go to work in a 7-11. If you're good with weapons or something in the Army, you're naturally gonna do something with weapons when you get out, whether it's being a cop or a criminal. These guys learned to do all sorts of things in the Army that just weren't considered *normal* by civilian standards."

After the war, Willeford found himself half-way toward a full pension and nowhere near a civilian job opportunity. He decided to stay in for another ten years and keep writing. He'd been doing poetry since he was a kid (*Proletarian Laughter,* a 1948 collection of poems published by Alicat Bookshop Press, was his first book), as well as the odd magazine piece and short story. Finding himself in Tokyo in 1948 with access to a radio station and a shitload of free time, he began writing a soap opera serial, *The Saga of Mary Miller,* and his devotion to narrative fiction was cinched. The following year, after moving to Hamilton Air Force Base in California, about thirty miles north of San Francisco near San Rafael, he started writing *High Priest of California.*

Willeford remembers well the push that got him going. "I'd been talking about it for a long time—writing a novel—and my roommate finally just got sick of hearing me gabbing. 'Aw,' he said, 'You ain't never gonna do it, so just shut up!' So, I had no choice after that, I *had* to start writing!"

Weekends, Willeford would drive his powder-blue Buick convertible into San Francisco and take a room at the Powell Hotel, located at the foot of Powell Street where the cable cars turn around. There he'd take a room for the weekend, and divide his time between writing and enjoying himself. "Being thirty years old, with a blue convertible, blue uniform, and blue eyes, I was just having the time of my life in San Francisco." It's amazing that the damn book got *done.* But it did, and Willeford mailed it off to a service in New York City that humped your manuscript around to different publishers for a buck a throw. First on Willeford's list was Gold Medal, probably the premier paperback-original publisher of the time (launcher of guys like John D. MacDonald, Richard S. Prather, David Goodis, Charles Williams, Bruno Fischer, and many, many others). Not surprisingly, they rejected it, as they did several of C.W.'s novels over the next few years, culminating in an editor's letter to the author's agent, saying: "I don't like this guy Willeford's hero. I don't like this guy Willeford's novel. In fact, I don't like this guy Willeford! Don't send me anymore of his books!"

Ridiculous as this response might seem, it's not really hard to understand, considering how against-the-grain most of Willeford's books were. *High Priest* was short (about 35,000 words, or a little more than half the length of most full-length novels of the time), carefully written, and lacking in the bloody-action climax most Gold Medal readers demanded. Paydirt was hit with the third publisher on the list—Beacon Books, a low-rent operation specializing in salacious sleaze (*Hitch-Hike Hussy*) that had begun operating in 1951. Beacon was owned by Arnold Abramson's Universal Publishing and Distributing, an outfit that survived through the mid-seventies, putting out novels under a dizzying assortment of names ("Intimate Novels" were digest-sized softcore porn, "Uni-Books" were also digest-sized and did stuff like *Loves of a Girl Wrestler,* while "Bronze Books" did so-called "negro" novels like *Hot Chocolate); the* Beacon imprint lasted into the early sixties, to be succeeded by Award Books, the closest UPD ever came to respectability.

The first edition of *High Priest* came out in 1953, as the second part of Royal Giant #G-20, a digest-sized (which means wider than regular "rack"-sized paperbacks) double-novel which featured Talbot Mundy's *Full Moon* ("Bold men fought and tortured—and so did their lovely women . . . !") as the opener. The cover copy for *High Priest* panted: "The world was his oyster—and women his pearls!" While over on the back we were told it was "A strange, shocking novel . . . as true as a Federal Reserve Note." (huh?) *Pick-Up,* Willeford's second novel (recently reissued by Black Lizard), came out under Beacon's imprint in 1955, sporting a cover painting UPD had already used for Royal Giant #G-21, something called *Highway Episode* by George Weller. This sort of thing was commonplace at

UPD—books, covers, and even a few particularly lurid cover blurbs were all used and re-used until the last possible bit of profit could be squeezed out of them.

When Beacon published Willeford's third novel, *Until I Am Dead* (1956), they changed the title to *Wild Wives* and slapped it on the end of a second edition of *High Priest*. This time, the cover copy screamed: "No woman could resist his strange cult of lechery!" and "Blind date with blonde bait!" (Hubba-hubba!) They also re-christened the author Charles "Williford," and misspelled the names of two of the main characters on the page-one blurb. Class.

Wild Wives/Until I Am Dead is a most uncharacteristic C.W. novel, in that it's the closest he's ever come to fulfilling the conventions of the hard-boiled detective genre. Smartass private dick Jacob Blake (a name that turns up again in *The Machine in Ward Eleven,* a 1963 story collection) is another dickhead Willeford hero, one who falls for a classically Cain-ian poison dame, and goes down in flames for his sin of weakness. The contrast it makes with *High Priest* is stark—Willeford calls that one "a reluctant lover" scenario, which he says is the predominant mode of modern American fiction, where the male will do anything to avoid commitment. Which is true enough, except Russell Haxby is a little spookier than your average red-blooded American male. There's a line past which reluctance becomes something a bit worse (though he's got a ways to go before entering Troy Louden's league).

The scenarios in Willeford's later novels became tougher, the people in them scarier. Beacon did a couple more books: *Honey Gal* (C.W. title: *The Black Mass of Brother Springer),* and *Lust is a Woman* (C.W. title: *Made in Miami),* while an outfit in Chicago called N-L Publishers did *The Understudy* (1961), and *The Director* (1960). *The Burnt Orange Heresy* in 1971 was his first hardcover, while a rewrite of his 1962 paperback original *Cockfighter* came out in stiff covers a year later (both are now Black Lizard paperbacks), and as a Monte Hellman film two years after that (Willeford also wrote the screenplay and appeared in it; it's called *Born to Kill).* Then there's a *completely* weird thing called *Off the Wall* (1980), a novelized view of David Berkowitz (Son of Sam, for you non-followers of big league mass murderers) from the view of Craig Glassman, the Yonkers Deputy Sheriff who lived below Berkowitz and helped arrest him.

Due next, probably not til early '88, is another Hoke Moseley, which Willeford says, "is more a picaresque novel than a crime story. Though there is a crime, and it is solved, that's almost incidental to the book." He seems comfortable writing unconventional crime novels, police procedurals where the procedure is secondary to the police. "I'm not really breaking the genre," he says, "just bending it a bit." Which is all Freddy Frenger does to the middle finger of that pesky Hare Krishna asshole in the beginning of *Miami Blues,* just bending it backward a little. Of course, the guy went and died of shock after that, but that wasn't Freddy's fault, was it?

—Lou Stathis, NYC, April 1987

"Isn't it illegal to carry a knife with a blade that long?"

Chapter One

I slipped a dollar under the wicket and a sullen-lipped cashier asked me for a penny.

"You're making the change," I told her. She gave me the ticket and four pennies and I bounded up the stairs. The man on the door tried to mark my wrist with a blue stamp, but I dodged it. It was one of those dance halls where men come to pick up something, and women come to be picked up. I was there because I was bored. I looked around.

There were twice as many women as men. Most of the women looked pretty bad, those that were sitting around waiting, but there were a few fairly nice ones on the floor. I edged through the crowd to the rope barrier and watched the dancers. The band (three saxes, a trumpet, piano and drums) was much too loud. The ceiling was low and there was a second listen to the music through reverberation. I looked for the bar and found it, but it only served beer. I ordered one at the bar, and then sat at a table facing the dance floor.

The place was noisy, hot, smelled of sweat, and the beer wasn't cold. I was ready to leave. Then I saw the woman in the red tailored suit.

It wasn't just a red suit, it was a created red suit. The woman lived up to it. She was a tall woman with shoulder-length brown hair, parted in the center. She looked as out-of-place in that smoky atmosphere as I would have looked in a Salinas lettuce-pickers camp. She had a casual air, but she was interested in what was going on. I got up from the table and tapped her on the shoulder.

"Dance?" I jerked my head toward the floor.

"Oh, yes!" she said, and nodded her head several times like she thought it was the best suggestion ever made.

I took her elbow and guided her through the crowd to the floor. We began to dance. She was a terrible dancer, and as stiff and difficult to shove around as a reluctant St. Bernard.

"Why don't you relax?" I asked her.

"What?" She looked at me with big brown excited eyes, and there were bright red spots on her cheeks.

"Relax."

"I haven't danced in a long time and I'm afraid of making a mistake."

"Don't be afraid. I made one."

"I didn't notice it."

"That's because you haven't danced in a long time. Come on. Let's get us a beer."

All the tables were occupied in the bar section, but a couple of young punks were sitting at one with nothing in front of them. I gave them a hard look and they got up and left.

"Sit down, Miss—?"

"Alyce. Alyce Vitale."

"Sit down, Alyce, and I'll get us a couple of beers."

I elbowed my way to the bar, caught the bartender's eye, bought two bottles of beer, and picked up a paper cup for Alyce. Back at the table I poured the beer and sat down.

"A man tried to take your seat," she said, "but I told him it was reserved."

"Thanks." I drank my beer and took a better look at Alyce. Her eyes were intelligent, but vague. In repose, her face had a wistful tragic look, but when she smiled it transformed her into a radiant beauty. She looked interesting. I flashed a smile back at her, my charming, disarming smile.

"Here's to you, Alyce," I said. She drank out of her paper cup and made a face.

"It's bitter."

"That's the way it tastes at first. This isn't your first beer, is it?"

"I've had home-brew before, but it never tasted as bitter as this."

"Home-brew? That dates you."

"Well, it was a long time ago. Do you work here, Mr—"

"No. I don't work here!" The question had surprised me. "I came up here to dance, just like you did."

"Oh." She was surprised, but not embarrassed. "I'm sorry, but I thought when you asked me to dance, and all—"

"Listen, Alyce. You're a good-looking woman. And a lot of men up here will ask you to dance. Once, anyway."

She didn't catch it at all, and I decided to take it easy with her. I don't like to waste good sarcasm. Besides, she was a new type to me. She must have been close to thirty, but she acted and talked as naive as a young girl.

"You don't have to drink that beer." I told her. "I'll get you a Coke if you want."

"I don't want anything, thanks. I'll smoke a cigarette."

I passed her my pack and we smoked for a minute or two.

"How did you happen to come up here?" I asked her.

"I was sitting in my apartment all alone, and just on impulse I felt like going out. Do you ever feel like that? Like you're not getting anything out of life?" Her voice was intense.

"No."

"This is the first time in my life I ever came to a public dance hall, but I just decided I had to have some fun, get out, do something. Haven't you ever felt like that?"

"No."

"That's why I'm here, anyway." She smiled. The smile did wonders for her face.

"Are you having fun?"

"Oh, yes!"

"In here?"

She nodded vigorously. I shook my head. This was San Francisco, with a million places to have fun. It didn't sound reasonable. I felt sorry for her if she had to come to a place like the Sampson Dance Palace to have fun.

"Come on," I said. "Let's get out of here. We'll go some place else."

"All right."

She got her coat from the checkroom and I waited at the door. The cold night air was a relief after the stuffiness of the dance hall. I had parked on the street, and I regretted not taking a better car off the lot than the Ford I'd picked. I should have taken a Buick. It would have been more impressive.

Alyce climbed into the car without asking where I was taking her, and seemed to be without curiosity.

"Have you had dinner, Alyce?" It was after nine, but I hadn't eaten since five and was hungry again.

"I don't eat at night, or at noon either."

"You don't?"

"Just breakfast. I'm hungry all the time, but if I eat I put on weight, so I just go hungry."

"Break a rule and have dinner with me."

"If you insist, Mr . . . ?"

"Haxby. I insist, and make it Russell. Not Russ, but Russell, and certainly not Mr Haxby." I was on Market and had to make a right turn and a block circle because of the No Left Turn law. The Ford climbed the hill easily, and I parked in the alley behind Antonio's.

Antonio doesn't advertise; he doesn't have to. He serves good food, and people who eat there once come back; that is if they can afford to come back. Antonio shook hands with me.

"Mr Haxby! How the hell are you?"

"Hungry, but not too hungry. This is Miss Vitale."

He talked to Alyce in rapid Italian, and she shook her head.

"I don't understand Italian," she said. Antonio shrugged and led us to a table. It wasn't necessary to place an order. He'd take care of it. I spoke to Alyce.

"Aren't you Italian?"

"No. Of course not. What makes you think so?"

"Vitale is definitely an Italian name."

"Well, I am definitely not an Italian." She blushed.

It didn't make any difference to me. If she wanted to lie, the hell with it. There was a bottle of Chianti on the table. I took out my knife, flipped the blade out and opened the wine.

"Isn't it illegal to carry a knife with a blade that long?"

"I never read the laws." I shrugged and put the knife

back in my pocket.

We had veal, cooked in olive oil and garlic sauce, with sliced, breaded, fried tomatoes, spumoni and coffee. Afterwards, I had a B & B. Alyce didn't want a drink. I signed the check and we left.

Neither of us had talked much during dinner. Alyce seemed happy enough just looking around at the people and concentrating on the violinist. The violinist was one of the features about Antonio's that I didn't like. There is nothing that sounds worse than one violin. Five, maybe even three, are all right, but one is completely miserable.

In the car I suggested that we go to the Top of the Mark. It was a clear night and the view would be worth the trouble. Luckily, I found a place to park in the hotel lot. In the lobby we waited in line for the elevator. Every stranger who comes to San Francisco has to check the view from the Top of the Mark, and there were a lot of out-of-towners in the lobby. I can spot them instantly.

In time, we stood at the glass window overlooking the city.

"You can see where I work," Alyce said.

"Where?"

She pointed and explained. Miller's Garage. I knew where it was and could pick it out. The auto lot where I worked was hidden by a hill.

"What do you do, Alyce?"

"Cashier. This is the best job I've ever had. It's six days a week, ten to seven. But I make eighty-five, after taxes, and that's good for a woman, even in San Francisco."

"Damned good."

We had a drink, Alyce drinking a Scotch and Soda, and me a stinger. She evidently didn't know anything else to order; I could tell by her hesitation. Anybody who knows something else will never drink Scotch anyway. It tastes like wood-smoke and weeds. I began to pump Alyce.

She had been born and reared in San Francisco. After graduation from high school she had stayed home with her parents till her father died, and then had been forced to work to support her mother. Her mother was now dead, and she shared an apartment with her cousin, Ruthie. Ruthie was in her early forties and a practical nurse, an occupation that kept her away from the apartment a great deal.

"This," I thought, "is going to be a very nice set-up."

I told her I worked for Tad Tate. She had heard of him. She began to chant:

Am I crazy?
You're right, you're right!
Will I buy your car?
You're right, you're right!

"I hear his commercials all the time. Who writes them, anyway? I think they're awfully funny."

"He has an agency," I told her.

I didn't think the commercials were funny. They were rather pitiful. The idea of a radio commercial is to keep repeating the same thing over and over, and the payoff is a long-range deal. When a person buys a used car he goes to a place he knows about, and if he's heard a name often enough, that's the place he will go. I didn't bother Alyce with my theory on radio advertising.

"Are you finished with that Scotch and Soda?"

She finished it.

"Do you want another?"

She shook her head. I helped her on with her coat, and we caught the elevator down.

"San Francisco," the elevator operator announced when we reached the lobby. Two tourists laughed. A man in overalls was standing by the Ford when we got outside.

"Is this your car?" he asked as I unlocked it.

"Yeah. What about it?"

"You aren't supposed to park here."

"All right. I'll move it."

"And don't park here again." He started to walk away. I opened the door for Alyce and told her to get in. I shut the door and caught up with the man in overalls. I signaled to him to come in between two cars.

"I've got something for you," I said. No one could see us between the two parked cars. I kneed him in the crotch, and as he bent over I clasped my hands together and brought them down on the back of his neck. He groaned and chewed on the gravel. I got into the Ford and drove down the hill. Alyce hadn't seen anything.

"Did you give him a tip?"

"Yeah."

I cut left toward the Marina District and could sense Alyce squirming in her seat. I looked in her direction.

"Russell," she said, "I have to get home. I know it's early, but I didn't tell Ruthie I was going out, and I'm afraid she'll worry."

"Where's home?"

She gave me the address. Without saying anything, I made a U turn and started climbing hills. She lived in a two-story duplex almost flush with the sidewalk, like so many San Francisco houses. Hers was the upstairs apartment. I cut off the engine and kissed her. The response was negative. Her lips were tightly compressed.

"Can you wait a minute?" she asked. "I'll run upstairs

and let you know if it's all right to come up."

"Sure."

"I'll only be a minute." She got out of the car and in a few seconds light flooded the upstairs picture window. I lighted a cigarette. She was at the door beckoning for me to come in. I got out and locked the car.

This was going to be a cinch.

I followed Alyce up the stairs. There was a musty odor about the apartment, the kind one finds in a zoo. I didn't like it.

Chapter Two

I followed Alyce up the stairs. There was a musty odor about the apartment, the kind one finds in a zoo. I didn't like it.

"Why don't you open a window, Alyce? This place smells like hell."

We were in the living room, a room that edged slightly over the street with a large picture window.

"That smell comes from the cats," she said. "I'll introduce you." She left the room.

It was a good-sized living room. Plenty of books. With a perfunctory glance at a few titles I could see she was a Book-of-the-Month-Club subscriber. Several ceramic ashtrays and an odd-shaped vase told me Alyce was a dabbler in ceramics, or else had a friend that dabbled. No one would buy anything as poorly made as the examples in the room. On the wall was a good print of Van Gogh's drawbridge, but it was spoiled by the picture hanging next to it: a wolf in the snow, howling at the moon. There was a television set, medium cost, and a three-speed record player-radio. A good brand. I looked out the window. She had a view of the Golden Gate Bridge that must have added twenty-five dollars a month onto the rent of the apartment. You could see part of the bay and a few piers. It was a nice room all around if you disregarded the picture of the wolf, and the single-winged mid-Victorian armchair facing the TV set.

Alyce returned carrying a large gray-striped alley cat.

"This is Ferdie," she said. She left, returning a minute later with a yellow-striped alley cat. "This is Alvin."

"Alvin?"

She nodded, departed, and returned with the third cat, a mean-faced charcoal-gray alley cat. The cats were enormous and stalked restlessly about the room, purring and meowing.

"Is that all?" I asked.

"That's all the cats. I have a dog, Spike. But he's asleep."

The cats explained the smell. I figured she was used to it, but it bothered me. I didn't plan to stay much longer. This woman was too weird for me. I looked at the cats. The mean-looking gray one rubbed up against my leg and I kicked at him. He dodged and stalked with dignity to the other side of the room.

"He likes you!" Alyce said.

"Well, I don't like him. How about a drink?"

Alyce gathered up two of the cats and took them out of the room, leaving the gray one. I got in another kick at him but I missed. Alyce returned with a half-pint bottle of vodka, handed it to me, and took the remaining cat from the room. I took a healthy swig out of the bottle. Alyce returned. She was carrying a glass and a bottle of orange soda pop.

"I looked," she said, "but there weren't any ice cubes. Ruthie must have used them."

"Aren't you going to have a drink?"

She shook her head.

I mixed a stiff vodka and orange pop. It tasted terrible.

"I'd rather drink coffee than this concoction."

"There's some in the pot. All I have to do is heat it." She hurried out of the room. I looked through her records. They were all pop stuff, mostly vocals. I stacked four instrumentals I found on the player and turned it on. It was warm enough to play Wayne King when Alyce returned.

"The coffee'll be ready in a minute. Please, not too loud, Russell. Ruthie's asleep."

I turned the volume down some. I took Alyce in my arms and attempted to dance a bit in the open space between the coffee table and the wall. It was no good. She was too stiff. I sat down.

"Say, Alyce, all of those cats are male, aren't they?"

"Uh huh."

"How come they don't have a girlfriend?"

"I used to have a female, Henrietta, but she kept having kittens all the time, and I had such a hard time finding homes for them that I had to find a home for her. She's living with a retired schoolteacher now and getting along fine. I go and see her once in a while."

"I'll bet she's glad to see you too. But how come all these tomcats are home on a Saturday night?"

"I never let them out. I keep them in a cage in the kitchen when I'm not home. Do you want to see—?"

"No." I started to kiss her and she turned away swiftly.

"The coffee's ready by now."

I took another shot of straight vodka. It was a halfway decent drink without the orange pop. Alyce brought a tray into the room holding a coffee pot and two cups. I poured us both a cupful. For reheated coffee it was all right. I took my cup to the Victorian armchair and sat down. The smell was unmistakable. Someone had been sitting in that chair who reeked with sweat. And it was a male. Men have a certain smell to them, a strong sweaty smell that is noticed upon entering a YMCA, a barracks or a man's room. It doesn't bother a man to smell it and he soon gets used to it, but it was odd to find on a chair in a girl's apartment.

"Do you keep men in your apartment besides the animals?"

Alyce looked surprised.

"Men?"

"Yeah. Men."

"Why, no. Would you like some more coffee?" As she warmed mine up I heard a noise in the kitchen. Utensils shifted around. "That's Ruthie. We must have wakened her."

"You got the coffee pot out there?" It was a man's voice.

"Ruthie has a nice bass." I said it as casually as I could.

"That's just Stanley," Alyce said. "I have it, Stanley!" she called.

Stanley came into the room. He was in his fifties, if not more, with a thatch of gray tousled hair and a stubble of gray beard. An ancient multicolored bathrobe covered his body, but left exposed a pair of skinny, wiry legs.

"Ruthie and I want a cup too." Petulantly. "You might have known that."

"You'll have to make some more then. We just had the last of it. Oh, Stanley, this is Mr Haxby. Russell, Mr Sinkiewicz."

"Charmed," I said.

"Pleased to meet you, sir." He picked up the pot and tottered from the room. I could hear him in the kitchen running water from the tap.

"Who's he?" I asked. A natural question.

"Stanley? Oh, he's a friend of Ruthie's." Alyce was

embarrassed. "I might as well tell you. I don't guess Ruthie would mind. You see, he's married, but his wife is an invalid. Ruthie worked for them, as a nurse, for a long time, and they got to be pretty good friends. Well, he goes with Ruthie now. That's about it."

"What about the wife?"

"She's an invalid. Paralyzed. But she has all the money and if Stanley were to divorce her, he wouldn't get a cent. So Ruthie and him . . . well, they're waiting, I guess."

"Doesn't look to me like they're waiting."

"He stays here sometimes." She blushed. "Then he gets up early and goes home. His wife doesn't know about Ruthie."

"Stanley has it made all the way around, doesn't he?"

"I don't like it and I know Ruthie doesn't, but . . ." She turned away. I could see she didn't want to talk about it. I got up from the chair and turned her around. Gently, I put my arms around her, moved in close. I kissed her, but it was no good. She held her lips together and held her body stiff. It was like kissing a piece of bronze. I released her, picked up my hat and stuck it on my head.

"Well, Alyce," I said, "I'll be seeing you around."

"You don't have to go yet, do you?"

"Yeah. Tomorrow's Sunday and I have to sleep late."

"How late?"

"Until I wake up."

"Why don't you come over tomorrow afternoon then. Stop by for a drink." She saw the look I gave the bottle of orange pop that was sitting on the coffee table. "I'll get some gin and vermouth for Martinis."

"What time?" Not that I particularly cared, because I didn't intend to be there.

"Two? Two-thirty? Will that be all right?"

"Sure," I said. "Two-thirty will be fine. Now let me try another one of those kisses."

She shut her eyes, stiffened, and clenched her fists. I kissed her, and though she obviously didn't like it she made no move to stop me. It was strange. When I let her go she turned on the hall light, and I started down the stairs.

"Goodnight, Alyce."

"Goodnight, Russell. And thank you for a wonderful evening. Two-thirty. Don't forget."

Downstairs, I shut the door to her apartment and climbed into the Ford. This Alyce was a new type. I couldn't figure what she was after or if she was after anything. The woman was good-looking but her personality was blah. Still, with a figure like she had there should certainly be something there. I might look in the next day, but then that was tomorrow and it would depend upon how I felt.

I drove crosstown to my apartment. It's a garage apartment behind an old house on Telegraph Hill. There is no view from my apartment except the backs of old houses all around me. And if you didn't know it was there you couldn't find it. The building was probably a servants' quarters at one time but it's fixed up now. The decorator's fees alone cost me a thousand bucks, but it was worth it. Just a living room, bedroom and kitchenette, but it was the kind of place I'd wanted all my life. And now I have it.

I took off my jacket and hung it in the wardrobe. I like to slide the door back on the wardrobe. Twenty suits. It made me glad I'm a used-car salesman and can afford to own twenty suits.

I wasn't sleepy so I fixed an onion and salami sandwich, a gin and quinine water, and sat down with my beat-up Kafka anthology. I reread *In The Penal Colony.* This is the best short story ever written. Kafka was one writer who had a sense of humor.

After I finished the sandwich and drink I went to bed. Almost asleep, I reviewed the evening in my mind, and just before dropping off I set the alarm for one o'clock.

I fell asleep.

"Who do you visit at the cemetery every Sunday?"
"Mother's grave. Fourteen months now since she passed away and I
haven't missed a Sunday."

Chapter Three

The alarm went off and I looked stupidly at the clock for a moment trying to figure out why it was ringing on a Sunday. I remembered Alyce and shut it off. I showered and shaved. This was a concession, because I never shave on Sunday. In the kitchen I fixed a sardine omelet and a pot of coffee. I read the Sunday papers while I ate, cleared the table, and added the dishes to the pile in the sink.

I dressed carefully, selecting a red paisley tie to wear with my powder-blue gabardine suit. Blue looks good on me: it sets off my hair. I backed the Ford down the narrow driveway onto the street and drove to the lot and parked it. In the office, I picked out the keys for the lone Buick convertible we had on the lot, checked the gas and drove to Alyce's apartment. It was 2:15. I pushed the doorbell.

Alyce opened the door. She looked sharp in a black faille suit and a double choker of imitation pearls.

"Oh!" Alyce said.

"What's the matter, didn't you expect me?"

"It was the car. I looked out the window when the car stopped, and saw it was a Buick, so I didn't think it was you."

I laughed. We climbed the stairs, Alyce leading. She was something to watch from behind climbing stairs. In the living room I sat down.

"Perhaps I'd better explain. I told you I sold used cars—well the lot is full of them. I have my choice, so I take any car I please."

"Don't you own your own car?"

"Why should I?"

"I guess that's right. I've got some Martinis mixed; would you like to have one now or would you rather wait for Ruthie?"

"Let's have one while we wait. Where's Ruthie?"

"Dressing."

Alyce poured us a cocktail and I sipped mine. It wasn't very good. Too much vermouth. She must have mixed them half and half. I drank it anyway. I looked at Alyce over my glass. Her eyes were bright and her cheeks were flushed. Excitement was very becoming to her. She looked even better to me now than she had the night before. I like a good-sized woman and Alyce is show-girl size.

"Alyce!" It was Ruthie calling. "Can you come in here a minute?"

Alyce put her glass down and got to her feet.

"That's Ruthie. Please excuse me. Pour yourself another Martini." She left the room.

I figured Ruthie was ready and wanted confirmation from Alyce before making an appearance. I looked around the room. There were two vases full of cut flowers that hadn't been there last night, and the room was well-straightened and dusted. If this was a two-bedroom apartment it must have rented for at least one and a quarter. That was steep rent for two girls to pay. The furniture was expensive; not imaginative, but respectable and solid. However, the place still smelled like cats.

Alyce and Ruthie came in. Ruthie was in her forties but her dyed red hair made her look older. Her mouth was full and generous and she looked like she was pouting with her upper lip. She wore tiny gold-rimmed glasses on a chain spring, the spool pinned to her violet dress. Plenty of fat jiggled on a heavy frame and her puffy fingers were adorned with several cheap rings. I liked her immediately.

"So you're the Russell Haxby Alyce has been talking about all morning?"

"I hope so," I said, "but then that depends on what she said about me."

"You don't have to worry. Pour me one of those, Russell." I poured a drink and handed it to her. She practically inhaled it, and held her glass for a refill. "I needed that. Sundays are miserable days."

Alyce sat in a straight chair, very erect, and fully conscious of her posture. I smiled. She smiled back, a very sweet smile.

"Alyce tells me you're a used-car salesman," Ruthie said.

"Every day except Sunday."

"I don't have a car, and neither does my boyfriend. So Alyce usually gets stuck on Sunday. We use hers."

"Everybody in California should have a car," I said.

"I don't mind letting you and Stanley use my car," Alyce said.

"I know. I know. It's just that it's inconvenient."

"You know I go to the cemetery every Sunday."

Ruthie smiled at me. Her mouth was very wide, the lips thicker. The smile made her look obscene.

"I know all about guys like you, Russell. You're the High Priest of California. That isn't original with me. It was a caption in *Life* about the used-car salesmen of California.

Did you see it?"

I shook my head. "I'm afraid not, but it makes a good caption."

"And it fits." She turned to Alyce. "Baby, go fill the shaker again, will you please? Stanley'll be here soon."

"And Alyce," I added, "one-fifth vermouth, four-fifths gin."

"I thought they were half and half . . ."

"No," I said. Alyce picked up the shaker and left the room. "All right Ruthie, what kind of a car do you want?"

"You're a smart bastard."

"Not exactly."

Ruthie leaned forward, put a damp fat hand on mine and lowered her voice. "I don't know what Alyce told you about Stanley and me, and I care less, but he doesn't have any money. His wife sees to that. I had a bigger allowance than him when I was ten years old."

"He might try working."

"No." She said it seriously. "His wife and I wouldn't like that, and I know damn well he wouldn't. He's a proud little bugger. You met him?"

"Last night. Slightly."

"Here." She took a roll of bills from her beaded bag and handed it to me. I counted it. One hundred even. "I want a car, and I want it to be Stanley's. He can afford a hundred dollar car by himself, but I want a better car than that. Let this make the difference between a lemon and a fairly decent automobile."

"That's easy." I pocketed the money.

"Fine then, Russell. Just sell Stanley a car and keep this under your hat."

"Of course."

Alyce returned with the shaker and we all had another round. About this time, Stanley showed. He unlocked the downstairs door with his key and started up the stairs. I raised my eyebrows in Alyce's direction and she blushed. Stanley entered. He had shaved, and looked a little better, but his suit was rumpled, his shirt unclean. He smiled an old man's reluctant grimace, revealing some haphazardly broken teeth.

"Having a little party?" he commented dryly.

I poured and handed him a cocktail. He downed it, shuddered, and spoke sharply to Ruthie.

"Did you get the car keys?"

"Where are they, Alyce?" Ruthie asked.

"On the telephone table in the hall."

"We'd better get going," Stanley said. When Ruthie left the room I gave Stanley one of my cards.

"Ruthie tells me you're in the market for a used car, Mr Sinkiewicz. Drop by next week, or give a call, and meantime, I'll look around for you and get you something halfway decent."

"I can't afford no expensive cars."

"You leave that to me."

Ruthie returned wearing her coat, and they left. Alyce and I were alone but she didn't look happy.

"What's the matter, Alyce?"

"Oh, it's just the inconsideration of Ruthie and Stanley. They both know I go to the cemetery every Sunday, and because you're here, they go ahead and take my car figuring you will have to take me."

"I don't mind. It's a nice day."

"You don't have to take me."

"How would you get there if I didn't?"

"I don't know. Take a bus, I guess."

"Go on, get your coat." I was exasperated.

I put the top back on the Buick and Alyce told me the name of the cemetery. She took a scarf out of her coat pocket and tied it over her head. The wind was icy, but liking the feel of the sun on my face I left the top back.

"Who do you visit at the cemetery every Sunday?" I asked.

"Mother's grave. Fourteen months now since she passed away and I haven't missed a Sunday."

"Why do you go every week?"

"I respect my mother, that's why." She was surprised at the question. "And I love her very much."

"Don't you think it's a little pagan?"

"To respect one's mother?" She shook her head. "No, I don't think so."

"Couldn't you respect her just as much without breaking up your Sunday every week?"

"I don't forget that easily. And as long as I'm living in San Francisco I intend to visit her grave every week."

That settled that. I turned on the radio, luckily catching the tail end of Beethoven's Ninth. Alyce closed her eyes to listen and I drove without speaking to the cemetery. Near the entrance we stopped, and Alyce bought flowers. I drove through the ornate entrance, followed Alyce's directions, and stopped at the place she indicated. We got out and I carried the flowers as far as her mother's grave, and placed them on the grass. While she meditated, threw away last week's flowers and drew water out of a spigot for the new bunch, I wandered around looking at headstones.

I was quite surprised to see the unadorned stone of Tom Mooney. I had forgotten him. Nearby, on another grave, there were fresh flowers. I removed them and put them on Mooney's headstone. The day wasn't a total loss. I rejoined Alyce.

I took her arm and we walked across the grass to the car. She was talkative, pointing out stones and fresh flowers; telling me of the people who came to visit on Sundays and what they had told her about the different deaths.

"This is Little Jackie," she said. "See the fresh American Beauty roses? He was only three years old when the Lord took him away. His mother comes every day. She is slowly eating her heart out over her poor lost little boy."

She smiled at me. I wasn't certain, but it seemed that Alyce was happy about it. I wanted a drink.

We got in the car and I drove back to the city. The almost full shaker of Martinis sitting in her living room occupied my mind on the drive back.

Two blocks away from her apartment she clutched my arm.

"Stop here, please," she ordered. I pulled into the curb and stopped.

"Why here?"

"I'll walk the rest of the way." She got out, closed the door. "It was very kind of you to take me to the cemetery, Russell. I know it was distasteful to you, that's why I doubly appreciate it. You're a very kind man." She started to walk away, and I let her go; then, suddenly angry, I got out and caught up with her. I took her by the arm.

"What's the matter with you, Alyce? What's the story?"

"Nothing." She looked into my eyes. I cooled off.

"Did I hurt your feelings? Is that it?"

"No. I can tell you don't like me, Russell, so we might as well let it go at that."

"What makes you think I don't like you?"

"Why should you? I'm a very dull woman."

I started to say, "No, you aren't," and realized how stupid it would sound, so I patted her on the shoulder instead.

"Sundays are terrible days, Alyce. I'll drop by tomorrow night and we'll go out to dinner. How's that?"

"Not at the house. Meet me at the garage. Miller's. Do you know where it is?"

"All right." I nodded.

"You don't have to meet me if you don't want."

"I want to."

"Thank you, again." She turned and walked rapidly away. I stared at her retreating figure. An odd woman for me to be fooling with, but I was puzzled, and that was enough to keep me interested.

I wondered if she was really mysterious, or just plain stupid.

Chapter Four

When the alarm went off on Monday morning, I shut it off and looked out the window. Fog. For breakfast I poached a half-dozen eggs and toasted some English muffins. Afterwards I drove down to the lot and parked the Buick. It was early. The colored flags and streamers hanging from the overhead wires were limp in the soft dampness of the air. There was no wind and the fog was so thick it was difficult to see from one end of the lot to the other. I crossed Van Ness and got a cup of coffee at the corner shop.

When I returned to the lot Tad Tate was there. Tad is a real salesman and a good guy to work with. He has a huge paunch and always wears a suit with a vest. Usually he has an unlit, well-chewed cigar in his mouth and a little black notebook in his hand. I like Tad. We understand each other.

"Well, Russell," he said, "we better get some soldiers from the Presidio down here for guard duty today. People will be stealing cars and we won't even know it."

"They always get a steal, don't they?"

"That's the idea. See if you can get rid of that 1938 LaSalle today, will you? I'm tired of looking at it."

"If you take the Cadillac price off it I will."

"Sell it for whatever you want. I'm sick of looking at it."

"Okay. Madeleine in yet?"

"She's in the office. I won't be back 'til around eleven. If you really need me—never mind. I'll be back at eleven."

He squeezed himself and his paunch into his MG and roared through the gravel of the lot and into the fog. I went into the office. Madeleine was already banging it out on the typewriter. We have twelve different forms to fill in on every car sold. She pounds the stuff out day after day and knows the business inside and out. I had never given her a tumble, because it doesn't pay in this business. But I intended to get around to it one day. She is a handsome woman, and so healthy she practically busts out of her clothes. When I'm around her I just keep my mind on other things.

"Good morning," I said.

"I see you found your way through the fog."

"You never knew me to miss a day, did you?"

"Just what do you do with all your money, Russell?"

"I spend it. Where's Andy?"

"Isn't he out there?"

"I didn't see him."

"He checked in. He probably went out for coffee."

"Okay." I went outside.

Andy was our colored mechanic. He had been with Tad for fifteen years. I looked around the lot. I found him removing a spotlight from a Buick super.

"Andy," I said, "when you get some time, work on that old Essex in the fourth row."

"Who's going to buy that?"

"I sold it yesterday."

"What kind of a job you want?"

"The best you can do with it. The engine's good, and with a little luck it'll last two or three years."

"I'll do what I can but it won't be much."

"And Andy, rub off the seventy-five dollar price and mark it two-fifty."

"Two hundred and fifty dollars?"

"That's what I said."

"Mr Haxby, I sometimes think you ain't got a conscience."

He took the spotlight and headed for his workshop by the office. I walked to the driveway and watched the traffic pound up Van Ness. It was heavy. The fog slowed them down. Once in a while you could spot an idiot going full speed up the hill passing people on the right. Two colored soldiers in a maroon Dodge crept along the curb. They wanted to park but were hesitant because the curb was painted red.

"Just pull on in!" I shouted and waved to them. After the car was parked they got out and walked over to where I was standing.

"We just wanted to look around," one said.

"Sure."

"You got any Caddy's?" the other one asked.

"Sure. Where are you men stationed?"

"We're out at Camp Stoneman. Just got back from Japan."

I sold them a Cadillac. It was easy. They were driving a borrowed car, but they had enough money for a down payment, and that was all I was interested in. The way Tad works it, it is foolproof. If we get the one-third down payment, we turn the buyer over to the AAA Acme Finance Company. They take up the loan and we get our money right then. The Triple A has to worry about collecting the other two-thirds. But they do collect.

These two soldiers were the kind I like to latch onto. With plenty of money in their pockets and just back from overseas, they like the looks of all the cars. After being away from the United States for two or three years, the model that was new when they left still looks to them like a new car. In fifteen minutes I had made two hundred dollars. The returning colored soldiers almost always buy a Cadillac.

After I finished my part of the paperwork, I handed the stack of papers to Madeleine, left the office, and cut across the lot to Thrifty's. There is a telephone in the office but I preferred to do my phoning elsewhere.

I called Miller's Garage and asked for Miss Vitale. I hardly recognized her voice when she answered the telephone. It was like a little girl's voice.

"Is that you, Alyce?"

"Who is this, please?"

"Russell. Russell Haxby."

"Oh! Russell! How nice of you to call me. I was just thinking about you."

"I just thought I'd call. Thought it best to confirm our date for tonight. You seemed a bit upset yesterday."

"I'm sorry. I can get off a little earlier than seven-thirty if you want me to."

"No, that's all right."

"All right." There was a period of silence. I broke it. "Seven-thirty."

"I'll be waiting." Again we hesitated, then we both hung up the receivers at the same time. I thought about Alyce for the rest of the day.

I sold the LaSalle to a veteran that afternoon. He had his insurance dividend check for $147.40. All I said was, "Even-Stephen." He signed the papers, endorsed the check, and drove the LaSalle off the lot.

At 4:30 I checked out and went home. The fog was just as thick as it had been in the morning. If it hadn't been for the Cadillac sale it would have been a bad day for me. I drove home in a Ford Victoria that had a working radio, and backed up my driveway. It would be dark soon and I didn't like to back down the driveway at night. I fixed a gin and cherry brandy, then took a shower. I took my time dressing and had another drink before I left. I put a lightweight trenchcoat on over my tweed suit. It was exactly 7:30 when I parked in front of Miller's Garage. Alyce was waiting for me.

I honked the horn and she got into the car.

"Where do you want to eat?" I asked her.

"I don't eat. Remember?"

"In that case we'll go down to Fisherman's Wharf. You can watch me eat fried shrimp and French fried potatoes."

"You're killing me," she said. Alyce was in a fine mood and gave me an account of her day. Some of it was amusing, but most of it was boring. After we were seated in a wharf restaurant I changed the subject.

"Do you know that shrimp salad is not fattening?" I surprised her.

"Shrimp?"

"That's right. Try one."

"What about the salad dressing?"

"It's fattening, but the shrimp isn't. Just put lemon juice on it."

She had a shrimp salad while I polished off my dinner. We sat smoking, drinking coffee. It was a pleasure to look at her across the booth. I got into a talkative mood myself and told her about the morning's Cadillac sale. She was impressed.

"Do you mean, Russell, that you made two hundred dollars on that one sale?"

"That's right."

"What do you make a week then?"

"On an average, it runs about two-fifty to three hundred. I'll make more this week."

"That's a lot of money."

"It goes."

"What do you spend it all on?"

"I'm spending some of it on you."

We left, and although it was still early I took her to the Commodore to catch the combo that was playing. The piano was good. The dinner, my drink, and holding Alyce's hand put me in a good mood. I was slightly happy and smoked one cigarette after another.

"What are you thinking about, Russell?"

"You."

"What about me?"

"That's what I want to find out."

She shook her head and smiled sadly. "I hope you never do."

"I will. Don't worry."

The room was getting smoky and we went outside, walked along Geary. I pulled Alyce into a storefront and kissed her. She tightened up, giving no response whatever.

"Why do you freeze up like that, Alyce?"

"I can't help it."

"You aren't afraid of me, are you?"

"No. Of course not."

"How old are you?"

"Twenty-nine."

"Then you're not a virgin." I made a statement.

"I was married for seven years. No. I'm no longer a virgin."

It must have been my fault. I was rushing her along too fast. There was no hurry. I could wait. I had a hunch she would be worth it. We walked back to the car. I started the engine, turned on the heater, and we sat and talked. She told me her husband had been dead for three years and that I was the first man she had gone out with since. I believed her.

"What do you do with your free time then? You must go out some."

"I do," she said. "I go to movies once in a while with my girlfriend. But I really don't have much time to myself. I work from ten till seven-thirty, and when I get home I have to take care of the animals and clean up the apartment. By that time it's time to go to bed. I get up at nine-thirty, and always just barely make it to work on time. That takes care of six days, doesn't it? Then on Sunday I go to the cemetery, and to a movie that evening."

It was a dull and horrible life she pictured.

"Do you like your work?"

"Oh, yes!"

"Do you stand or sit?"

"I stand, but I don't mind because I'm so busy."

"I see. Well, Alyce, maybe I can make life more interesting for you."

"That's what I'm afraid of."

I could see her face in the faint light from the streetlamp. She wasn't smiling. The lines from the wings of her nose to the corners of her mouth were deep and tragic.

"Mother used to tell me to go out all the time. But I couldn't really leave her when she was home. She was ill, and couldn't bear to be alone. And now, since she died, there hasn't been much meaning to my life."

"You're a young woman, Alyce. You shouldn't brood over things like that. There are a great many years ahead of you."

"I know it and I hate it. I don't feel very good, Russell. Will you take me home?"

"All right," I said. I drove toward her apartment and we didn't speak. She looked out the window at the fuzzy neon lighting that wavered through the fog. Again, two blocks away from her home, she asked me to stop.

"I'll walk the rest of the way," she said.

"What for?"

"It was nice of you to take me out, Russell, and I had a wonderful time. But I don't want to see you anymore."

"Why?"

"I think it would be best."

"I don't. And I intend to take you out again tomorrow night." She thought that over for a moment.

"Please don't!" She put her face in her hands and began to cry.

"What the hell are you crying for? I haven't done anything to you."

"It's what I've done to you." She continued to cry.

"You haven't done anything to me. You just don't feel good, that's all. Your stomach is probably indignant over the load of shrimp."

"No, that isn't it." She blew her nose and dabbed at her eyes with a postage-stamp handkerchief. I handed her mine.

"We'll talk about it tomorrow," I said.

"All right then." She started to get out of the car.

"I'll drive you the rest of the way."

"No. I'll walk. Goodnight, Russell." I watched her walk down the hill.

She had a beautiful posture.

I sat there for a few minutes smoking a cigarette. I flipped the butt out the window, then drove to a business district. I parked and went into a bar. I ordered a straight gin with a dash of bitters. Sipping it, I looked over the customers. The man next to me was my size. I put my drink down, raised my elbow level with my shoulder, and spun on my heel. My elbow caught him just below the eye. He raised a beer bottle over his head and my fist caught him flush on the jaw. He dropped to the floor and lay still. I threw a half-dollar on the bar and left. No one looked in my direction as I closed the door.

I felt a little better but not enough. I drove home, and dug through my LP albums till I found the *Romeo and Juliet Overture.* There are three speakers rigged up around the walls of my living room, and when I put the music on full volume it filled the room like the symphony orchestra was right there. I poured a glass full of gin and played the overture several times while I finished the drink. After this emotional bath I felt wonderful. I went to bed and slept soundly all night. Like a child.

Chapter Five

By nine a.m. the next morning the sun decided to burn its way through the clouds and let San Francisco take a look at it. I took my coat off, put my cuff links in my pocket, and rolled up my sleeves. Business picked up.

Not that I sold any cars that morning, but people appeared on the lot and I talked and talked to them. I like to talk about anything to anybody when I feel good and I felt great with the sun on me and the ready listeners crowding the lot. By 11:30 I was in such a good mood that when I went into the office to check out for lunch, and saw Madeleine twitching her behind around, I asked her to have lunch with me. She jumped at the chance.

I took her to Kang's Eastern House. I lapped up some Chicken Chow Mein and Egg Foo Young while she ate almost half of her Chicken Fried Rice. Women don't eat much. Foolish, foolish. I believe a person should take advantage of anything that gives him pleasure. When you figure that this rock we're living on is spinning around once a day every day, 365 spins a year, and with each day you get a day older, what the hell does an extra inch or two around the waistline mean? An extra inch or two. Period.

Madeleine was pretty sitting there across the table. She wore her bleached hair short and practical. The suit she had on was smart, and she was eating with her gloves on. I didn't remind her to take them off because I had an idea she had spilled ink on her hands or had changed a typewriter ribbon.

I smiled at her, a tolerant smile.

"Well, hello!" I said.

"Are you finally coming up for air?" She laughed.

"I was hungry." I lighted a cigarette. "We're going to have to do this again, Madge."

"I don't like to eat alone, either." She took one of my cigarettes and I tossed her the book of matches I was holding. She was ready. Definitely. I opened my mouth to ask her for a date that night and just as suddenly thought of Alyce. I changed my mind. Madeleine would be around for a while. It would be best to continue on with Alyce. There was something there, something intangible perhaps, but something interesting.

"If you're through counting the number of grains of rice on your plate, let's go back to work," I said.

We returned to the lot. That afternoon I settled down and sold used cars. A guy showed up in a crummy pair of overalls and paid $1300 cash for a Chevy. Before I tossed the roll to Madeleine, I removed my commission. She shook her head in surprise at the bundle of cash.

I sold a jalopy worth twenty-five bucks for eighty to two high school kids, and knocked down twenty of it on Tad Tate. What he didn't know wouldn't hurt him.

A man I'd been calling for a week showed up at 4:00 and I managed to convince him that a Pontiac convertible was the only car in the world for him. It was a good day. I checked out, driving home in a Studebaker Champion.

The apartment was in rough shape. Dust balls as big as my head rolled around the floor. The sink was full of dirty dishes. There were no clean towels. Every ashtray was full to overflowing. I picked up the telephone and called Mrs Wren. She's been doing my cleaning for two years and does a good job. I don't like to have her come at a regular time, but just call her when I need her, and happen to notice how lousy everything looks. She said she'd be over the next day, so I put a twenty in an envelope, wrote her name on it, and weighted it with a bottle of ink on my desk.

I gathered my dirty laundry all over the apartment and piled it on the bed. I pulled the sheets loose and tied the four corners around the laundry. I called the Chinaman and he was knocking on the door in five minutes.

"Hello, Tommy," I said. "Can you get this stuff back by tomorrow morning?"

"Sure thing, Mr Haxby."

"Fine. Put it on my bill."

"Sure thing, Mr Haxby."

After all that slave labor I was hungry so I went into the kitchen. There were no clean plates. I opened a can of beans and dumped them into a pie tin, chopped a few wieners and shoved the loaded tin under the broiler. I made coffee and buttered some rye bread. The beans and wieners timed out to the coffee. I ate the mess and threw the tin in with the dirty dishes. Finding the creme de cacao, I filled a jelly glass half full, filled it the rest of the way with canned milk, and dumped in a half-dozen cherries. I killed this concoction listening to the news. Nothing was new. My eyes caught T.S. Eliot's *Collected Poems.*

I took the book out of the stacks and flipped through the pages to *Burnt Norton.* I put Bartok's *Miraculous Mandarin* ballet suite on the record player and read *Burnt Norton* aloud. This is a real esoteric kick. The doom of doom in that long poem combined with the exhilarating effect of Bartok is so exciting that it drains your blood right into your feet and makes your heart beat like a Chinese gong. I finished reading the poem and turned off the player. I had to rest for a few minutes until the blood returned to my cheeks.

I showered and dressed, selecting a blue gabardine suit and a knitted yellow tie, and crumpled a yellow silk handkerchief into my breast pocket. It was a good effect. Before I left the apartment I had a brandy.

It was now after eight, so there was no use trying to pick Alyce up at Miller's Garage. I drove into the middle of town. The streetcars weren't running that week because of the strike so I parked in the middle of Market. The sidewalk was crowded. It had been a long time since I had drifted along with the window-shoppers on Market Street. I entered a bar. It was jammed with servicemen and barflies. Loud, noisy, and full of smoke. I shoved my way in between two people at the bar, and ordered a shot of straight gin. I had to pay for the drink before the bartender would release his hold on the glass. I liked the noise of the place. There was a jukebox playing a hillbilly number and wrestlers on the TV screen. A young soldier on my right was wearing the blue ribbon for Korean service. I bought him a drink, drank my shot of gin and left.

A few doors down I entered a liquor store and bought a fifth of gin and a fifth of vermouth. I spotted a strangely shaped bottle of peach liqueur and bought it too. I opened it and took a drink. It had a sweet sickening taste.

"Hey!" the man shouted, noticing me. "You can't drink in here! You want me to lose my license?" He was a small ferret of a man in his balding thirties.

"I can't?"

"It's the law. I didn't make it." He was smug.

I threw the bottle at him. Startled, he ducked, and the bottle broke on the concrete floor, flooding a three-foot square with yellow sticky goo.

"Oops," I said.

It was worth the eleven bucks the bottle cost to see the expression on his face.

I got into the car and drove to Alyce's apartment. There was no room in front to park, but I noticed the light was on in her upstairs window. At the same time I got a knotted feeling in the pit of my stomach. A premonition. I was used to getting them. My back got a chill in it. It was like getting a toenail caught in a wool blanket. I parked up the street and walked back to Alyce's apartment.

I pushed the bell and waited.

When Alyce opened the door there was fear in her eyes.

Her eyes were large and brown anyway, but now they were wider and flecked with dancing gold spots. She tried to slam the door but I saw her intention and held it open with my hand. I stepped inside.

"You don't seem happy to see me," I said.

"Russell," she whispered it. "You can't come in!"

"I am in."

"I told you not to come here, but to meet me at the garage."

"I had to work late," I lied.

"Please go." She tried to shove me but I didn't budge. "Meet me at the garage tomorrow and I'll explain."

"I'd better shut the door. We're in a draft." I closed the door behind me and climbed the stairs. Alyce climbed them behind me pulling on my coat. She got a free ride up the stairs. The kitchen was the first door on the right from the stairwell. I went to the sink and took the gin and vermouth out of the sack. Alyce closed the door. She was close to tears.

"Please, please, please, Russell! You can't stay!"

"Don't get excited, Alyce. I'm sorry I'm a little late, but I'm here now. Right? Let's have a drink and talk things over. Everything's going to be all right."

I mixed two Martinis and handed one to Alyce, but she wouldn't take it.

"No," she said. "Please drink yours and then go. Can't you see I don't want you here?"

"Why?"

"I'll explain tomorrow. Right now I can't."

"Here's to you, Alyce. Woman of Mystery." I drained my glass, picked up the drink I'd made for Alyce, pushed her away from the door, opened it, and walked down the hall to the living room.

There was a barefooted man sitting in the Victorian chair watching cowboys gallop across the television screen.

He was wearing a once-white terrycloth bathrobe. His hair was composed of black and white pinstripes, and his beard looked like spilled salt and pepper. He didn't take his eyes off the screen. Something was the matter with him. I couldn't put my finger on it for a moment, then it struck me like a jab under the heart. He didn't have his marbles. No one had to tell me. It was one of those things you know instinctively. But perhaps I was wrong. I turned and looked at Alyce.

She was leaning against the door. Her smile was a sickly twisted grimace; the sort a prisoner gives the judge when he's asked if he has anything to say before he's sentenced. She stood away from the door and held her chin a shade too high.

"Mr Haxby," she said, "I'd like you to meet my husband, Mr Salvatore Vitale. Salvatore, Mr Haxby."

Salvatore wrenched his deep-set eyes away from the television screen and looked into my face, but not my eyes.

I knew he was crazy.

Chapter Six

 was startled.

This was the kind of a deal that men pulled on women—not women on men. Alyce had been very clever. I raised my glass to Mr Vitale.

"How do you do?" I grinned, and poured the drink down my throat.

"Mr Haxby is a used-car salesman," Alyce said.

"I'm watching television," Salvatore said.

"That's nice," I said.

"Salvatore likes television," Alyce said.

"That's nice." I said.

"Hop, Hop, Hopalong Cassidy." Salvatore explained and he pointed to the screen.

"Yes," I said. Salvatore returned his attention to the set and I looked at Alyce. I raised my eybrows. She averted her eyes and left the room. I followed her into the kitchen and closed the door behind us.

"How long did you think you could get away with it, Alyce?"

"I don't know." She was close to tears. I wanted to make them flow.

"What you've pulled on me, Alyce, I wouldn't have done to a dirty yellow dog. A person who is married has a sacred trust. To go out with an upstanding fellow who had the best of intentions and to take advantage of his ignorance is a rotten dirty trick."

"I'm sorry," she said. She was properly contrite, and covered her face with her hands.

"I suppose that makes it all right. You're sorry."

"You just don't understand, that's all."

"I understand that a good way to get killed is to go out with a married woman. Especially when you don't know it and aren't on your guard. Well, Alyce. I won't be seeing you around." I screwed the caps on the two opened bottles and put them in the paper sack. I started to leave and Alyce blocked the door.

"Please, Russell. Let me explain. I'll make Salvatore go to bed, then we can go into the living room and talk."

I shrugged with pretended indifference. I was anxious to hear the story.

"If you don't think he'd mind. He seemed to be quite interested in Hopalong Cassidy."

"I'll make him go to bed." She left the kitchen and I mixed myself another drink.

I was very happy at the turn of events. What a fascinating situation to be in! I hadn't suspected for a minute that she was married. I listened to her argue with her husband in the living room. He was quite reluctant to go to bed.

Of course, there had been a few clues, had I been sharp enough to catch them. The smell of the chair I had noticed the night I brought her home. And after that, meeting her at the garage instead of the aparment. Letting her out of the car two blocks away instead of in front of the door. It shaped up in my mind. I was glad I hadn't paid any attention to the clues. It was much more interesting this way.

Salvatore's bare feet flapped through the hall and disappeared somewhere in the rear of the apartment. Alyce opened the door. Her face was drawn, the lines from her nose to her mouth deeper, nose white. She forced a brave sad smile.

"Come into the living room, Russell."

The television set was off. After Alyce closed the door we sat together on the sofa. She looked at me. I attempted a hurt expression, but I couldn't hold it. Suddenly we both burst into laughter. It was a funny situation.

"I'm sorry, Russell, really I am," she said when she had quieted down. "It was such a shock to see you at the door downstairs. I fully intended to tell you about Salvatore, but in my own way, and in my own time. That is, when I could think of a way."

"I should have been put on my guard the first night. Was he here when you brought me home?"

"I took a chance. Salvatore was in bed, and he sleeps like a dead man once he goes to sleep. I tried to get away with it, and I did. Honestly, Russell, you're the first man I've gone out with since I've been married, and I couldn't bear to see you get away. I think," she turned her head away from me, "that I'm in love with you."

The admission came hard to her. It must have been the first time she had ever said it to a man. However, it was easy for me to say it.

"I know I love you, Alyce." I pretended to get a lump in my throat.

She kissed me then, a girlish unskilled kiss, but wet and sincere.

"Salvatore," I jerked my head, "is right down the hall."

"Salvatore!" She said it bitterly.

"He's off his rocker, isn't he?"

"Yes." She nodded.

"How long?"

"Almost four years now. You see, he's twenty years older than I am."

"He looks more than that."

"He didn't used to. He was a friend of my father's. The whole thing is so stupid, yet it's simple too.

"I was at home with mother all the time. Mother never let me out unless she went along. Even when I was in high school, she took me, and picked me up afterwards. Father died when I was still in school. Salvatore was a successful man then and used to come around after father died, ostensibly to see mother, but he really had his eye on me. We were hard up too. Just the insurance and not much of that. Salvatore would give me candy, money, take me to movies, buy me clothes, and even let me drive his car. Mother didn't see through him either; just thought he was being nice, you see, because he had known and liked my father. All of a sudden I was in pretty deep. He asked me to marry him. I was just nineteen."

"Were you sleeping with him at the time?" Alyce was shocked.

"Oh, no!" She smiled wryly. "I was ignorant then. Stupid! I didn't even know about such things. When we did get married and he took off his clothes, and I realized what he wanted to do to me I went out of my head with fear. He had to get a doctor to come to the hotel and give me a sedative."

"Just a minute, Alyce. You mean to tell me that you went to high school here in San Francisco and didn't even know the facts of life?"

"I didn't have the slightest idea even. Mother never told

me anything and I didn't have any close girlfriends to tell me. I was terribly fat in high school and not very popular."

"It seems funny."

"It wasn't at the time. It was horrible. He didn't touch me then for another year. He kept bringing books home on the subject and making me read them. I couldn't hold out then. It was my duty as a wife so . . . I steeled myself, then I, well, I worked out a schedule for him. You wouldn't be interested in that."

"Sure I would." I was, too.

"He wasn't. After a few weeks he told me to take the schedule and do something with it."

"I'm not surprised." I laughed.

"Why? It seemed fair to me. I was doing my duty and being just as fair as I knew how. It was miserable for me, yet I was willing. I don't see why he couldn't meet me halfway . . ." She shook her head. She still didn't know why. "We were living in a house then. Mother was with us and Salvatore was making twelve thousand a year. The shipyard. He's working there now for a dollar thirty-five an hour as a common laborer."

"How did it happen? When did you first know he was losing his mind?"

"One night after supper. He sat down in his chair and didn't move for twenty-four hours."

"Did you have a television set then?"

"No. He just sat staring at the wall with a sort of blank look and I couldn't budge him. He wouldn't talk or anything. We called a doctor and he said that Salvatore was merely overworked and then he left. He wouldn't eat. Nothing. Just sat there. I finally called an ambulance but when we got to the hospital they wouldn't admit him. I had to pay for the ambulance coming to the house even. I tried three more hospitals before I could get one to take him and then they only kept him for two days. I took him to doctors and they'd examine him but none could say what was wrong. At last, he was given a blood test and that was it. Paresis."

"Syphilis?"

"Quite advanced. The doctors said at least ten years or more. It was too late to do anything hardly. We had ten thousand dollars in the bank. I spent it all in the next year on specialists and treatments. Then I had him put in an institution upstate. I had to go to work."

"You committed him?"

"No. I could never do a thing like that. I would never stand up in an open court and say my husband was crazy. It wasn't easy to get him in the institution but I did get him in. He didn't recognize me for six months."

"Did you visit him there?"

"Every Sunday. Mother and I. We'd leave San Francisco at six a.m. and we wouldn't get back till late Sunday night. Then when Salvatore got so he knew me I brought him home. The doctor said I'd bring him back in a week but I didn't. He's been home ever since, and gradually getting better. He can read the newspaper a little, but he still can't write very well. He's working though. He works too hard, but he doesn't get tired."

"Who takes care of him when you aren't here?"

"Mother used to before she died, and then I got Ruthie to come and live with me. He does lots of things for himself now but I still have to make his lunches. I hate to make lunches." She was trying to make me understand what a hard time she'd had. "Russell, you have no idea how hard this all was for me. I didn't know how to get a job or what to do if I got one. I worked all over the city in all kinds of jobs. No one knows I'm married. I've kept it a secret. Not even down at the garage or anyplace."

"I guess you've had a rough time all right."

"Especially since mother died." She put her head on my shoulder and began to sob quietly. I put the story together in my head. It was screwy enough to be the truth. Evidently she was just about as sexy as a Tierra del Fuegian. But maybe all that could be changed. I played it tenderly.

"Darling, darling Alyce. Don't cry. Everything is going to be all right. We'll work something out. You'll see."

She brightened. "Do you really think so, Russell?"

"Sure. Wait till this agile brain of mine starts working. I'll think of something."

"I love you, Russell. I think you're just wonderful."

"I am. Remember, Alyce: 'Love will find a way.'"

"'Love will find a way.' I'll remember that. You see, I'm still married. I never got a divorce. It didn't seem fair to get a divorce until Salvatore was well again, so I've just drifted along in a rut. So I can't even think of getting married till I've got a divorce."

I didn't like the change in the tone of the conversation. I got to my feet. Alyce was getting way ahead of herself.

"Where's Ruthie?" I said.

"She's on a case. She won't be home till tomorrow morning sometime, I guess."

"What shipyard does Salvatore work for?"

"The Pittman. Why?"

"I just wondered, that's all."

I looked at Alyce, half-sitting, half-reclining on the sofa. She was wearing a housecoat that had a zipper down the front. Her figure under the sleazy material was well defined, heavy breasted, deep soft hips. All I had to do was pull the zipper down. Maybe ... It would be too easy. I didn't want it that way. I put my hat on.

"I'll leave the gin and vermouth here, Alyce. What are you going to tell Salvatore about me?"

"I'll just tell him you're a used-car salesman who wants me to trade in my car on a better one."

"Fine. That way I can come here to the apartment."

She shook her head. "You'd better not. He does everything I tell him to do, but he gets awful jealous, and that makes him hard to manage. He's a lot like a pet. He even gets jealous of the cats when I make over them. So it would really be better if you didn't come here except when he's out. At a movie, or at work, or something."

"All right. I'll pick you up at the garage tomorrow night."

"That will be wonderful."

I lifted her to her feet and kissed her. She was still inflexible. She couldn't help it. It was just distasteful to her. I cut the kiss short. As I turned to leave she did a peculiar thing. She stuck her hand out. I took it in mine and we shook hands gravely.

"Good night, darling." She said it like she meant it.

I left.

Chapter Seven

I kicked the Champion across town. My mind was busy and I drove unconsciously. There were foreign thoughts in my head. Alyce was the kind of woman that men married. And a man could do worse. But a man like me, thirty-three years old, who had never been married, could never marry. There's a time in a man's life when it's possible. But when that time goes by it's too late. What was making me sore was the thought that I might have missed something. As I put the car in the garage I came to the conclusion that if I had met Alyce ten years before I would have married her. She was the perfect type for it. Simple-minded, loyal, and kind. The type that doesn't worry you, who takes what is offered, and expects nothing. It was too bad I hadn't met her ten years before. Too bad. Too bad for me and too bad for Alyce.

I made a cucumber and avocado sandwich and brewed a pot of coffee. While the coffee perked I changed to pyjamas and a dressing gown. It was early. I thought of my project. It had been a long time since I'd written anything. I got out paper, took the cover off the portable and inserted a piece of paper in the machine. James Joyce's *Ulysses* and Stuart Gilbert's *Study* were side by side in the bookstacks. I took the books to the desk and started to work.

As a rule, *Ulysses* never fails me. I worked for an hour

taking archaic words from the text and converting them to words in current usage. After changing the words in a paragraph, I would rewrite the paragraph in simple terms. I'd been doing this for years as a form of relaxation and had a good-sized pile of manuscripts stacked up. Someday I planned to write a book describing the system I worked by, and would utilize my converted text as an appendix. It was a brilliant idea and it would pay off some day, plus bringing a great book to a simple-minded audience. There was no hurry. It was a hobby more than anything else, and when I finished *Ulysses* I could do the same thing with *Finnegans Wake.*

But after an hour I was tired of it. I was restless and didn't want to work. I didn't want to read and I didn't want to drink. The radio couldn't hold my interest. After a boring newscast I shut it off.

I relaxed in a chair and thought of ways to get rid of Salvatore. The bastard. A syphilitic bastard like that marrying an innocent girl like Alyce. I leaped out of the chair.

Her name was in the telephone book and she answered.

"This is Russell, Alyce."

"I was asleep."

"Alyce. Listen, did you get . . . were you infected? Did you have any checks made on you after you found out about Salvatore?"

"Do you mean did I get anything?"

"Yes. Of course that's what I mean."

"It was sweet of you to think of that, Russell."

"Well. Did you?"

"No. I don't know why but I didn't. I had every kind of test they could think of."

"How come you didn't take tests before you got married?

It's a state law."

"I know it is. I thought it would be more romantic to go to Reno. Over there we didn't have to take any tests."

"That's right. I'm sorry I woke you up, Alyce, but I had to know."

"It was nice of you to call."

"No it wasn't. I love you, that's why."

"And I love you."

"Where does Salvatore sleep now?"

"He sleeps in the bedroom behind mine. Why, you didn't think—?"

"I just asked, that's all."

"He sleeps in the bedroom behind mine and I lock the door as soon as he goes to sleep. I make him go to the bathroom first, before he goes to bed, and then he sleeps all night."

"He can't get out at all?"

"Not unless I unlock the door."

"Well, I'm sorry I woke you. Go on back to bed. I'll see you tomorrow."

"Goodnight, dear." She hung up. I slammed my receiver on the cradle. Russell Haxby: Jealous Lover! I had to laugh. But just the same I was glad I called. A man should never let anything bother him or prey on his mind.

I dialed Mary Ellen. She would be available for the night. Her roommate answered the telephone.

"Hello, Diane. This is Russell Haxby. Is Mary Ellen home?"

"No she isn't, Russell. And I don't know when she'll be back either."

"Oh. What are you doing at home, anyway?"

"Just sitting here."

"Listen, Diane, don't get the idea you're playing second fiddle, but I'm giving a little party and I'm short a girl. So I happened to think of Mary Ellen. Do you think you can come over?"

"Who all's there?"

"You know everybody. Don't worry."

"I don't know a soul on Telegraph Hill and you know it."

"You know me."

"Oh." The line was silent while Diane thought it over. She wasn't stupid. "How do I get there?"

"Call Eddie at Domino Cab. He knows the way. It's easier than trying to tell you."

"All right. Give me fifteen minutes."

"Fine. Tell Eddie to put it on my bill." I hung up.

I made a shaker of stingers. The cigarette boxes were empty and I filled them. I stacked the record player with LPs and smoked a cigarette. The doorbell rang. I shoved the buzzer and Diane came up the stairs. She had made it in twelve minutes. I helped her off with her coat. All she had underneath it was a nightgown. I laughed like hell. We drank the shaker of stingers and went to bed.

Diane slept soundly beside me. Every once in a while she gave a gentle snore. I couldn't sleep at all. My mind kept turning Alyce's story over and over looking for flaws. I had her on my mind and it was keeping me from my sleep. And that irritated me. I finally dropped off but the last time I looked at my watch it read 3:30.

Diane woke me in the morning. She was standing in the doorway with my dressing gown on. The hem was dragging the floor.

"Want some breakfast?" she said when my eyes were open.

"Sure. Four eggs over light and twenty slabs of bacon."

"What's the matter—aren't you hungry?" She went into the kitchen and I went into the bathroom. As I took my wristwatch off I noticed it was a quarter of eight. I grabbed a towel and rushed into the kitchen.

"Diane, you've got to get out of here right now."

"Before breakfast?"

"As soon as possible. The cleaning woman is coming this morning and I forgot all about it."

"So what?"

"I don't want her to see you, that's all."

"All right, if you say so, but it looks funny to me."

The doorbell rang.

"Goddam it," I said, "that's her now. Too late." I pushed the buzzer and instead of Mrs Wren the Chinaman came up the stairs with my laundry. I took it away from him and tossed the bundle on a chair. I got the keys to the Champion out of my pants and shoved them at Diane.

"Here," I said. "Take my car. I'll drop by and get it this evening."

"Have we got any plans for tonight?" She put on her coat.

"Go on. Beat it. I'll talk to you tonight." I gave her a dismissal kiss and she went downstairs. From the window, I watched her back down the driveway. She was a good driver. I suddenly smelled the bacon burning and rushed into the kitchen and shut off the stove. Toast was burning in the oven. I threw the charred bread onto the sideboard. Mrs Wren let herself in with her key and came right into the kitchen. She stood in the doorway with her thick hands folded on her considerable stomach and shook her blue dyed curls.

"The bachelor breakfast," she said. "When are you going

to get a wife, Mr Haxby, and start living a decent life?"

"If I could find someone like you, I would get married."

"Aah! There's plenty of nice girls in San Francisco would give their eyeteeth to get you, Mr Haxby."

"Who wants a girl without any eyeteeth?"

"Go on. Get dressed. I'll fix your breakfast."

"Fine. If I had a wife, Mrs Wren, do you know what I'd have for breakfast?"

"A decent meal."

"No I wouldn't. I'd have an argument."

I showered and dressed, taking my time. I wore a grey tweed suit with a green-and-gold striped tie. I had to open my laundry before I could run down a white handkerchief with a green border for my breast pocket. I went into the kitchen.

Mrs Wren kept up a running tirade while I wolfed the sausages and eggs. It was music to me. I loved to have her bawl me out. It reminded me of my mother when I was a boy. That sort of noise had fallen on my deafened ears throughout childhood. It was nice to hear again.

"All right, Mrs Wren. You find a girl for me and I'll get married. Okay?"

"I know plenty, don't worry. You come to church this Sunday. I'll introduce you to some nice girls."

"Okay. I'll be there this Sunday. Have them all in line."

"Aah! First off I would have to use dynamite to get you in a church."

I laughed at her. She was a character.

"How are the boys, Mrs Wren?"

"Both are fine. They write me. Not as often as I would wish but good for them. Tommy is in Tokyo now and Daniel in Germany. You would think the army would keep brothers together, wouldn't you?"

"The army does funny things, Mrs Wren. They even made me a captain."

"I didn't know you were ever in the army, Mr Haxby. You never told me that before."

"Sure. I'll show you a picture of me in a uniform." I went into the living room, unlocked the desk drawer, and showed her the photograph taken when I received the DSC from Patton. "There you are."

"You looked so handsome in your uniform."

"Yeah." I locked the photo back in the drawer and drank another cup of coffee. Mrs Wren was now elbow deep in dishwater at the sink. I took a ten dollar bill out of my wallet and put it on the shelf in front of her.

"Here. You send your boys some extra cigarettes. They get enough to smoke but they need extra sometimes."

"Is it all right?"

"Sure it is. Your money's in an envelope on the desk. I got to get moving."

"Thank you, Mr Haxby. I'll tell the boys it was from you."

"You do that."

I left the house and walked three blocks before I could catch a cab for the used-car lot.

Chapter Eight

I didn't feel like working. To kill time I sat in a car and listened to its radio. It had been a long time since I'd listened to early morning radio programs. The programs were good. There was more music for one thing and it was better music. Andy came by and moaned about me using the radio without the engine running.

"Listen, Andy," I told him, "if you don't like it keep your face shut about it. Otherwise, I'll give you a fatter lip than you've already got."

He walked away muttering. I jumped out of the car and caught up with him. I spun him around.

"What'd you say?"

"I didn't say nothing, Mr Haxby."

"You better not, Andy." I let go of his shirt. My hand had grease on it. "Just a minute." I took a clean rag out of his pocket, wiped my hand and gave it back. I returned to the car and sat down again. Looking down the length of the lot I spotted a man wandering about. I snapped the radio off and walked down to see what he wanted. It was Stanley Sinkiewicz.

"Well, Stanley. Made up your mind, huh?"

"Hello, Mr Haxby." He had a shy grin on his wrinkled face. "To tell you the truth, I've been studying buying a used car for a long time now. But I just been putting it off."

"Now is the time to buy. In another month they're going sky-high. The Government, you know."

"That's what I figured."

"You're figuring right. When Ruthie told me you were thinking about a car, I came down here the next morning and put one away for you. I could have sold it twice yesterday."

"She said you'd give me a good deal." He was hesitant.

"That's what friends are for."

"I know. But business is business."

"I don't own this business." I got confidential. "I just work here. It don't come out of my pocket." I winked slowly, punched him in the ribs.

"I know what you mean." He laughed. "What kind is it?" He rubbed his hands together.

"I'll show you." I took him to the fourth row, where we kept the heaps, and showed him the Essex I'd marked up from seventy-five to two-fifty. He admired the ancient vehicle. Then he noticed the price and shook his head.

"I can't do it, Mr Haxby. That's too much."

I stepped into the cleared space between the rows of cars and looked carefully all around to see if anyone was looking. Nobody was. I marked out the fifty on the windshield.

"There you are, Stanley. Two hundred. And as far as I'm concerned the hell with my commission. Give me one-eighty and you can drive it off the lot."

"That's a real buy."

"Sure it is."

"All right. I'll buy her." He pulled an old-fashioned purse from his pants and opened it. It was bulging with tens and twenties. Somehow, I wasn't surprised. He counted out $180 and handed it to me. It didn't make a dent in the wad in the purse. I took him into the office and we filled out the papers. Afterwards, I walked him back to the Essex and showed him how to start it. He was like a six-year-old with a new electric train.

"Russell," he said (after this first-class bargain I was now in the first-name class). "I want you to do me a favor. If Ruthie asks you how much I paid for this car, I'd like to have you tell her one hundred dollars."

"What for?"

"Just for a favor, that's all."

"Sure. Why not?"

"I'll appreciate it. It's a favor to me. Another one." He patted the steering wheel.

"Be glad to do it."

"Why don't you and Alyce have dinner with me and Ruthie?"

"All right."

"It's on me," he added.

"Fine. I'll see you over at the apartment around eight."

"That's a good time. I'll go over early and put the dummy in a movie so he'll be out of the way." His wrinkled features took on a mysterious look. "You know about the dummy, don't you?"

"Sure."

"I didn't want to let the cat out of the bag, but you'd have found out anyways."

"Don't worry. I know all about him."

"Good. See you tonight then." He drove the heap off the lot.

It was the easiest hundred I had ever made. What Ruthie didn't know wouldn't hurt her. And if she asked me how much the Essex cost I'd just wink and keep my mouth shut.

I called Alyce from Thrifty's and told her about the dinner invitation. She wasn't happy about it.

"I can't leave Salvatore at home all alone."

"Stanley said he'd put him in a movie. Don't worry about it."

"All right. I can't let Salvatore tie me down all my life. Can I?"

"I hope not. I'll see you around eight." I hung up.

Tad Tate drove his MG onto the lot and we talked business for a while. I told him about selling the Essex for one-eighty and he laughed like hell.

"You're a no-good bastard and I love you," he said.

We matched half dollars for about half an hour and Tad took me for nine bucks. He offered to buy me a drink and I told Madeleine we'd be gone for awhile. We drove to his hotel for the drink so he could show me the new vicuna sport coat his tailor had made for him.

"Where's the vest, Tad?" I asked him.

"Whoever heard of a vicuna vest?" He laughed. He had a rich phlegmy laugh and always had to spit afterwards. When he went into the bathroom to spit I mixed a Scotch and soda for him and a gin and quinine water for myself. He had a nice room. All of the hotel stuff had been thrown out and a good decorator had fixed it up. It wasn't modern like my apartment, but it was comfortable and suited his personality. I'd asked Tad once why he liked to live in a hotel and he had said it was the security. I didn't blame him. Someday, I'd be just as rich; then I'd live in a hotel for the security.

We finished the drink and I went back to the lot. I skipped lunch and pushed the iron all afternoon. I didn't make any sales but did line up some prospectives. At 4:30 I told

Madeleine to lock up, and I took the keys off the rack for the lone Lincoln Continental we had on the lot. This is the best and most beautiful car ever made. If I were to buy a car, this is the kind I would buy.

After I drove home I had plenty of time so I took it. I soaked in the tub reading *Time,* dressed with care, finally choosing a gray pinstripe suit, and a blue shirt with a darker blue-and-gold striped tie. After dressing, I finished the *Time,* then worked a couple of chess problems. I got intrigued with the second problem and when I looked at my watch it was a quarter after eight.

I drove to Alyce's apartment and parked in her garage-way. They were waiting for me: Stanley in his wrinkled suit, Ruthie in a beaded dress, and Alyce lovely in a rose pinafore and Swedish blouse that must have cost her a week's pay. There was a shaker of Martinis on the table and I poured one. It tasted halfway decent for a change.

"Sorry I'm late," I said, "but I had a couple of problems that came up at the last minute."

"I'm crazy about the car," Ruthie said.

"It's old," I said, "but it'll give Stanley a lot of service."

"It ain't a bad car," Stanley said.

"Where do we eat, Stanley? I'm hungry," I said.

"Suit yourself, Russell. It's my treat. Any place you say."

"How about Antonio's? Do you like Italian food?"

"I love it," Ruthie said.

Stanley and Ruthie went downstairs, but I hung back to kiss Alyce a couple of times. I messed up her lipstick and when she went into her bedroom to fix it I followed her, checking the bedroom where Salvatore was supposed to sleep. She'd told me the truth. Stanley and Ruthie were sitting in the Essex when we joined them downstairs and I made them get out and get into the Lincoln. I wanted to get to Antonio's.

After parking in the alley we went inside. Antonio fawned over me as usual and gave us a good table. I ordered a special non-fattening salad for Alyce, then spoke to Ruthie and Stanley.

"Suppose we just let Antonio fix us up with a dinner? What do you say?"

Stanley nodded gravely. Ruthie wasn't so sure.

"This place looks like a dump to me."

"I'll give you a good dinner, don't worry." Antonio didn't like the crack about the place looking like a dump. He left in a huff.

"You hurt his feelings, Ruthie," I said.

"The hell with that greaseball. Can we get a drink or not?"

I signaled a waiter and ordered drinks. It was an excellent dinner. Minestrone, ravioli, chicken cacciatore, hot garlic bread and a hot maple pudding of some kind for dessert. Alyce watched wistfully as the three of us wolfed it down. I ordered brandy all around and when it arrived poured mine into my coffee.

"I'll take care of the waiter, Stanley," I said. "He's a good boy." I threw a five dollar bill on the table. He looked at the tip strangely and waited apprehensively for the check. I watched his face as he read it. His chin dropped eight inches. I couldn't see how much it was but I knew it would be close to thirty dollars. It was. Ruthie's eyes read TILT when Stanley reluctantly opened his old-fashioned purse and laid three ten dollar bills on the table. The waiter picked them up, plus my five, and didn't bring back any change. We left.

The pair in the backseat was a silent pair as we drove back to the apartment. They got out of the car and I thanked Stanley for the dinner. He grunted and got into the Essex. Ruthie kissed me on the cheek.

"Thanks for opening my eyes," she said. She got into the car with Stanley and they pulled away. He'd have a nice time explaining where he got the purseful of folding money. I turned to Alyce.

"Well, baby, where do you want to go? The night's getting started."

"I think I'd better go to bed. It's been a miserable day and I'm just dead."

"All right." I kissed her a couple of times, but it wasn't any fun. "You do love me, don't you?" It was hard to tell.

"Oh yes! I love you more than anything else in the world." It was hard to believe.

"You're just tired, I guess."

"I'm just dead, honestly." She sighed. "I could sit here and talk all night, but I'd better go to bed."

I reached over and opened the door for her.

"Goodnight, baby." She got out of the car, opened the apartment door and disappeared. I watched the lights flood on in the upstairs window. I gunned the engine and drove away. After circling the block I parked about fifty yards up the street and cut my lights.

I didn't have to wait long.

Alyce opened the door, got into her Chevy and headed it downtown. I followed. She parked on Market and went into the Paramount. I passed her car, double-parked a few cars down and watched through the back window. In a few minutes she came out of the movie leading Salvatore by the hand. He was gesturing wildly with his free hand, evidently unhappy about being dragged out of the movie. They got into her car. I followed her again and this time she drove directly home.

So did I.

Something would have to be done about Salvatore.

Chapter Nine

The next morning I started clicking the delicate tumblers in my agile brain. I'd had a good night's sleep, and I was slurping down my third cup of coffee. The radio was on and I listened to Don McNeil's Third Call To Breakfast. The sun was shining and it was a beautiful day.

I called the lot. Madeleine answered.

"Is Tad there?"

"Are you kidding?"

"Well, when he gets there, tell him I won't be in today."

"Did you have a bad night, Mr Haxby?" she asked sweetly.

"That's none of your business." I hung up.

I went to my desk and unlocked it. Somewhere among the mass of papers, photos, theater programs, bills and other junk, I knew I'd find my library card. I found it but it took me more than an hour. I also found my membership cards to the Legion and other veterans' organizations. When I was separated from the service I'd joined every veterans' group that asked me. This was to make sure I didn't get cheated out of any possible veterans' rights. I found that none of the organizations were any good, but the loss was nominal. I put my Legion card in my billfold and slipped the library card into my shirt pocket.

I looked up the Pittman Shipbuilding Company in the telephone book. As I suspected, their main offices were downtown and not at the docks. I made a note of the address and left the apartment. I didn't drive the Lincoln because I didn't feel like coping with the parking problem downtown. The sun felt nice on my back as I walked down the hill. Four blocks was enough and I hailed a passing cab. The driver let me off on Market when I tapped his shoulder. It was too early to go to the Pittman offices, so to make time pass I caught up on some shopping. I bought a stack of flaming sport shirts, some argyles and a new hat. I wore the hat and made arrangements for the other clothing to be delivered at my apartment after three.

The Pittman Shipbuilding Company was on the seventh floor of the Lazrus Building. It was a classy layout with thick wall-to-wall carpets and current magazines on the tables. The receptionist, a bleached blonde doubling on the switchboard, smiled in my direction.

"Good morning, sir," she said.

"I'd like to see the president, if I may."

"Mr Callahan?"

"That's right."

"Do you have an appointment?" She looked at her desk calendar.

"No. However, I'll take very little of his time. I'm the chairman of the Legion Subversive Committee."

She stared at me for a second, and I showed her my Legion membership card. She examined it closely, then disappeared behind a door marked PRIVATE. I didn't have to wait long. She reappeared and smiled again.

"Mr Callahan will see you in a few minutes. He's on the telephone."

I lighted a cigarette and watched her shuffle papers until the call was broken. She opened the door marked PRIVATE and closed it behind me. Mr Callahan, a beefy red-faced man in his fifties stood up as I came in.

"Russell Haxby," I said, and we shook hands. He indicated a chair with his forefinger.

"Sit down, Mr Haxby. You're from the Legion Subversive Committee? Is that right?"

"Yes. I'm the chairman. I know that you're a busy man and I don't like to take up much of your time, but this is a matter of vital importance to you. And, I might add, the nation."

"Yes?" I held his interest.

"It's about one of your employees."

"One of the Pittman employees?" He caught on fast.

"That's right. A certain Salvatore Vitale."

"Oh, yes." He looked at the ceiling. "I know all about him. It's a very sad case. At one time he was very high with the company."

"We know that. We also know that he held a membership in the Communist Party in 1937." His eyes left the ceiling in a hurry and looked sharply into mine.

"Salvatore Vitale?"

"That's right. We didn't think you knew that."

"But I've known Vitale for years. Do you have any definite proof of this?"

"Unfortunately, we haven't." I forced a wry smile and shook my head sadly. "That's the way these birds are. It's almost impossible to pin them down. We piece this bit of information together, another little bit, and so on, but when it comes to getting what you call definite proof—we run into a stone wall. Our laws, Mr Callahan, are designed to protect the innocent. But they also protect the guilty." I shook my head sadly again.

"I just wish I could show you some of our files, Mr Callahan. Gosh! It would open your eyes. All I can say is this: we have several leads that point to Vitale as far back as 1937. In the past few years, of course, there is almost nothing. I'm not an official Government representative. I'm a Legionnaire, and all the Legion can do is call to the attention of the employer certain bits of information we obtain. It's no more than any good citizenship organization can do. If you wish to retain Mr Vitale in your employ, knowing now what I've told you—well, then, it's strictly up to you."

I stood up. It would be best to let it go at that.

"You don't give us much to go on, Mr Haxby . . ."

"And neither do they, Mr Callahan!" I looked straight into his eyes, spun on my heel, walked to the elevator and pushed the button. I could feel his eyes on my back. As the elevator door opened I heard him ask the blonde receptionist to get him a glass of water.

I caught a cab to the Public Library. There was some research I wanted to do.

I found the books I wanted and sat down to pore over them. Smoking wasn't allowed, and I disliked the mustiness of the room and the scholarly faces on the people at my table. My books were heavy but I carried them to the desk. The librarian peered up at me from her stack of index cards. Her eyes looked like the eyes of a doll behind her thick-lensed glasses.

"I want to check these out, please," I said.

She looked at the books and shook her head. I noticed her scalp was dirty and flaked with dandruff.

"I'm sorry, sir," she said. "Those books can't leave the library. We don't have duplicates and we have to keep these here for research."

I smiled, opened my wallet, and put a ten dollar bill on the desk.

"Look, Miss, I have a thesis I have to finish by next week. Suppose you make an exception this once?"

She folded and unfolded the ten dollar bill. It was a hard decision for her to make. But she made it.

"Where's your card?" she asked. I took it out of my shirt pocket and tossed it on the desk. After she checked the books, I left the library, caught a cab and went home.

I studied the thick medical books for the rest of the afternoon. There was an interruption when my purchases of the morning arrived, but the rest of the time was spent in concentrated study. By five that evening, for all practical purposes, I could consider myself an expert on *dementia paralytica,* galloping paresis and stationary paresis. What Alyce had accomplished with Salvatore was quite remarkable in view of what I'd discovered in the medical texts. However, no matter how well he seemed to be on the road to recovery, there would be a relapse. There was bound to be. It was just a question of time.

It was up to me to hasten it.

The place for that guy was an institution anyway. He shouldn't be running around loose in San Francisco and lousing up my love life.

I found two frozen chicken pies in the refrigerator and tossed them in the oven. While they heated I perked coffee and made a salad. I ate dinner, had a drink and a cigarette and stretched out on the couch. The telephone woke me out of a deep dreamless sleep. I jerked to consciousness and answered it. It was Alyce.

"Oh, Russell, I'm so glad you're there! Can you meet me right away?"

"Sure. What's up? You sound excited."

"I'll tell you when I see you. I'm phoning from home. Will you meet me?"

"Sure. In fifteen minutes at Sammy's on Powell. Know where it is?"

"I can find it, I guess."

"Right. Fifteen minutes." I hung up.

I undressed and showered, singing *Old Man River.* Sometimes when I sing in the shower my voice sounds a lot like Billy Eckstine's. It's the resonance bouncing off the walls. There wasn't any hurry. It would take Alyce at least fifteen minutes to find Sammy's, and another five minutes to find a place to park in that congested area.

I dressed well in shades of gray, topping my appearance with a gray homburg and matching doeskin gloves. I looked like a man on his way to Washington to argue a case before the Supreme Court. Before leaving the apartment I lighted a piece of incense and the rose lamp over the radio-phonograph. When I brought Alyce to the apartment I wanted it to look and smell exotic.

I put the top back on the Continental and headed downtown for Powell.

Chapter Ten

It isn't easy to find a parking place on Powell Street after eight in the evening. I circled around for fifteen minutes, settling finally for a slot half in and half out of a red zone a block away from Sammy's Bar and Grill. I walked down the hill to Sammy's and stopped at the entrance for a moment to watch the rainbow trout swimming around in the tank. When you order trout at Sammy's you get fresh trout.

Alyce was sitting in a booth, wearing her red gabardine suit and an air of aloofness. She didn't see me and I looked admiringly at her from the archway that divided the bar from the restaurant. She has the best posture I've ever seen, a proud full bosom and a chin held imperiously high. I slid into the opposite seat. The room was dimly lighted and she looked sharply across the table. I took my hat off and put it on the seat beside me.

"Oh, I didn't recognize you for a second. I thought it was Dean Acheson." She smiled softly.

"Did you order anything?"

"No. I told the waiter I was waiting for somebody."

"Fine." I signaled the waiter. He scuttled sideways over to the table and tried to force the menu into my hand.

"No, thanks," I said. "A shot of gin and a Pink Lady." He left.

"What's a Pink Lady?" Alyce asked.

"Drink it and see. Now, what was all the secrecy about?"

"Russell, it's terrible. I got home tonight absolutely bushed. I don't remember ever working so hard. Ruthie wasn't there, and Salvatore was sitting in the living room with all the lights out bawling like a baby."

"You mean he was crying?"

"Like a child. It upset me quite a bit. He's been getting along so well lately. You know I went down to the shipyard only two weeks ago and asked the foreman how he was getting along. I wanted to know if Salvatore was doing his share. The foreman was very nice and told me that Salvatore worked harder than any man he had. He was well pleased with him. Of course, he couldn't give him any complicated jobs or anything like that, but on the jobs he knew how to do Salvatore did very well."

The waiter arrived with the drinks and I put a dollar bill on the table. He cleared his throat. It wasn't enough so I gave him another. He went away.

"What happened?"

"That's what I can't figure out. For awhile I couldn't get anything out of Salvatore at all. Then he handed me his paycheck. That surprised me, because I'd made arrangements with the company to have them make his checks out to me and mail them. I was afraid he'd lose one of them on his way home, you see. And he couldn't even write his name when he first went back to work down there."

"I didn't know they were allowed to do that."

"I don't know about that, but that's the way they did it after I talked to them. But this check was made out to Salvatore and marked 'Separation.' It had this week's money and two weeks' more."

"They just let him go, that's all."

"I know that now. But why?"

"Why don't you call and find out?"

"I did call. I called his foreman and he said he wasn't allowed to tell me. He told me he was sorry, but he also said that he didn't want Salvatore to come down there again under any circumstances."

"That certainly is unusual. Do you suppose Salvatore got violent and had a fight with somebody down there? He's a powerful man, you know."

"I thought of that. You know how men tease people like him. But the foreman would tell me nothing."

"It certainly is strange," I said, and I drank the shot of gin in one movement to keep from laughing.

Tears welled in Alyce's eyes, but she quickly checked them. She sipped her drink. I could tell it was too sweet for her by the way she pursed her lips. I lit two cigarettes and passed her one.

"Come on, Alyce," I said, "pull yourself together. I don't believe it's anything serious. He probably sassed the foreman or somebody complained about having to work with him. Something like that. It's nothing to worry about."

"I don't care about that. I mean, I do care, but I don't know what I'm going to do about Salvatore."

"There are other jobs."

"You don't understand, Russell. He's a sick man and has to have security. Security in doing the same things every day; finding the same things in the same place every day. He can't jump from job to job like ordinary men. That's why I've kept such an expensive apartment: to keep a home for him. And I had to have three bedrooms. Now, I'll be at work and he'll be around the house with no one to watch him. I don't know what to do."

"What about Ruthie? She's there, isn't she?"

"She used to be home a lot, but lately she's been working a great deal and she doesn't have any patience with him anyway. They argue all the time. He doesn't like to take orders from her—it's just a mess." She dragged heavily on her cigarette and let the smoke coil from her nose.

"There is something more important to me, Alyce. What about us?"

"Yes, what about us?" She said it bitterly. "Here I am, piling all my troubles on you. It certainly makes me attractive, doesn't it?" She made a pitiful attempt to smile. "Russell, I love you more than anything else in the world and couldn't bear to lose you now. Please try and understand the position I'm in."

"I understand all right. I think you're very noble."

"Don't say that. I'm not noble, I'm trapped. But I have to get out of it by myself. It isn't fair to drag you into it."

"It affects me. I'll help you find your way out. You see, Alyce, your whole life is a living lie. You have to tell the world you aren't married and put up a front; then you go home at night and face an impossible situation. You can't go on like that, you know. You need to live a normal happy life like other women." I used a bantering tone then. "Here you are, a young woman, and you're pouring out all the affection that should belong to me, on three cats, a dog and a nut!"

She laughed. "The way you put things." She shook her head. "Did you ever meet a woman like me before, Russell?"

"Frankly, no."

"Do you think you can put up with me?"

"It's easy to put up with you. Do you know why?"

The shake of her head was barely perceptible. I said it simply and sincerely.

"Because I love you. That's why."

That did it. The tears that were waiting in those big brown eyes began to flow freely. I handed her my handkerchief. She dabbed at her eyes and blew her nose with a refined honk.

"Darling, darling," she said, "life is pretty wonderful after all, isn't it?"

"Sure it is." I slid out of the booth. "You don't have to drink that Pink Lady. I'll get us something else." I crossed to the bar and told the bartender to send us two Gibsons. In the bar mirror I watched Alyce repair her face. There was a Magic Voice jukebox set into the wall. I dropped a quarter into the slot and waited for the voice.

"You have three selections," the Magic Voice informed me.

"Play *Claire de Lune* three times."

"Thank you, sir." The voice clicked off and the familiar piano music began to swell into the room. It sounded like Iturbi. I should have asked specifically for Erroll Garner. I returned to the booth. Alyce had her face fixed and looked like she'd stepped from the pages of *Harper's Bazaar*. Her face was radiant. The drinks arrived. I gave the waiter a five and told him to repeat the order in five minutes.

"To us, Alyce!"

"To us!" We drank them down chug-a-lug.

On her perennially empty stomach, two king-sized Gibsons would make her like putty. I lighted cigarettes for us again, and we sat quietly, looking lovingly at each other, and listening to *Claire de Lune*. The second set of Gibsons arrived.

"To us," I said again.

"I'd better not. I have to go home. Salvatore and the cats haven't had any dinner yet." She was back to reason again.

"Go ahead and drink it down. It's already paid for."

"You drink it, darling." She reached across the table and patted my hand. "I'd better not."

"Suit yourself." I drank both of the Gibsons. "Why don't you get going? You said you had to go; why don't you go?"

"You aren't angry with me are you, darling?"

"No. Go ahead. You said you had to go. Go!"

"I can't stand it if you're mad at me."

"I'm not mad but I will be if you don't get going."

She got up from the table reluctantly. I watched her as she left, not taking my eyes off her as she moved to the archway and stopped. She wanted to come back but she didn't. Her duty called. She disappeared.

I called the waiter over.

"Didn't I give you a five dollar bill awhile ago?"

"Yes, sir."

"Then where the hell is my change?"

He flushed to the roots of his hair.

"I'm sorry, sir. I thought . . ."

"Never mind what you thought. Give me my change."

He reached in his pocket and put the dollar bill on the table.

"Keep it," I said.

"I don't want it.'

His voice broke. His red face turned pasty.

"You're not too proud to steal but you're too proud to beg. Is that it?" He walked stiffly away from the table. I let the dollar stay on the table and left.

There was a ticket on the Lincoln. It was for parking in

the red zone. I tore it up and scattered the pieces in the street. The police would have one hell of a time tracing the owner. By the time they did the car would be sold.

Although it was early I drove home.

The apartment smelled of incense. I thought of Diane.

I looked through the telephone book and found Andy's home number. I dialed it.

"Andy," I said, when he answered, "I let a prospect take a '50 Champion the other day. She isn't going to buy it. Pick it up at her house first thing in the morning."

"All right, Mr Haxby. What's her name and address?"

I told him, hung up the phone and went to bed.

Chapter Eleven

Friday was a dreary overcast day. It was as good as any other day to drive to Sausalito.

I parked the Lincoln on the lot and checked in at the office.

"Hello, stranger," Madeleine said.

"I miss one day and I'm a stranger."

"You never miss a day, remember?"

"Where's Tad?"

"He went across the street for coffee."

I left the office and started across the lot. Andy was sitting cross-legged on the ground with a can of white paint and a brush making whitewalled tires where none had been before.

"Did you pick up the Champion, Andy?"

"Over there." He jerked his thumb toward the car.

"Did the lady give you any trouble?"

"She said you was supposed to pick it up."

I laughed and crossed Van Ness to the coffee shop. Tad was sitting with a cup of smoking coffee in front of him, and writing in his little black book.

"The same," I told the waitress, "with milk."

Tad growled at me. "Where the hell were you yesterday? I was busy as hell."

"I was trying to sell the Lincoln Continental."

"You should have been at the lot then. It was advertised

and six different people wanted to look at it."

"If any of them were really interested they'll be back. It is a rare and lovely car." The waitress brought my coffee and I heaped three teaspoons of sugar into it.

"Tad, I've got to go over to Sausalito today."

"Okay. When will you get back?"

"I don't know."

"All right. Take another day off. What the hell do I care?"

"I'll be in tomorrow for sure."

"That's damned white of you."

I finished my coffee and got off the stool. I pointed to Tad. "He'll take care of it," I told the waitress.

"You're a no-good bastard!" Tad shouted at me as I closed the door. I waited for a lull in the traffic and dashed across the street. I checked the gas on a Pontiac. It had enough and I took the keys from the rack in the office. I drove into the traffic stream and after a few blocks took the left turn for the Golden Gate.

Sausalito is a small town hugging a cliff a few miles the other side of the bridge in Marin County. Fishing parties use the docks and some of the haves of San Francisco keep their yachts at the various piers. There are a few hotels and a few motels. The townspeople claim that Rita Hayworth made a movie there once. Sausalito also has a commanding view of Angel Island.

My Aunt Clara has a rooming house there that she inherited from her second husband. She's my mother's oldest sister and has always been overly fond of me. Maybe I remind her of her second husband.

I crossed the bridge and took the cut-off into the town. I found my aunt's street, put the Pontiac in first gear and climbed for ten minutes. Stopping in front of her house I twisted my front wheels back into the curb and got out of the car. By this time Aunt Clara was at the door to see who had the nerve to climb her street. I waved and grinned at her. Two old women rocking on the porch stared at me curiously.

"I could stand a cup of coffee," I said.

"Russell!" Aunt Clara opened the door, kissed me, then dragged me by the hand through the house and into the kitchen.

Over coffee we discussed the family, what there was left of it. Her boys were fine, although she seldom heard from them. I told her that as far as I knew, mother was still married to the producer in Los Angeles.

"That was a sad thing," she said.

"I don't think so. She seems to be happy enough."

"But to live in Los Angeles must be terrible."

"Yeah. There's that, all right."

"When are you going to get married, Russell?" She changed the subject.

"As soon as I can find a producer." I grinned at her.

"You aren't getting any younger, you know." She was serious now. It's an odd thing how women worry about men that aren't married. It was my turn to change the subject.

"How are you making out these days, Aunt Clara? Do you have enough money?"

"I don't need much money."

"Everybody needs much money. That's what I came to see you about. There's a man over in the city who lost his son, and he's a friend of mine. He kind of went off his rocker a little bit, what with his grief and all, and I wanted to see him in a quiet spot for a few weeks till he gets his health back. Do you think you could take him in?"

"Be glad to. I only have those two on the porch. And I probably wouldn't have them if they could hobble down the hill."

"He can work, you know. In fact it would be good for him. Nothing complicated; but let him mow the lawn, chop weeds, beat rugs, and stuff like that."

"Knowing you, and I think I do, I spot something phony in this." She smiled, but she meant it just the same.

I laughed. "Not at all. Here." I opened my wallet and counted out fifty dollars. "He lives with his daughter, but she works all day and can't take care of him, that's all."

"I see. But never mind, bring him over." She put the money into her apron pocket.

"Atta girl. You're my favorite aunt."

"I know I am. When are you going to be over with this bereaved old man?"

"This afternoon." I kissed her and left the house. As I went down the porch steps I smiled at the two old women. "And how are you young girls this morning?" They cackled at me. Salvatore would be right at home in this atmosphere.

I drove back to the city and pulled the car into Miller's Garage. Alyce was busy in the change booth. She was surprised when she looked up and saw me.

"Take the rest of the day off," I said.

"I can't, Russell. The boss won't just let me leave."

"Sure he will. Tell him you have to go to the dentist."

"He'll dock me a day's pay."

"It'll be worth it. Come on. I'll be over there in that green Pontiac." I pointed to it.

She joined me in a few minutes and got into the car. I headed for her apartment.

"I've found Salvatore a job," I told her.

"But I told you that he was my responsibility."

I explained that my aunt needed a handyman and would pay him fifty dollars a month and provide room and board. After telling her how nice and quiet it was in Sausalito she began to get interested.

"Maybe it would be the best thing in the world for him."

"Sure it would," I said. "Get him out into the open, working in a garden, and he'll be like a new man."

Salvatore wasn't so easy to convince.

This was the first time I'd seen him to catch his reactions. He was a sick man all right. Alyce had only talked to him for a few minutes when he began to stutter in protest.

"Listen, Salvatore," Alyce continued over his protest. "You're going to like it over there. Russell's Aunt Clara has an interest in you, and will make life just as pleasant for you as possible. You can work in the garden and have a fine old time."

"I, I, I, I'm not going." He returned his attention to the TV screen and tried to ignore us. Alyce signaled for me to leave the room. She followed me into the kitchen.

"It's no use, Russell. I can't make him go if he doesn't want to go, can I?"

"It's for his own good. You go into the bedroom and let me talk to him."

"If he won't listen to me I know he won't listen to you."

"Let me try anyway." She shrugged and went down the hall and into her bedroom. I shut the living room door behind me. Salvatore had his eyes riveted on a platoon of marching cigarettes. They were performing a complicated drill upon the screen. I went directly to the screen and snapped it off.

I stood in front of the set and faced him. He glared at me. His eyes looked into my face without looking into my eyes. They weren't shifty eyes, but they were alert, like the eyes of a sparrow.

"Salvatore," I began, "how did you like the asylum?"

"I, I, I didn't like it."

"You wouldn't want to go back up there then, would you?"

He shook his head and lowered his eyes. It was strange to be talking to a man as old as he was as if he were a child. Although he wasn't a tall man, his shoulders were wide and powerful, his hands small and work-marred, and his fingers had a definite tremor to them. He was badly frightened.

"You see, Salvatore, everybody has to work. It's one of the rules we live by." I offered him a cigarette. He didn't take it. I lighted one and blew the smoke at the ceiling. "Do you know why you were fired from the shipyard?" He didn't answer. "It was because you're crazy."

"I, I, I did more work than anybody!" he protested in a rush.

"Nevertheless," I stopped him, "you're crazy. Nobody wanted to work with you. They want you to go back." I pointed dramatically in the general direction of North. "Now Alyce and me, we don't want you to go back, so we found you a job where nobody knows you. After a few weeks, when things quiet down, we'll get you another job at another shipyard. You'd like that, wouldn't you?"

"I can do more work than anybody!" Just like a broken record.

"Sure you can. But if you don't take this job with my aunt, men with white coats will come here to the house. They'll put you in a big black car and take you back. Up there." I pointed again. He shuddered. "Up there you'll be put in a little room with bars on the window. No television. No radio. Nothing. It'll be dark in there. No lights. Nothing. Do you understand?"

"Be, be, be, before there were lots of men with me. In, in, in a big room, and—" He wanted to convince me.

"Not this time. That was before. This time you'll be put in a little room. All by yourself."

I let him think it over while I puffed on my cigarette.

"Remember, Salvatore. To keep from going back, you have to work. You can't lie around without working. It's the rule. My aunt will take good care of you. You'll like it."

"C, c, can I take my television?"

"Sure you can. You take the wires loose and I'll tell Alyce." I left the room and shut the door.

In the bedroom, I told Alyce to pack his clothes.

"Does he really want to go?" Alyce was incredulous.

"Sure he does. Pack his clothes. He's disconnecting the TV set."

Salvatore didn't have many clothes; mostly working garments: blue jeans, T- and work shirts. He had one good expensive suit and Alyce made him wear it. It didn't fit him very well. At the time it was made he was a desk man, with a sizable paunch, evidently, because the trousers were loose on him, and the coat was tight across his shoulders. His hard outside work at the shipyard had been good for him. Even though his mind was shot with spirochetes, he was probably in better physical condition than he'd ever been in his life.

Downstairs, I threw the loaded suitcase in the back of the car. With some difficulty, Salvatore sat on the back seat holding the television set in his lap. He'd never be able to use it in Sausalito without an aerial, but I didn't remind him of that. On the drive to Sausalito, Alyce kept a running commentary going about how well he would like it at my Aunt Clara's. She was trying to convince herself but didn't realize it. Salvatore paid little attention to her. He was more interested in the scenery and pointed to ships in the bay as we crossed the bridge.

As I swung onto the cut-off from 101 into Sausalito, a light rain began to fall. By the time I'd made the slow crawl in first gear to Aunt Clara's house it was raining hard, and the three of us got wet running the short distance from the car to the front porch.

Aunt Clara took charge of things immediately and installed Salvatore in a front upstairs bedroom. I got Alyce away from there as fast as possible before she could ask too many questions.

On the way back to the city the rain fell in heavy sheets and there was a strong wind on the bridge. Alyce broke down. It was the letdown after all the excitement. She cried intermittently all the way back to her apartment. I tried to comfort her.

"You have to admit it's for the best, Alyce. And he isn't too far away. From time to time you can drive over and see him, gradually cutting your visits down. In a few months he won't need you any more. The first break is always hard, but it's for his own good, and certainly for yours." I was logical about it but she was womanlike.

"He looked so pitiful waving to us from the window." This remark brought on a fresh surge of tears. I was glad to pull up in front of her apartment.

Ruthie was home. She made coffee and we sat around the living room drinking it while I explained the situation for her. She was delighted.

"This is the smartest thing you've ever done, Alyce," she said. "It's about time you had a life of your own. I have to congratulate you, Russell. You've put a little sense in her head." She nodded her dyed red locks.

I said nothing. Alyce had calmed down.

"I don't know. I hope it's for the best. It's all happened so fast. I don't know what to think." Alyce looked into her cup like an insect was in it.

"Why don't you let Russell do your thinking for you?" Ruthie said. "It took me long enough to realize that a woman needs a man to run things for her."

I got to my feet. "I think I'd better go." In the emotional stew Alyce was in it would be best to leave her alone to think things over. With Ruthie on my side I didn't have to worry.

Alyce went downstairs with me. I kissed her. She smiled bravely.

"Can I trust you to run my life?"

"Forever. You know you can."

"I should feel like a load has been lifted from my back. But somehow it feels heavier than it ever has."

"You just have a letdown, that's all. Take a nap for the rest of the afternoon. Eat a big dinner, play some records this evening and keep your mind off things. Go to bed early and I'll see you tomorrow after work. Remember one thing: you're starting your life all over again. From scratch."

"I'll try."

"That's the idea." I kissed her again, gently. For the first time I got the feeling that she was trying to respond. At least she was relaxed.

As I drove away in the rain she was standing in the doorway waving.

Chapter Twelve

Once home I sat in a chair facing the window. I watched the rain beat into the messy backyard that was my view. The apartment was neat and cheery with everything in place. Mrs Wren had done a good job. With luck it would stay that way for a week or so. When I was alone like this life was very pleasant. There were no complications. Life was so simple.

I called my grocer and ordered groceries. While I waited for the delivery boy I changed into pyjamas and a dressing gown. I filled my pipe, selected a stack of Oscar Peterson records and put them on the player. I listened to his fine piano, smoking my pipe, feeling very happy about everything. It was all going my way.

The delivery boy pushed the button. He was soaking wet.

"Where do you want these, Mr Haxby?"

"Just bring the box into the kitchen." He put the soggy cardboard box of groceries on the breakfast nook table.

"It's really raining, Mr Haxby," he said.

"Don't you have a rain hat?" His thick brownish hair looked like the working end of a mop.

"No, sir."

I went into the bedroom, took a five out of my wallet and gave it to him.

"Here. Buy yourself a rain hat, for Christ's sake."

"Thanks a lot, Mr Haxby."

"Do you want a drink?"

"I don't think I'd better, Mr Haxby. But thanks, anyway." He left, dripping his way down the stairs. It's tough to be a kid. I was glad that I was thirty-three years old and didn't have to struggle through those miserable years again.

I put the groceries away. It was really too early to eat so I took my time preparing dinner. There were some frozen strawberries in the stuff I'd ordered and I made a strawberry pie. The dinner turned out well. Pork chops, grits and gravy, topped by the pie with plenty of whipped cream.

After eating I sat down with my copy of *Ulysses* and reread the Penelope episode. I finished the chapter and threw the book across the room. Joyce is so damned clever that sometimes it irritates me to read *Ulysses*. The brilliantly selected words, twisting and turning, force their way into your consciousness and coil like striking snakes.

I drank a double shot of gin and went to bed.

At first I thought it was the alarm clock, then realized it was the telephone. I let it ring for a while, hoping it would stop, but it continued to ring persistently. It was Alyce. Glancing at my watch I saw it was five a.m.

"Yes, Alyce. What's the matter?"

Her voice was tearful over the wire.

"Salvatore's home!"

"How did he get back from Sausalito?"

"The police just brought him in."

"Suppose you tell me about it." I tried not to sound irritated.

"He walked all the way. In all this rain. Evidently, he waited till your aunt was asleep, then he left the house

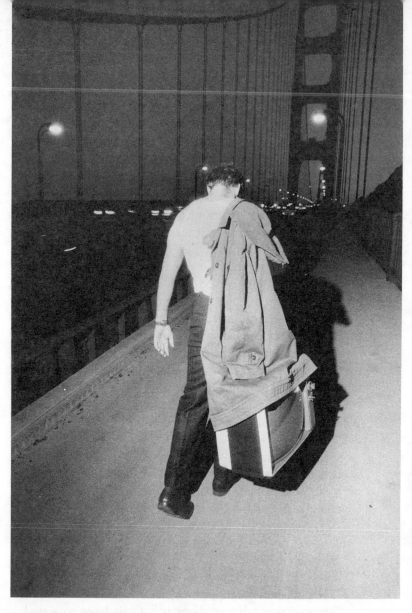

"How did he get back from Sausalito?"
"He walked all the way . . . he left the house carrying his television set . . . then he carried it in his arms, walking all the way across the bridge."

carrying his television set. He took his coat off and put it over the set so it wouldn't get wet. Then he carried it in his arms, walking all the way across the bridge. At the tollgate they stopped him and of course he didn't have any money. Salvatore must have looked strange to the gateman, I guess, and they held him there for the police. The police just brought him home."

"Is he all right?"

"He's sneezing and coughing. He was wringing wet. I gave him a hot lemonade and a codeine tablet and put him to bed."

"I'll come over and get him. If I don't get him back to Sausalito my aunt will be worried."

"Oh, no! Not now! He'd better stay here. I'm not even going to work tomorrow. He may get pneumonia."

"I'll be over in a few minutes." I hung up.

Sometimes that is the way things go. Aunt Clara didn't have a telephone so I called Western Union and sent a wire telling her that Salvatore Vitale was all right, signing it "Love, Russell."

I got dressed, threw my trenchcoat over my shoulders, and pulled on an old felt hat. I raced the Pontiac through the wet empty streets to Alyce's apartment.

Ruthie opened the door for me and I followed her up the stairs and into the living room. Stanley was sitting in a chair, fully dressed, drinking coffee. Alyce was pacing the floor. She wasn't wearing makeup and there were tear streaks on her face. Her upper lip was thin. It was strange I'd never noticed it before. Ruthie went into the kitchen to get me a cup of coffee.

"I don't like this police business," Stanley said. "It worries a man to see policemen at four-thirty in the morning."

"Why?" I asked him. "What have you done you shouldn't?"

"Don't forget. I'm a married man." He shook his head sadly.

Alyce clutched the lapels of my trenchcoat and looked into my eyes.

"Oh, Russell. What shall we do now?"

"Sit down. He'll be all right." I put her in a chair and removed my coat. Ruthie returned with my coffee. She handed me the cup and laughed.

"You should have been here, Russell. Stanley could get a job with the Fire Department. I never saw a man get dressed so fast in my life." She laughed again.

"There's nothing funny about it," Stanley said.

"Maybe you'd better go home," I told him.

"I think I'd better." He was grateful for the out. Stanley and Ruthie left the room. I sipped the coffee, set the cup on the mantel, and sat in a chair facing Alyce.

"What's the matter, baby?"

"It was such a mistake. I know you meant well, Russell, but it was just too fast. Before any major decision like that there should have been all kinds of preparation. I shouldn't have let you rush me along. I didn't have time to think. You just don't know, that's all. He's a sick man."

"He's not going to get any better staying here in the apartment and being treated like a baby. How do you expect him to get on his feet again?"

"Maybe it would be all right for him to be at a place like your aunt's, but we can't rush it the way we did. If it takes a few weeks, conditioning him to the change, preparing his mind to accept it, well, then it might be a different story. Right now, security is the most important thing in the world to him."

"I'm going to tell you something right now I was saving for later, Alyce. Security is important to me too. To both of us. I want to marry you—and just as soon as possible."

Her eyes widened.

"Do you actually think I could give you any happiness?"

"You're everything I've ever looked for, Alyce. I want to marry you as soon as we can. I want to take you out of that damned garage down there, put you in an apron and have you smile at me with that sweet tragic smile when I come home from work."

She smiled the tragic smile.

"It sounds wonderful." She turned her head away. "But I don't see how we . . ." Her voice trailed away into nothing.

"We can do anything we want to do."

Ruthie entered.

"Well, Stanley's gone home to his wife." She said it bitterly.

"Ruthie," I said, "get Salvatore in here."

"What are you going to do?" Alyce asked.

"I'm going to talk to him, and he's going back to Sausalito this morning, not three months from now."

"Russell, I can't let you do this. You don't know how to handle him. You'd better let me do it my way."

"You'd better let Russell do it his way," Ruthie said. She left the room.

"Please, Russell," Alyce said, "don't frighten him like this."

"I'm not going to frighten him. I'm going to explain things to him."

"But he can't understand! All you'll succeed in doing is . . ."

I looked into her eyes. It was a silent duel. "Go give Ruthie a hand," I said.

"All right!" She got up from her chair and left the room. I finished my coffee. It was cold.

In a few minutes they brought Salvatore into the living room sniffling and protesting. He was dressed in flannel pyjamas and slippers. When he saw me he stopped his mumbling and backed against the wall, staring and afraid.

"I want to talk to him alone," I said. The two women left, Alyce giving me a last imploring look. I shut the door.

"What's the matter with Sausalito, Salvatore?" He didn't answer. I took my knife out of my pocket, flicked out the blade and began to pare my nails. "Didn't you like it over there? What's the matter: didn't your television set work? Do you remember what I told you yesterday? You don't? Well, I'll tell you again. You don't have to go back to Sausalito. You're going back to the institution instead."

I smiled at him. His body was shaking violently.

"Don't you want to go back up there, Salvatore?" I pointed with my knife.

He shook his head uncontrollably, but finally got it out. "N, n, n, no!"

I pointed to the picture window.

"Then, JUMP!" I shouted.

He reached for me instead. His hands were outstretched and reaching for my throat. I jabbed my blade through his right palm, twisted it, and stepped back. It took all the fight out of him. He held his hurt hand against his chest and watched the blood beginning to spread on his flannel jacket like ink on a blotter.

I pointed to the window again.

"Jump!" I shouted. He didn't hear me. Slowly he walked

to his favorite chair and sat down heavily. I moved my hand rapidly up and down in front of his eyes. He didn't see it. I leaned close to his ear.

"Fire!" I shouted. He didn't hear it. I felt his pulse. It was pounding along about sixty per. Salvatore would live forever, probably, but he'd do his living at an institution.

I put my knife away, walked to the window and kicked out the glass. The glass rattled, part of it falling to the street, the rest to the floor. Alyce and Ruthie entered the room.

"He tried to jump out," I said.

Alyce saw his cut hand at once and darted from the room for the first-aid kit. I put on my coat and hat.

"Ruthie," I said, "get him in an asylum for Christ's sake, and be sure that this time he's committed."

"It should have been done a long time ago."

"I'm going home. Take care of things."

"I know what to do."

"All right. Get Alyce in bed."

I drove the Pontiac down to the lot, left it there, and caught a taxicab home. I undressed and got into bed after I closed the drapes to keep out the early morning light. I could get at least two hours sleep before I had to go to work.

Chapter Thirteen

I didn't see Alyce for two weeks. Why, I don't know. But then I didn't analyze my actions. After work every night I was dead tired. Being tired, I went to bed at 7:30 and slept soundly all night. She may have telephoned during that two-week period. I don't know. The phone was off the cradle.

But two weeks later, on a Sunday morning, I got out of bed rejuvenated. I showered, shaved, put on my powder-blue suit and a straw hat.

The sun was shining into the apartment. The sky was pale blue and stippled with flecks of fleecy clouds. I got into the Rambler I'd driven home in the evening before and drove to St. Patrick's. I was in time for ten o'clock mass and took communion. After church I drove to the Sea Cliff Restaurant and ordered an enormous breakfast. It was perfect. I washed it down with four cups of coffee. It was such a beautiful day I felt like singing. I tipped the waitress a little too much, got into the Rambler and slid the top back.

It was time to evaluate my relationship with Alyce.

It had cost me money, time; and had contributed, I felt sure, to my two-week period of inactivity. I had to bring the situation to a head. Alyce was very much a woman and didn't know it. If I could prove it to her, I could prove to myself that all my effort hadn't been wasted. It would be nice to see her again. I drove to her apartment.

I parked the Rambler and pushed the bell. Looking up I could see that the window had been replaced. Ruthie opened the door.

"Russell!" She was surprised to see me.

"May I come in?"

"I'll say!" She took me by the arm. We climbed the stairs together and entered the living room. I hadn't noticed Ruthie was in black until I saw Stanley. He was wearing a new Oxford-gray suit and a mourning band. He got up and shook hands with me solemnly.

"I appreciate you getting me out of here the other night before . . ." He jerked his head at the window.

"I didn't think he'd try that," I said.

"It was a terrible thing." He held his hat in his right hand, spinning it in a circle. I got the impression he wanted to leave.

"Stanley's wife died day before yesterday," Ruthie said.

"Is that right? I'm sorry, Stanley," I said.

He cleared his throat. "We've been expecting it for some time. I have to go pretty soon. The funeral."

"Stanley doesn't think I should go with him."

"He doesn't?" I tried to seem surprised.

"It isn't that, Ruthie." His voice had a whine to it. "But all the relatives will be there and it won't look right." He turned to me. "Would it?"

"Where's Alyce?" I asked.

"Alyce!" Ruthie said. "I haven't told her you were here." She left the room and I patted Stanley on the shoulder.

"I'll get you out of this, Stanley. You go ahead. I'll bring Ruthie out to the cemetery with me."

"If she stands over with you, they won't notice anything,

will they?''

"Of course not. After all, Ruthie used to be your wife's nurse.''

"That's right!" He must have felt a lot better.

Alyce entered the room followed by Ruthie. She was wearing her black faille suit and it made her face look pale under her makeup. She reminded me of a little girl being introduced to company for the first time.

"Hello, Russell," she said weakly.

"Hello, baby," I said. I walked over and kissed her on the cheek. She blushed. I took her hand in mine. It was similar to holding a piece of dry ice.

"You got here just in time. Alyce was just leaving for the cemetery," Ruthie said.

"Fine! I'll take both of you girls out with me. We'll meet you out there, Stanley.''

"That's a great idea!" he said. "Well I'd better get going." He started to leave.

"By the way," I said, and I put my arm around Alyce's shoulders, "when are you two getting married?"

Stanley ran his forefinger around the neck of his collar. "Well, we're going to have to wait awhile. A decent period, anyway."

"In about three weeks." Ruthie was more definite. They left the room.

"I didn't think I'd ever see you again," Alyce said slowly.

"You knew better than that."

"No. I didn't."

"I thought it would be better if I waited awhile."

"You could have called."

"I thought it would be best if I didn't. Were you going to the funeral, or to put flowers on your mother's grave?"

"To see mother—like every Sunday."

I kissed her. She was like a stone.

"Let's get going then. You'd better get your wrap. The top is back." She left the room. I looked out the window and saw Stanley pull away from the curb in his Essex and Ruthie re-enter the apartment.

It was a silent drive to the cemetery. I should have taken a car with a radio. We stopped at a florist's and all of us bought flowers. The caretaker at the gate told Ruthie where the funeral was being held. I inched up the curving path and stopped to let her out. I climbed the hill again, and remembered the correct spot to park.

"When I die I'll be buried here too," Alyce said, when we reached her mother's grave.

"Do you have it paid for already?"

"I pay so much a month, but my insurance will take care of the rest."

"How about Salvatore? Do you have insurance on him?"

"They don't give insurance to men in his condition."

She removed the wilted flowers, refilled the cans with water and arranged the fresh bouquets. I didn't help her because I felt she enjoyed the work. I placed the flowers I had bought on the stone of Tom Mooney. When I returned Alyce was finished. We stood there quietly for awhile and I smoked a cigarette.

"It should be about time to pick Ruthie up," I said.

We got into the car and I drove down the path to where the cars for the funeral were grouped. It was just breaking up, and we didn't get out of the car. Presently, we saw Stanley and Ruthie walking across the grass. He was crying into his handkerchief and she was guiding him. She put him into the Essex, took the driver's side and drove down the hill.

We left the cemetery. I cut left before we reached the city and headed for the beach. We parked by the sea wall and watched the breakers flash in the afternoon sun. There were a lot of people at the beach. For San Francisco, it was a beautiful spring day.

Alyce turned in her seat and looked me in the eyes.

"Russell," she said, and her voice was husky, "there's something I want to ask you. I don't want you to lie, and if you do lie I'll be able to tell it."

"What is it?"

"Do you love me?" She was deadly serious.

"Sure I do."

"No. Not that way. Say it."

"I. Love. You." I didn't smile.

Her eyes flowed like Niagara Falls. Like rivers. She put her arms around my neck and buried her face in my coat. Her muffled voice said over and over again, "I love you."

Somehow, I wasn't surprised.

Alyce had a good time that afternoon. At Playland by the beach we went on all the midway rides, ate hot dogs and for dinner we had a steak at Bob's Blue Steer, back in the city. After the steak I ordered brandies for both of us.

Alyce was comfortable and well loosened up. She told me that now Salvatore was committed to the asylum, she was not only resigned, she was happy about it.

"I feel like a new woman," she added tritely.

"That's fine," I said. "Let's go for a ride."

When we left Bob's it was quite dark. We got into the Rambler and I made straight for the Golden Gate. Alyce was happily singing all of the old songs she could remember. When we were in the middle of the bridge she asked me

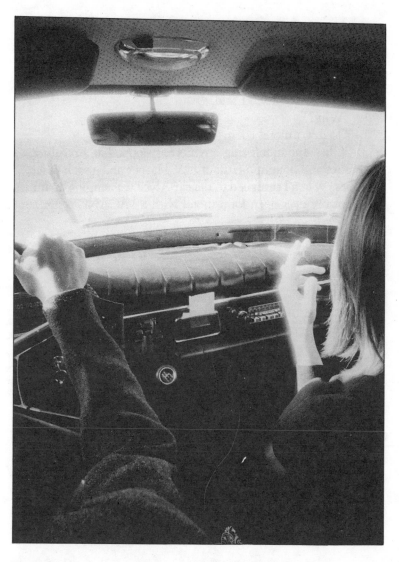

We parked by the sea wall and watched the breakers flash in the
afternoon sun . . . For San Francisco, it was a beautiful spring day.

where we were going.

"Marin County," I said.

"Why?"

"To get a motel room for the night."

"Oh." She didn't sing anymore. I stopped at a roadside market and bought a fifth of I.W. Harper and a sack of ice cubes. When I returned to the car Alyce was singing again. I kept my eyes open for a motel with a VACANCY sign.

Chapter Fourteen

I got out of bed and lighted the heater. Sunlight was filtering through the cheesy, grayish burlap curtains but the room was cold. It was one of those concrete-brick rooms, whitewashed for Spanish effect, with black wrought iron curtain rods and cheap Monterey furniture. There was one good-sized drink in the bottle. I looked at Alyce. She was still asleep. I drank it.

I took a shower and returned to the heater to towel myself. Alyce was awake and blinking at me. Her modesty had completely left her now and she sat up in bed, exposing herself in the filtered sunlight.

"Good morning, darling." She stretched and it was suddenly called to my attention that she was at least three days overdue to shave under her arms.

"Good morning. How's your head?"

"I feel wonderful. Is the water hot in the shower?"

"Scalding. In fact you can't adjust it properly."

"That's for me then." She got out of bed and threw her arms around me and gave me a kiss. I would have been happier about the kiss if her teeth had been brushed first. I put my clothes on. I hated the feel of my socks, worn the entire day before, but I had no clean ones. I was smoking my second cigarette when Alyce came out of the bathroom. She stood shivering in front of the heater drying herself with the motel bath towel.

"I hope I didn't get my hair too wet," she said.

"Just a little bit around the edges."

"I should have brought a shower cap."

"I should've brought some clean socks."

I watched her dress. It was like we'd been married for ten years. I thanked the Lord and all the stone gods on Easter Island that we weren't married! I wanted another drink. She shimmied into her girdle. A roll of fat protruded a good inch over the top. All women had that roll; why should I have been surprised? It was merely because I hadn't noticed it before. That was all. She combed and combed her hair. She put on makeup, adding the extra above her upper lip to make it even with the lower. She put on her jacket and turned, placing a hand on her hip, throwing her pelvis up and forward like a model.

"How do I look?"

"Just the way you're supposed to look," I said. "Come on."

She started to kiss me, remembered her lipstick and changed her mind. I opened the door and we went outside. In spite of the carport, a fine film of dew covered the seats of the Rambler, and I regretted not putting the top up before we'd gone inside. But last night I'd been in a hurry. It was understandable. I returned to the room and brought out the unused face towel and wiped the seat. Alyce got in and I started the engine. I let it warm up for a full minute, backed out and eased down the driveway in first gear to the office. I threw the key at the office door as we went by. It missed the door and landed in a geranium bush.

I looked at my watch again. It was still early, just 7:30. I drove slowly, enjoying the contrast of hot sunlight and cold air. It was another beautiful day. I was hungry.

"How about breakfast, Alyce?"

"Do we have time?"

"It's only seven-thirty. You have to eat."

"All right."

There was a drive-in a mile down the road. I pulled into the slot reserved for the patrons who wanted to eat inside. We entered. I had sausage and eggs while Alyce drank a glass of orange juice and a cup of coffee. We were both silent during breakfast. I didn't want to say anything because I wanted to delay telling Alyce it was all over. Alyce acted like she was afraid to speak. I finished with two cups of coffee and two cigarettes. As I lighted the second cigarette I looked at Alyce. Her eyes were too bright. The tragic lines were sharper and were etched deeply from the wings of her nose to the corners of her mouth. She was a woman built for suffering and tragedy. It was written in every line of her face. My expression must have been distasteful. Her lower lip began to quiver. It looked funny, like it was the only nerve she had left.

"Are you sorry?" I asked her.

"No. Are you?" Her voice had a catch in it. It wasn't that the catch in her voice was practiced: it was just that I knew it would always be there. It would be there if a man came home drunk; if he missed coming home one night; if he put ashes on the rug or raised his voice. I knew it. In that moment I pitied every married man I'd ever known.

"Of course not, baby," I said. "I just don't talk much in the morning. It was a wonderful night."

"You do love me, don't you, Russell?"

"Of course. Do you want another cup of coffee?"

"No, thanks. I want you to know that last night was the

"I love you, Russell." She sighed.
"I love you too. Now let's get the hell out of here."

most wonderful thing that ever happened to me. You're the kindest, the sweetest—I love you, Russell." She sighed.

"I love you too. Now let's get the hell out of here."

I paid the cashier and we went outside. I put Alyce in the car, walked around and got in myself. She was smiling at me, a brave smile that said, "As long as you love me nothing else matters!" I'd seen that type of smile before. Too many times.

I rode along with the traffic stream. The highway had filled with commuters from Marin County going to work in the city. I took my time. Within a few minutes we were on the swooping downgrade that led through the tunnel and onto the approach to the bridge. A few scattered whirls of fog hugged the ground but the sun was bright and the bay glittered. I got into the center lane and held it to the tollgate. I paid the forty cents and as we left the tollgate I looked at Alyce. She didn't look so good. Her face was pale and her eyes were on the handbag she was twisting in her lap.

"Do you want to go home first or to the garage?" I asked her.

"I guess I'd better go home first—to see how things are."

"All right."

"Russell—" She hesitated.

"Yes?"

"Have I done anything wrong?"

"Not unless you think so."

"What I mean is—are you mad at me?"

"No. Should I be?"

"You've acted so funny this morning. Did I say anything, or—"

"For Christ's sake!"

It seemed to be the only way they could end. In tears,

always in tears. I was right. Big juicy tears bubbled up and streaked down her cheeks. The tragic lines caught them, turned them under her mouth and they dropped from her chin. I let her cry for a moment. It was completely noiseless. Then I handed her my handkerchief:

"Here. That isn't going to do you any good."

"Then you are mad at me?"

"No. I'm not mad. I'm just taking you home. You have a job, I have a job. We have to go to work and the time to play is over."

"Will I see you tonight?"

"No. Not tonight."

"When then?"

"Don't try to pin me down, Alyce!" I was getting sore.

"That's all you wanted then, just to sleep with me and that was all. Now it's over, isn't it?"

I'd hoped to avoid all this, but she'd asked for it.

"That's right. You catch on quick. We're approaching your corner; or do you want me to drop you in front of the house?"

"Here will do." She handed my handkerchief back to me, got out and slammed the door. "This is pretty hard to take, Russell."

"I guess it is. Well, Alyce, I won't say it's been nice because it hasn't. See you." I put the car into first gear.

"Just like that." She was staring at me like she couldn't believe it.

"Just like that." I let the clutch out fast and the car leaped away from the curb. I looked back once in the rearview mirror. Alyce was walking up the hill and she looked tired.

It wasn't quite nine yet. Instead of going to my apartment I drove to the lot and parked the Rambler. Tad was standing by the office chewing the end of a cigar.

"I'm going to get a shave," I told him. "Be back in a few minutes."

"Okay, Russ. You ought to shut your eyes before you bleed to death."

"You ought to see them from this side," I said. I entered the office and tossed the car keys on the counter. Madeleine twitched herself up from her typewriter, took the keys and put them on the rack. I took a good look at her. I wondered if she'd appreciate me. A well-built, uncomplicated woman, Madeleine.

"You know what, Madeleine: we ought to go down to the beach and catch Kenton tonight. What do you say?"

"I have a date."

"You could break it."

"Not this one. I'll take a raincheck."

"Suit yourself."

I cut across the lot and went into Thrifty's and bought a pair of socks. Bruno's Barber Shop was next door. There was a man in the chair, and while Bruno finished cutting his hair I changed socks, throwing the dirty pair in the towel hamper. I doubt if Bruno liked it but he didn't say anything. I was next.

I lay back in the chair. The hot towel felt wonderful on my face. I thought of Madeleine. She didn't have a date. She'd come around before the day was over with some story about how her date was called out of town unexpectedly or something like that. I must have sighed.

"Towel too hot, Mr Haxby?" Bruno asked.

"No. Not hot enough." It was an effort to answer. He changed the towel. I was tired. I could have slept all day right in that chair. I was almost asleep, then I didn't fight it

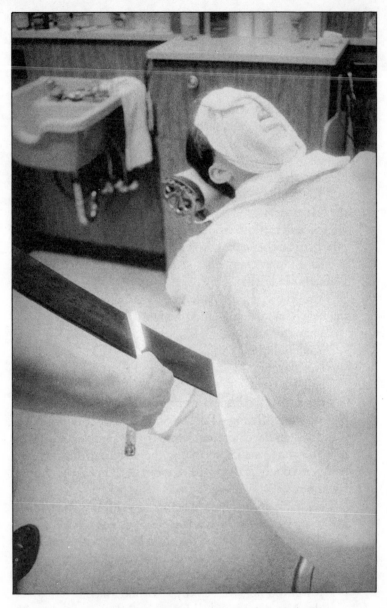

*I could have slept all day right in that chair. I was almost asleep,
then I didn't fight it any more. I drifted down . . . down . . .
what the hell, Bruno'd wake me when he was through.*

any more. I drifted down ... down ... what the hell, Bruno'd wake me when he was through.

The End

HIGH PRIEST OF CALIFORNIA

A Play in Three Acts
By Charles Willeford

PLACE: San Francisco

TIME: Winter, 1953

CAST OF CHARACTERS

Blackie Victor
Alyce Victor
Russell Haxby
Stanley Sinkiewicz
Ruthie Mansfield
Police Officer

ACT I

SCENE: The living room in Alyce Victor's
San Francisco apartment, on the second floor,
overlooking the bay and part of the city.
TIME: Two a.m., Sunday morning.

ACT II

SCENE: Same as Act I.
TIME: Two p.m., the following afternoon.

ACT III

SCENE 1: Same as Act 1.
TIME: Two a.m. One week later.

SCENE 2: Same as Act 1.
TIME: Two p.m. One week later.

ACT I

SCENE: *The living room of Alyce Victor's apartment in San Francisco. The "wall" facing the audience is a huge window overlooking part of the city, the bay, and a section of the Golden Gate Bridge. A double doorway with practical sliding doors, upstage left, leads to a hallway (a telephone on a small table is visible when the doors are open), the stairway down to the ground floor, and to the rest of the apartment. The doors are painted a peculiar shade of yellow-white. Against the wall, stage right, is a radio-phonograph console with two stereo speakers. On top of this cabinet is a small (17") portable TV set. The room is furnished with moderately good taste; unfortunately Alyce Victor, a course-taker in adult education classes, has scattered the evidence of this activity—ceramic ashtrays, watercolors, needlework, and pottery—throughout the room. Side by side above the imitation fireplace, upstage center, are two framed reproductions: Van Gogh's "L'Arlesienne," and "The End of the Trail."*

As the curtain rises Blackie Victor is discovered seated in a red womb chair facing the television set. The set is on, but there is no picture. Blackie Victor, a man in his early fifties, looks much older: his hair is almost white, and there are deep lines in his forehead. His chin is on his chest, his eyes are closed, and his long arms dangle over the chair. He wears an old black bathrobe; faded yellow felt letters on the back spell out:

BLACKIE

VICTOR.

A car stops in the street below. Blackie shakes his head, goes to the window and looks down. A car door slams. He exits, closing the door behind him. His bare feet are heard shuffling down the hallway. Below, the front door is audibly closed.

A moment later, Alyce Victor and Russell Haxby enter. Alyce is 29 (actually). She wears a tailored suit, and beneath her tailored figure, a girdle and "chafies." Alyce walks swiftly most of the time, and the "swish-swish" sound of her "chafies" are audible enough for Russell Haxby to become acutely aware of the sound. Russell Haxby, thirtyish, wears a topcoat and a plain but expensive business suit. He carries a gray fedora. Haxby has a tendency to listen to the sound of his own voice. Russell strips off his topcoat, drapes it over a chair, and puts his hat on top of the coat. As he crosses directly to the "window," Alyce softly closes the double doors.

ALYCE: *(Brightly)* Well, how do you like my view?

RUSSELL: I like the red neon horse. On a night like this he rides without the support of the building, just hanging up there. And the lights on the bridge are like radioactive Crackerjacks. *(He points)* Come and look.

ALYCE: I've seen it. How about some coffee?

RUSSELL: A view like this must add twenty-five bucks a month to your rent—

ALYCE: Forty—according to my neighbor next door. Shall I make some coffee?

RUSSELL: D'you have any bourbon? With a little water.

ALYCE: I'm sorry, but I haven't got any whiskey at all. I think there's some wine, though. Would you like a glass of wine?

RUSSELL: What kind?

ALYCE: Muscatel, I believe.

RUSSELL: *(Shudders)* Never mind. I'll settle for coffee. Half a cup, the rest hot water.

(Exit Alyce, leaving one door open. Russell examines the room, shaking his head at the pair of pictures above the mantel. He goes to record player, kneels, hauls a stack of records out of the cabinet, and glances briefly at each title as he drops the record on the floor.)

Hey! D'you mind if I play some music?

ALYCE: *(Off)* Of course not! But not too loud; it's awfully late.

RUSSELL: Why not? Music should be heard to be believed. Here's one.

ALYCE: *(Off)* What's that?

RUSSELL: It looks like all pop stuff, for Christ's sake.

ALYCE: I'll be there in just a second.

(Russell puts on a symphonic-popular arrangement, all instrumental, of "How High the Moon." Crosses to "window," lights a cigarette, and looks out. Enter Alyce with coffee pot, cups, etc on tray. She places tray on a coffee table, and plugs in the cord to a socket near the base of a standing lamp.)

I couldn't hear you very well from the kitchen, Mr Haxby.

RUSSELL: *(Shrugs)* I was just wondering how many cars each day go in and out of Marin County both ways across the Golden Gate. And about how many of them I sold, and if I sold them all—every damned one of them—how much my commission would be . . .

ALYCE: Oh! Is that what you do? Sell automobiles?

RUSSELL: *(Shaking his head)* I don't sell them; I *give* them away! Used cars, not new ones. One year old to one turn of the century. I've never sold a new car and I don't believe I could. I'm the tin-can pander of Van Ness Avenue.

ALYCE: What company do you work for?

RUSSELL: My commission. Period. Here. Let's have our coffee over here.

(Russell moves the coffee table over in front of the divan and sits. Alyce sits on the divan, but as far away from him as she can get.)

ALYCE: I don't believe it's hot enough yet; I just plugged it in. But it doesn't take long with instant—

RUSSELL: *(Pours a cup, tastes it, and makes a face.)* Not only is it cold, but it's so damned weak it won't pour out of the cup!

ALYCE: *(Apologetically)* You said half hot water, and—

RUSSELL: *(Leaping up)* Come on, let's dance!

ALYCE: We'll have to be very quiet. Ruthie's home. I saw the light on under her door.

RUSSELL: *(Frowning)* Ruthie? Who's Ruthie?

ALYCE: My cousin. She lives here with me. We share the apartment; I thought I told you—

RUSSELL: I thought we were going to be alone here, otherwise—

ALYCE: *(Primly)* Do you think I'd invite a gentleman I met at a dance for the first time to come home with me at two o'clock in the morning if—

RUSSELL: If you weren't chaperoned? As a matter of fact, that's what I did think.

ALYCE: No. *(She shakes her head)* I wouldn't do anything like that. You just don't know me very well, that's all.

RUSSELL: I don't know you at all, but I had intended to know you much better. And now I learn that you are a woman of mystery. An enigma. An enchantress. A beguiling nymph with a tree house on the seventh hill of San Francisco. A lady who goes "swish-swish" as she walks, who lures innocent, unsuspecting used car salesmen to her tower—and then says, "Shhh, don't make no noise. Ruthie's home!"

ALYCE: Shhh! Not so loud. No, Mr Haxby. I'm not like that at all. I was just reluctant to see you go, that's all. We were having such a good time, and—

RUSSELL: *(Looking at his wristwatch)* It's almost two a.m. Time *to* go. *(He turns off record player.)*

ALYCE: I suppose it is; I don't know what happened to the time, it went so fast. Would you believe, Mr Haxby, that tonight was the first time in my life that I ever went to a public dance hall? And alone, besides.

RUSSELL: Sure, I believe it. It was another first for me, too. Except for close friends on a party, I've never had a strange woman approach me and ask me to dance with her before. How come you picked on me, anyway?

ALYCE: *(Embarrassed)* I saw you dancing, earlier, you know, and you danced so well I just thought you were one of the hosts—you know, someone who danced with the unescorted girls, or something.

RUSSELL: I don't know whether that's a flattering comment or not, but I'll let it go. But I noticed you were frightened when you asked me. Did I look so formidable?

ALYCE: No, that wasn't what bothered me. What I was thinking about, you see *(giggles)* was how much I was supposed to tip you . . .

RUSSELL: *(Taken aback slightly by this confession)* How much *were* you going to tip me?

ALYCE: *(In a high voice)* A dollar.

RUSSELL: If I had only known! I missed my chance, didn't I? I could've got the dollar first, before I bought you a drink.

ALYCE: You're a simply marvelous dancer, Mr Haxby.

RUSSELL: I guess I am at that. You aren't, you know. You're pneumatic enough to float, but you're as stiff to push around the floor as a Mack truck.

ALYCE: *(Nodding eagerly)* I know it, and I'm sorry. It's just that I haven't danced in a long time—maybe six or seven years.

RUSSELL: I didn't mean to be critical. At one time I wanted to be a professional dancer, when I was much younger, you know. But the *barre* got me down.

ALYCE: You started to drink?

RUSSELL: The *barre,* not a liquor bar! It's a horizontal wooden rod along a studio wall. And you hang onto it with one hand for hours at a time doing this,

> *(Russell demonstrates several ballet positions, using the back of a chair as a handhold)*

and this, and this, and this . . . and that's what you have to do every single day. I wanted to soar, to fly above the stage like a masculine Peter Pan.

> *(He takes a long run and leaps over the chair. He pulls down his jacket, straightens up, and shrugs.)*

A man makes more dough selling used cars.

ALYCE: I think I know what you mean, and I guess dancing is just like everything else. You have to walk before you can run. When I first started to take ceramics I wanted to do the hardest design they had, but Mr

Hawkins—he's our ceramics teacher—wouldn't let me. I had to make ashtrays instead but it turned out to be the best thing anyway. I made scads of ashtrays and gave them away for Christmas presents.

(She hands him an oddly designed piece.)

I made this ashtray.

RUSSELL: I wondered what it was—

ALYCE: I made it big on purpose. People usually like large ashtrays, Mr Hawkins says, and it can be used for cheese and crackers, or candy, or—

(There is a rattle of utensils offstage.)

RUSSELL: Who's that?

ALYCE: *(Apprehensively)* Ruthie, I suppose . . .

STANLEY: *(Off—Loudly)* You got the coffee pot out there, Alyce?

ALYCE: *(To Russell)* It isn't Ruthie, it's Stanley. *(Calling)* Yes, Stanley! We're using it!

RUSSELL: Do you take in boarders?

ALYCE: I'll tell you in a minute.

(Enter Stanley Sinkiewicz. He is wearing an undershirt, trousers, and slippers. His looped white suspenders hang to his knees. His gray hair is touseled and uncombed. He is a thin wiry man in his early fifties, with a dour expression.)

STANLEY: *(Grumpily)* I don't see why you can't leave the coffee pot in the kitchen where it belongs. *(Nodding to Russell)* Howdy, Mister.

ALYCE: This is Mr Russell Haxby. Mr Sinkiewicz.

STANLEY: *(Nodding acknowledgement. Russell merely stares.)* Me and Ruthie want a cup. *(Stanley unplugs the pot and shakes it by his ear.)* I guess there's enough in here. *(Exit Stanley.)*

RUSSELL: I think I'd better go. *(He puts on his topcoat.)*

ALYCE: You don't have to go on account of Stanley. It's all right. Stanley's Ruthie's boyfriend. He stays here sometimes, but then he always has to get up early and go home. He's married, you see, and he has to get home before his wife wakes up.

RUSSELL: I understand. He isn't married to Ruthie, but to somebody else who is asleep.

ALYCE: That's right. He wants to marry Ruthie, and they are sort of unofficially engaged. But his wife's an invalid. That's how Ruthie met him; she's a trained nurse and she takes care of Mrs Sinkiewicz. Mrs Sinkiewicz has been in bed for a long time now, more than two years, and she has all the money. So if Stanley divorced her he wouldn't get a cent. So I guess he and Ruthie are sort of waiting around to see what's going to happen—

RUSSELL: It doesn't look to me like they're waiting.

ALYCE: Well *(turning away)* you know what I mean.

RUSSELL: Sure. *(Shrugs)* It's an affair of their own and certainly not one of mine. Now that the coffee's gone, shall we have a nightcap?

ALYCE: I don't have anything except the muscatel, as I said—

RUSSELL: Never mind. It just so happens that—

(Russell takes a flask from his topcoat pocket, unscrews the cap, and offers it to Alyce.)

Here, you first; you can take the fusel oil off for me.

ALYCE: No thank you. I hardly ever take a drink.

RUSSELL: *(Drinks, screws the cap on, and puts the flask away)* And that's a nightcap, Alyce. I'll be on my way.

ALYCE: Tomorrow is another day. You don't have to hurry off.

RUSSELL: It is tomorrow. This has been a nice evening, Alyce. You aren't going with somebody, are you? I mean, are you engaged or do you have an understanding friend like Mr Sinkiewicz?

ALYCE: Engaged?

RUSSELL: Do you have a special friend, some guy who takes up the majority of your free time?

ALYCE: Oh, no! *(Breathlessly)* Why, you're the first man I've had a date with in years, at least five years! I never go out! I'm home all the time after work. I gave you my phone number, didn't I? I know I meant to. Just a second, I'll write it down for you.

(Alyce opens her purse, finds a ballpoint pen and writes her name and number on the back of an envelope. She tears off the piece of paper and hands it to Russell. He slips it casually into his pocket.)

RUSSELL: *(Dryly)* Thanks.

ALYCE: And in case you lose it, I'm in the telephone book. Alyce Victor.

RUSSELL: That's an odd name. Victor? What is that, Italian?

ALYCE: Oh, no!

RUSSELL: It isn't?

ALYCE: Well, maybe it is, I'm not sure. On my father's side, maybe.

RUSSELL: But not on your mother's?

ALYCE: No. Mother was Scotch-Irish.

RUSSELL: Is that right? I'm Scotch-Irish myself. Also English, and maybe a little French.

ALYCE: My, that's interesting! How do you get to be three nationalities?

RUSSELL: It's very difficult, Alyce. I was lucky enough to be born that way, although I doubt if I could do it again.

(*Enter Stanley, dressed for the street, and carrying the pot.*)

STANLEY: The coffee was too weak, but here's the pot back if you want to make some more.

RUSSELL: What nationality are you, Mr Sinkiewicz?

STANLEY: I'm a Polack. Born in New Jersey and then emigrated to California. Why? With a name like Sinkiewicz, did you think I was a Spaniard?

RUSSELL: (*Yawning, and covering his mouth with a hand*) I just asked to be impolite. Can I drop you off somewhere, old man?

STANLEY: No. (*Exit Stanley.*)

RUSSELL: Mr Sinkiewicz isn't very friendly.

ALYCE: Oh, don't pay any attention to him. Nobody's very friendly anyway at this hour, not after just getting up.

RUSSELL: I suppose you want to go to bed, too? (*He glances at his wristwatch.*)

ALYCE: Oh, no! I'm as wide awake as a cat after drinking all that coffee.

RUSSELL: (*Glancing at her full cup.*) All of what coffee?

ALYCE: I had a lot before I left the house, earlier tonight.

RUSSELL: Sure. (*He picks up his hat.*)

ALYCE: Wait! Before you go I want you to meet my family.

RUSSELL: You know, it's getting pretty damned late, Alyce—

ALYCE: No, no, no! You just wait.

(*Exit Alyce, walking rapidly. Russell listens to the swishing sounds, and follows her progress with keen attention.*)

RUSSELL: (*Puts on his hat, sits down, pours some coffee into his cup, adds whiskey from his flask. He lifts the cup in a toast.*)

To a cup of lousy coffee, Mr Sinkiewicz, and an irate family. (*He drinks.*)

ALYCE: (*Enter Alyce. She has an alley cat in a chickenwire-covered crate. She places the box in the center of the floor.*) This is Ferdie. (*Exit Alyce.*)

RUSSELL: To you, Ferdie. (*He drinks.*) Sorry to get you up so early.

ALYCE: (*Enter Alyce with another boxed alley cat. She places the box atop the box containing Ferdie.*) This is Alvin.

RUSSELL: Al-vin?

ALYCE: (*Nods.*) Uh huh. (*Exit Alyce.*)

RUSSELL: (*Adds more whiskey to his cup.*) Well Alvin—here's to you! (*He drinks, and shudders slightly.*)

ALYCE: (*Enter Alyce. She places a third boxed cat on the stack.*) And last, but not least, is Seymour.

RUSSELL: Is this what you meant by your family?

ALYCE: *(Proudly)* Uh huh! Aren't they pretty? There's one more. Spiky. My dog. He's a little fox terrier I got at the pound. Both of poor Spiky's front feet were cut off by a cable car. Long before I got him, of course. But he hasn't been feeling well lately, and I've got him in the vet's hospital.

RUSSELL: *(Leaping up)* Look, Alyce, I've got to go home!

ALYCE: You don't have to rush right off. Have another cup of coffee.

RUSSELL: *(Goes to top box, raises the lid, reaches in and quickly withdraws his finger. He drops the lid shut and latches it.)*
They're all tomcats, are they?

ALYCE: That's right. I wouldn't have any other kind.

RUSSELL: Then what are they all doing home on a Saturday night?

ALYCE: Oh, I never let them out. What with the traffic and all, they'd be killed. When you take the responsibility for animals you have to be a responsible person.

RUSSELL: *(Nodding)* And therefore you don't let them out on Saturday night—

ALYCE: Or any other night.

RUSSELL: Then why don't you get a female cat?

ALYCE: Oh, I used to have one. Henrietta. But I had to give her away. She kept having kittens all the time.

RUSSELL: I think I understand, now, why you haven't gone out. You have to stay home to take care of your cats.

ALYCE: Did you know that cats drank a lot of water?

RUSSELL: No, I *didn't* know that. How much do they drink?

ALYCE: Only this morning—to give you an idea—I filled the saucepan with water and it's almost all gone. Come on out to the kitchen with me, and I'll show—

RUSSELL: Never mind, never mind. I believe you. I'm going to have to go now. Tomorrow's Sunday and I have to sleep late.

ALYCE: How late do you have to sleep?

RUSSELL: As late as possible.

(He moves in on Alyce; she steps back, stops, and bravely holds her ground.)
Do I get a goodnight kiss, Alyce—or do I know you too well?

ALYCE: Well . . . I only met you tonight . . .

(She clenches her fists, closes her eyes, and prepares for the worst. Her body is still and tense. Puzzled, Russell makes a circle about her and stops. He kisses her very gently on the mouth, without touching her with his hands.

Alyce relaxes, sighs, and opens her eyes.)

RUSSELL: That wasn't such an ordeal, was it?

ALYCE: *(Shyly, unable to meet his eyes)* No . . . *(in a small voice)*

RUSSELL: You're an interesting woman, Alyce. You seem to be blessed with an odious honesty, however. Ordinarily, even if a girl hadn't had a date in five years she wouldn't say she hadn't had a date in five years. But for some uncanny reason, I'm beginning to believe you.

ALYCE: Why would anyone lie about something like that?

RUSSELL: I don't know. Perhaps they wouldn't; they just wouldn't mention it, that's all.

ALYCE: *(Rattles through these lines)* I wouldn't. I just wouldn't. I haven't been interested in going out. Not really. I work six days a week and I don't get home until seven. Then, when I come home I have to fix dinner and eat; and then I'm tired or else I work on my watercolors. Then there are my cats to take care of—and Spiky, when he isn't at the vet's—and I painted the hallway all by myself, mixing the paint and all. Did you notice how nice it looks on the doors? The color is called sugar-cream. I invented it.

RUSSELL: *(Turning away)* I'll look at it closely on my way out. *(Stops)* Are you working tomorrow? Sunday?

ALYCE: Oh, no! I don't work Sundays. I go to the cemetery every Sunday morning, of course, to put flowers on Mother's grave. Then the rest of the day I stay home.

RUSSELL: Why "of course"?

ALYCE: I promised.

RUSSELL: Okay. I'll tell you what I'll do. I'll come over for awhile, then, tomorrow afternoon. Two, two-thirty, like that. Okay?

ALYCE: That would be wonderful! If you sleep late and have a late breakfast, then it'll be about lunchtime when you get here and you can have lunch with me. What would you like for lunch? I can stop by the store on my way to the cemetery, and—

RUSSELL: Anything. Anything at all. Don't worry about it. I think I'll try another one of those kisses. *(Alyce assumes the tense, rigid position, fists clenched. She closes her eyes. Slowly, not unkindly, Russell takes her into his arms and kisses her hard. He releases her, turns away.)*

Goodnight, Alyce. *(Exit Russell)*

ALYCE: *(She collapses onto the couch and sighs. She gets up suddenly and rushes to the door.)* Two o'clock, Mr Haxby! Don't forget!

RUSSELL: *(Off)* Right. *(The downstairs door slams.)*

ALYCE: *(She collects cups and puts them on the tray. She sniffs Russell's cup, shakes her head and smiles. She sees pile of records on the floor, crosses to cabinet and, kneeling, begins to put them back into the cabinet. Enter Blackie. Pouting, he shuffles into the room. Alyce turns.)*
Blackie! What are you doing out of bed?

BLACKIE: *(Childishly)* You were talking to somebody and making noise and you woke me up.

ALYCE: Even so, you didn't have to get out of bed. I was talking to Mr Haxby. He's a real estate agent and we were discussing some property I'm interested in. Suppose you had walked in while he was here? How would that have looked?

BLACKIE: *(Sullenly)* He's gone now.

ALYCE: But that isn't the point. I know he's gone now. But how could I have explained it if you had walked in while he was here?

BLACKIE: I didn't, though.

ALYCE: *(She feels the top of the TV set.)* How late did you stay up watching television?

BLACKIE: Not very long.

ALYCE: How long? Ten? Ten-thirty?

BLACKIE: Eleven, maybe.

ALYCE: I thought so. You stayed up until sign-off, didn't you, even though I told you to go to bed early.

BLACKIE: *(Eagerly, placatingly)* There was a cowboy movie on, really good; and you wouldn't want me to go to bed right in the middle! It was real good. The good guy was all dressed in white and he had a white horse that could count all the way up to ten. The horse was pretty, too. And real smart. When the cowboy asked him a question he would nod his head and paw with his foot. He knew every single thing the cowboy asked him!

ALYCE: *(Calmly)* I'm glad you enjoyed the movie, Blackie. But you're simply going to have to get to bed earlier. You can't stay up all night watching television and then go to work the next day. Did the foreman ask you to work tomorrow—on Sunday?

BLACKIE: He said I could work if I wanted and I said that I wanted. But then he said maybe I'd better take the day off and work double-shift on Monday.

ALYCE: *(Shaking her head)* No. You aren't working any double-shift. Monday, or any other day. So forget about it.

BLACKIE: Why not? The foreman depends on me. I'm the best sweeper he's got!

ALYCE: No. One shift on Monday, and tomorrow you don't work at all. Did you know that you put in more than sixty hours last week? No man can work like that, day in and day out.

BLACKIE: *(Flexing his biceps)* I can. I'm strong.

ALYCE: Well, we'll see. But no work tomorrow. I want you to sleep late in the morning. Then, in the afternoon, you can go to a double-feature movie uptown.

BLACKIE: Will you go with me?

ALYCE: I can't. I have to go to the cemetery. But you can see the double-feature twice if you like.

BLACKIE: You don't care if I see it twice?

ALYCE: Not if you stay in bed and sleep all morning.

BLACKIE: I'll stay in bed . . . But I can't help it if I wake up, can I?

ALYCE: If you wake up, stay in bed and practice your reading. Did you read any tonight?

BLACKIE: *(Sheepishly. He describes a circle on the floor with a foot.)* I didn't have time.

ALYCE: What you mean is, you didn't take the time. I told you to practice reading when I left for at least a half-hour. And then you could watch television.

BLACKIE: *(Eagerly)* I practiced my writing instead!

ALYCE: Let me see it.

BLACKIE: No. It isn't any good.

ALYCE: I'll be the judge of that. Hand it over and let me see it.

BLACKIE: *(Reluctantly he takes a piece of crumpled paper from his pocket.)* Here. I told you it wasn't any good.

ALYCE: *(Frowning, as she studies the paper.)* Uh huh. *(Nods approvingly.)* This is much better. Much much better. But you just wrote "Blackie." Why didn't you practice writing your last name as well?

BLACKIE: It's too hard.

ALYCE: No it isn't. Why last week you were writing it fine!

BLACKIE: It's too hard.

ALYCE: I don't understand it. You can write it easily enough when I'm here watching you. Why not when I'm away?

BLACKIE: It's too hard.

ALYCE: No it isn't. All it takes is practice. One of these days you'll be able to read and write almost anything—

BLACKIE: You went away tonight and left me.

ALYCE: I simply can't stay home with you every night. And I didn't leave you alone. Ruthie was here.

BLACKIE: I don't like Ruthie. She calls me "Dummy" all the time.

ALYCE: *(Sighing)* All right, I'll speak to her about it again. It's time for you to get to bed. Right now.

BLACKIE: Can't we play some records?

ALYCE: Of course not. It's early in the morning. We should be in bed.

BLACKIE: *You* were going to play some!

ALYCE: No, I wasn't. I was merely putting these away. Now go on; go to bed.

BLACKIE: *(Moves reluctantly toward the doorway. Stops and turns.)* I'm hungry.

ALYCE: No you aren't, either. You're just stalling. Go on, now.

BLACKIE: I am *too* hungry. I guess I know when I'm hungry.

ALYCE: All right. What would you like to eat?

BLACKIE: *(After thinking it over)* A glass of milk?

ALYCE: Pour yourself a glass in the kitchen. Drink it over the sink, and then go to bed.

BLACKIE: I don't think I want any milk. I want an orange instead.

ALYCE: *(She takes an orange from the bowl, and tries to hand it to Blackie. He puts his hands behind his back.)* Here. Take it.

BLACKIE: Peel it for me.

ALYCE: *(Her patience is sorely tried.)* Listen, Blackie, I'm tired and I'm sleepy, and you know that I can't go to bed until you've gone to sleep. If you want this orange, take it. If not, go to bed. Now.

BLACKIE: I don't see why you won't peel it for me. You know I can't peel it.

ALYCE: You could if you tried; besides, I know that you peel and eat oranges when I'm not here to do it for you.

BLACKIE: You don't care nothing about me! You think I'm a dummy, too. And you're going to send me back. I know you are!

(He sits on a footstool and buries his face in his hands—then looks slyly at Alyce by peeping through his fingers.)

ALYCE: Now, now! Don't start that again. I'm not sending you anywhere. I'll peel the orange for you.

(Alyce peels orange as she talks.)

You're going to have to stop all of this petty foolishness. You don't realize how hard you're working at the shipyard, that's all. All you're supposed to do down there is sweep the floors. But anytime somebody has something too heavy to carry they hand it to you. That's the sort of thing you aren't supposed to do; the other workers are taking advantage of you, simply because you're physically strong. Then, by the end of the day you get overly tired and come home and take it out on me. I'm not going to let you work any more double-shifts, either.

BLACKIE: *(Proudly)* I can do more work than anybody.

ALYCE: Not if you don't get enough rest, you can't. Here. All peeled.

BLACKIE: *(Shrugs)* I don't want it.

ALYCE: *(Drops orange and peelings onto the tray.)* I didn't think you did in the first place. Honestly, Blackie, I don't know sometimes where I get the patience . . .

(Blackie stares sullenly at the floor.)

Are you going to bed or not?

BLACKIE: No!

ALYCE: Well, I am!

(Starts to leave)

But remember this: You can stay up all night if you want to, but if you do you can just forget about the double-feature tomorrow.

BLACKIE: Why? You said I could go . . .

ALYCE: Not if you don't go to bed.

BLACKIE: I want to practice my writing. That's why I want to stay up. You told me I should practice writing my last name—

ALYCE: No, you don't. You just want me to stay up and talk to you.

BLACKIE: *(Argumentatively)* I was in bed. Before. Then you came in real loud and everything and woke me up. Now I'm not sleepy and you want me to go to bed. Besides, I'm hungry, and you won't give me anything to eat.

ALYCE: I peeled an orange for you and you wouldn't take it.

BLACKIE: But I want a glass of milk. Warm milk. Not too hot, and no skin on top.

ALYCE: Will you go to bed, then, if I fix it for you?

BLACKIE: *(Trapped)* That's all I asked for—just a glass of milk.

RUTHIE: *(Off: Screaming)* Do you people know what time it is?

ALYCE: *(Calling)* We're going to bed now, Ruthie!

RUTHIE: *(Off—Still screaming)* You might as well! You won't get any place arguing with the Dummy.

(She appears in the doorway. Ruthie has on a flowered muumuu, furry slippers, and her red hair is in curlers. She is in her middle forties, and quite plump.)

See; now you've got *me* shouting and raising *my* voice!

ALYCE: *(Intensely)* Listen Ruthie, I don't want you calling Blackie "Dummy."

RUTHIE: *(Shrugging)* All right! I'll call the Dummy Einstein if you want me to. But you'll never win an argument from him.

ALYCE: That's what I mean. You called him "Dummy" again! He's my husband, whatever else he is, and I won't have it! And besides, we weren't arguing—

RUTHIE: *(Contritely)* I'm sorry, sweetie. My god, it's three o'clock in the morning, and we're discussing semantics. Good night, Alyce. Good night, Blackie.

(Exit Ruthie. Blackie sticks his tongue out at her as she leaves.)

ALYCE: Good night, Ruthie. We're going to bed. *(To Blackie)* All right. Go on into the kitchen, and I'll turn out the lights. Then I'll warm you a glass of milk . . .

BLACKIE: *(Surprised)* Milk? I don't want any milk. I'm going to bed. *(Exit Blackie)*

ALYCE: *(Turns out wall switch. Light source is the small TV lamp. She goes to window, looks out for a long moment, suddenly hugs herself, whirls about once, squeals happily. Recovers her composure, picks up two crates of cats and exits as the curtain falls.)*

ACT II

SCENE: *Same as Act I.*
TIME: *Two p.m., Sunday afternoon.*

(As the curtain rises, Alyce, wearing a black tailored suit, is dusting furniture. A fresh bowl of fruit is on the coffee table. Two crudely-wrought ceramic vases containing fresh cut flowers brighten the room. A cocktail shaker and six glasses are on the coffee table. The divan and coffee table are as Russell saw them the night before.)

ALYCE: *(Surveys the room, puts the dustrag into a drawer. She calls.)* Ruthie! What time is it, Ruthie?

RUTHIE: *(Off, but enters in the middle of her speech.)* It's two o'clock! The last time you asked me it was two minutes *until* two, and the next time you ask me it'll be two minutes *after* two.

(Ruthie wears a long red flannel nightgown, with U.S. OLYMPIC SLEEPING TEAM in white letters on the back. Her hair is still in curlers, and her feet are encased in furry slippers. She carries a cup of coffee on a saucer. She sprawls heavily on the divan and spreads her legs wide, completely relaxed.)

I am really and truly beat, kid. Don't expect that pick-up of yours to show up exactly on time.

ALYCE: I didn't pick him up.

RUTHIE: So he picked you up instead. It's all the same in the end. *(She looks at the flowers.)* What did you do, sweetie, buy out the flower shop on way out of the cemetery?

ALYCE: No. I got them on sale at the little shop near the gate, where I always buy flowers for Mother's grave. They're old and won't last long. The living room needs a good cleaning, but the flowers help, I think.

RUTHIE: They look nice, kid. How did the grave look?

ALYCE: About the same, I guess. I get awfully disheartened sometimes, Ruthie. I wish I could get out there every day. When I leave it looks just beautiful. Fresh flowers, clean water, and I pick out all the weeds and gather up all the leaves. And then, the next Sunday, I have it to do all over again. For what I pay each year for perpetual care, you would think the caretakers would do more than just water the grass. Every time I see last week's flowers, all wilted and brown, I feel just terrible.

RUTHIE: It'll look a lot worse a hundred years from now. Let the dead lie. You can't win a battle with a grave, Alyce, and your mother will never know the difference. If I were you I'd start cutting these trips down. Try going every other week, then every other month, and then once a year, maybe—

ALYCE: You know I couldn't do that! If I died, Mother would've visited me every single day; I know she would. And flowers help keep Mother's memory alive. There's one little old lady who comes out there every Sunday, and I talk to her sometimes. Her little boy died of pneumonia thirty-five years ago, and she still brings him fresh roses every Sunday.

RUTHIE: (*Shudders*) How morbid can you get! Your mother lived her life, Alyce; and she managed to live yours, too, while she was alive—if you don't mind my saying so. Now, I think you're getting onto the right track with this boyfriend you've picked up, whether anything comes of it or not. You've been wasting all your good years on the dummy, and—

ALYCE: (*Wearily*) Please Ruthie. I don't want you calling him that anymore.

RUTHIE: As punch-simple as he is his head is just one great big callus. So he can't be as sensitive as he pretends. Seriously, Alyce, you should never have taken him out of the sanitarium. With the genuine brain damage he's had, he could be dangerous as hell. To be brutally frank, he gives me the goddamned creeps.

ALYCE: I think he's a lot better; I really do. And he's getting better all the time. If I sent him back, he'd soon be just like he was when I brought him home two years ago. And besides, I couldn't afford to keep him there any longer.

RUTHIE: The state hospital costs nothing—

ALYCE: Let's not go into that again. I will not, I cannot, go to a judge and tell him that my husband is crazy—

ALYCE: The judge makes the decision, not you. *You* aren't the one who commits him—

ALYCE: No! I don't want to discuss it, Ruthie.

RUTHIE: Well, it's your funeral, not mine. But how're you going to explain Blackie to your boyfriend?

ALYCE: He isn't any boyfriend, he's just a man I happened to meet. And I'm not going to explain Blackie. He's at the Paramount's double-feature, downtown.

RUTHIE: You'd better hope he stays there. One look at Blackie and this used car salesman of yours'll be long gone. Believe me.

ALYCE: *(Sadly)* He may not even come . . .

RUTHIE: Don't worry, sweetie. He'll be here. I'll bet he's never run into anyone like you before. What does he look like, anyway?

ALYCE: *(Sits)* I don't know; it's kind of hard to say, exactly. He isn't exactly handsome, but he has a pretty smile. And he talks funny. Well, not really funny, but in short sentences, like. You know what he means and you don't know what he means, both at the same time. He talks as if he were laughing—not at you, but at himself sort of. I can't explain it. I hope he likes me.

(Alyce stands, turns in a circle, thrusting out her ample breasts, with her chin held high.)

Do I look all right?

RUTHIE: You look like a million 1935 bucks, kid. But a black suit isn't the gayest outfit in the world—unless you're planning on taking him to a funeral.

ALYCE: It's the dressiest outfit I've got.

RUTHIE: You look better in a suit than most people. But let me put a flower in your buttonhole.

(Ruthie rises, breaks off a flower and puts it into the lapel of Alyce's jacket. She stands back.)

There, that's better. And if you like, you can wear my pearls—they're on my dresser somewhere. But watch yourself with this guy, Alyce. You don't know anything about men, and I know too damned much. Either way, you can get into serious trouble. Women are funny that way. No matter how lousy a man is, they somehow get attracted to the same type every time. Look at me, for example. Two husbands, and both of them bastards. And I had to support both of them till they died. And now, when I should know better, I pick another loser like Stanley.

ALYCE: I don't see anything wrong with Stanley.

RUTHIE: Neither do I, kid. He's a real sweetheart. But he's a bastard, too, and he's never done a day's work in his life. At least he's healthy, and that's a switch. I'd better get dressed myself.

(Ruthie crosses to doorway.)

Stanley should be over pretty soon.

(Turns and hesitates)

I hate to ask you, Alyce, but if you aren't going to use your car this afternoon, how about letting Stanley and me take it?

ALYCE: I don't know, Ruthie . . . I have to pick Blackie up at the movie later on, and—

RUTHIE: Can't you forget about Blackie for one day? You've got yourself a date, remember? It's about time that you thought of yourself, Alyce. I mean it! This martyr crap gets old after awhile. Look at what's happening to Stanley and me. The months we waited. Me nursing his wife, and Stanley telling me to hang on, hang on! His wife'll probably outlive both of us; the guiltier I feel about everything, the better I take care of her. She's no good to herself or to anyone else, paralyzed that way, and yet she hangs onto life day after day after—

ALYCE: You shouldn't talk like that! It isn't her fault.

RUTHIE: And it isn't mine, either. I'm sorry. Yelling doesn't do any good. The point I was making is that Stanley and I are getting *something* out of life. If she dies, fine; we get married. If she doesn't, well—I really don't believe that she'll live forever. Come on, Alyce, how about the car keys?

ALYCE: They're on the telephone table in the hall. I don't see why Stanley doesn't buy a car for himself. He could buy a secondhand car pretty cheap, couldn't he?

RUTHIE: *(Patiently)* He doesn't have much money, Alyce. I had a bigger allowance than Stanley when I was twelve years old. Even if he had a car, I'd have to buy the gas for it.

ALYCE: Why doesn't he find a job and go to work?

RUTHIE: Stanley isn't that kind of a man. His wife doesn't want him to work and neither do I. If he had a job I don't know when I'd get to see him. Like tonight. I'm supposed to report to the hospital that I'm available again this evening—but I don't think I will. If the Nurses Registry calls, tell them I'm still out on a case. Will you?

ALYCE: *(Smiling)* Uh uh. No, I'll just do as I always do. I let them talk to Blackie.

RUTHIE: *(Laughing)* Well, he's good for something, isn't he? I never thought of that.

(Starts toward door, turns.)

Say, Alyce. About this boyfriend—he sells used cars. Maybe, if you work it right, you could get Stanley and me a good deal. If we both chipped in we might be able to buy something—at least some transportation. Do you want to talk to him, or do you want me to ask him?

ALYCE: I only met him last night. It somehow doesn't seem right to—

RUTHIE: Right? He's a businessman, isn't he? He gets a commission, and with those guys business is business. I know how used car salesmen operate. When they die they don't bury 'em. They just screw them into the ground like this—

(Ruthie makes gesture)

ALYCE: Not Russell. He's honest. I know that much, and I'll bet he would give you a good deal, too.

RUTHIE: Talk to him, then. See what he says. We ought to be able to manage something—

(The doorbell rings)

Is that Stanley or Mr Haxby?

ALYCE: *(Runs to window, looks down)* It's Russell; you'd better run back to your room!

RUTHIE: Let him in. Did you think I was going to hang around in my nightshirt?

ALYCE: Well, hurry! I've got to let him in!

RUTHIE: Go ahead, kid. I'm leaving.

(Exit Alyce. Ruthie pours a cocktail, raises glass in mock salute, and looks at ceiling)

To the innocent lamb!

(Sips, and exits with rest of the drink.)

ALYCE: *(Off, and entering ahead of Russell)*

You're right on time, Russell.

(Enter Russell behind Alyce.)

RUSSELL: Yeah. I couldn't sleep. Jesus, why don't you open a window? The whole apartment smells like cats.

ALYCE: It does? I don't notice anything.

RUSSELL: What's in the shaker?

ALYCE: Martinis. Do you want one?

RUSSELL: Yeah.

(Alyce pours two glasses; Russell crosses to window and looks out.)

A nice view in the daytime, too.

ALYCE: When it isn't too foggy it is.

(She hands him a drink; he sips it and makes a face.)

RUSSELL: God, that's awful. How'd you mix these, anyway?

ALYCE: Just like the recipe said: half gin and half vermouth.

RUSSELL: You don't make martinis that way, Alyce. Listen. First, you take an olive, and then you put a single drop, a single drop, mind you, of vermouth on the olive. Do you follow me so far?

ALYCE: Yes. I think so. A single drop of vermouth on an olive.

RUSSELL: Right. Then you take your gin and pour it into a shaker of big ice chunks. Not cubes, but chunks. Revolve the shaker counter-clockwise. Now you take the olive, and dry it off with a bar towel. Drop it into the full shaker. That's a martini. Understand?

ALYCE: That isn't very much vermouth for a full shaker.

RUSSELL: Now you've got it. Exactly. Not very much vermouth. Is there anybody home?

RUSSELL: Ruthie. She ought to be out in a few minutes. She's dressing.

RUSSELL: (*Sets glass on the coffee table.*) Come here.

(*Alyce approaches warily. Russell takes her stiff figure into his arms.*)
Relax, can't you?

(*He kisses her competently, releases her, pours another martini, and resumes his station by the window.*)

Do you know what, Alyce? I've just sold myself to a riverboat captain! His boat will struggle upstream against the current floating downstream. And when the captain reaches Pennsylvania, I'll be put to work in the coal mines. Anthracite. Forever and a day, and one more besides.

ALYCE: What do you mean, Russell?

RUSSELL: I don't mean anything. Things just happen to me, and sometimes I can't get them under control. See if you can get rid of Ruthie.

ALYCE: Oh, she's going out. Stanley'll be over pretty soon and they're going out for a drive. She's taking my car—

RUSSELL: (*Pouncing*) Ruthie doesn't have a car? Stanley doesn't have a car?

ALYCE: No. In fact, I was going to ask you about—

RUSSELL: Don't ask. I'll sell him one.

ALYCE: That's certainly nice of you, Russell. I hated to ask you, but they're always using mine and I hate to turn Ruthie down. But sometimes, I need the car myself—especially on Sundays.

RUSSELL: Of course you do! Everyone should own his own car. Why live in California if you haven't got a car? That is, a used car, never a new car. Take one of those shiny, brand new, fastback anythings—do you know what's wrong with them?

ALYCE: I don't know very much about cars, I'm afraid.

RUSSELL: I'll tell you. I was going to tell you anyway. A new car has no verisimilitude. Like a virgin. What good is a virgin? No verisimilitude, you see. But a used car, a well broken-in used car with a respectable number of miles on the odometer, well, that is something else again, you see. It has more than virtue; it has verisimilitude! Am I right?

ALYCE: I don't think you're talking very nice.

RUSSELL: You don't?

ALYCE: No, you're implying something, something dirty, I think.

RUSSELL: I prefer the indirect approach, I suppose. My, but you look *nice* today, Alyce!

ALYCE: *(Pleased)* Thank you. This is a new suit.

RUSSELL: Do you always wear suits? I never see you in anything else?

ALYCE: Oh, no. I have some dresses, but I don't like to wear them. I work as a cashier, you know, and I think suits look more businesslike.

RUSSELL: Yeah. How do you look in a bathing suit?

ALYCE: All right. I've got a new black bathing suit with yellow shoulder straps and a net midriff. But I've never worn it yet.

RUSSELL: Tell me something, Alyce. Did you expect me today?

ALYCE: *(Seriously)* Yes. That is, I did, but I wasn't sure. I hoped you'd come, but if you hadn't I wouldn't have been surprised. I would've been awfully disappointed, though.

RUSSELL: I almost didn't make it. I came because there's something different about you. Or odd, I don't know. I don't know exactly what I'm going to do about you, and in a way I'm sorry I came.

ALYCE: You're sorry for me? Is that it?

RUSSELL: Of course not. I'm sorry for myself; these things are always such a drag, at least in the beginning.

ALYCE: What things?

RUSSELL: The whole bit, I guess; but maybe we can shorten the process. It would be so simple if you'd just say, "I love you, Russell," and let me take it from there.

ALYCE: But I hardly know you—

RUSSELL: That's what I mean.

> *(Takes cigarette from his case, lights it, exhales.*
> *Sings:)*   Filter, Flavor, flip-top box.
>   This is a real cigarette
>   Right out of Marlboro country
>   Mmmn, good!

Tell me, Alyce, do you think I'd look good with a tattoo on the back of my hand?

RUTHIE: *(Enter Ruthie, dressed for the street.)* Hello there. You're Russell Haxby. I'm Alyce's cousin, Ruthie. And you may call me Ruthie.

RUSSELL: Okay, Ruthie. I just told Alyce that I loved her.

RUTHIE: I don't blame you. Anything left in the shaker?

RUSSELL: Some ice cubes, I think, and the bitter dregs of the worst martini I ever drank.

RUTHIE: I'll fill it again.

RUSSELL: That would be nice. Try some gin this time; the vermouth that's left will do without adding anymore. I'm going to sell a car to Stanley, if you don't mind.

RUTHIE: That's wonderful, Russell. All he needs is transportation, of course, but he needs a car that'll run. Don't hook him now; he has very little money.

RUSSELL: Money isn't a problem.

RUTHIE: It is to Stanley.

RUSSELL: I'll treat him as if he were my own son. I thought you said you were going to fill up the shaker?

RUTHIE: Sure. One shaker of martinis coming up.

   (Exit Ruthie)

RUSSELL: Let's hope not.

ALYCE: *(Puzzled)* Why did you tell Ruthie that you said you loved me?

RUSSELL: Because I did and I do. After she leaves I'll show you how much.

ALYCE: *(Doorbell rings)* That's Stanley. *(Calling)* Want me to let him in, Ruthie?

RUTHIE: *(Off)* I'll get it.

ALYCE: *(Russell stalks slowly toward Alyce; she backs away.)* I'll—I'll go get the shaker . . .

RUSSELL: Come here, damn it. Am I your dream prince?

ALYCE: *(Nodding)* Yes . . . I think so.

RUSSELL: And do you love me?

ALYCE: I—I—I think so . . .

RUSSELL: Good. Go get the shaker.

   (Exit Alyce, brushing by Ruthie and Stanley as they enter.)

STANLEY: *(Dourly)* You're still here, I see.

RUSSELL: Yeah—one big happy family. Alyce went for the shaker, Ruthie, in case you're interested. I know *you* are interested, Señor Sinkiewicz.

STANLEY: I don't drink—or smoke.

RUTHIE: The doctor told Stanley not to drink anymore.

RUSSELL: You're very wise to take care of yourself, Stanley, and because Ruthie asked me to, I'm going to save you five hundred dollars.

STANLEY: *(Frowning at Ruthie)* What's this? Five hundred dollars?

RUSSELL: Just give me your phone number, Señor Sinkiewicz.

STANLEY: I don't understand; how can you save me five hundred dollars?

RUTHIE: For god's sake, give him your phone number and quit arguing with a man who's trying to save you some money.

STANLEY: Adams 12533.

RUSSELL: I'll call you early in the week.

   (He writes number in his memo book, puts the notebook away.)

STANLEY: What *is* all this?

RUSSELL: Hard sell, Ruthie? Or soft sell?

STANLEY: Why don't somebody let me in on all this?

RUTHIE: Hard sell, definitely. I'll tell you later, Stanley, after you've been prepared psychologically.

ALYCE: *(Enters, with full shaker.)* Hello, Stanley. Do you want a cocktail, Ruthie?

RUTHIE: Well, I don't know . . . well, I guess *one* won't hurt me.

   (Alyce pours four glasses, drops an olive in each glass.)

RUSSELL: *(Alyce serves him first; he takes a glass and raises it in a toast.)* Here's to rural electrification!

RUTHIE: I'll drink to that.

   (They all drink, except Stanley.)

STANLEY: Let's go. *(Rises)* Did you get Alyce's car keys like I told you?

RUTHIE: Sure. Well, nice to have met you, Russell.

RUSSELL: Yeah. I'll call you next week, Sinkiewicz.

   (Exit Stanley. Ruthie hurriedly pours and downs another quick drink, puts down the glass, and exits after Stanley.)

RUSSELL: A nice fellow, Stanley.

ALYCE: *(Surprised.)* Do you really like him?

RUSSELL: No. I don't like him. Sit down, kid.

   (He pats the divan, and Alyce sits beside him.)

You see, Alyce, the way I look at it is this. A man who is married is married. He should make the best of it, or even the worst of it. I suppose that's why I never got married. I like to look around, see what I can find here and there, d'you know what I mean? Does that frighten you? Me being the permanent bachelor type?

ALYCE: No. Why should it?

RUSSELL: Women usually don't see eye-to-eye on such things. But a man like me, thirty-two years old, who's never been married—well, he's a pretty selfish guy. Set in his ways and unable and unwilling to change. Do you follow me?

ALYCE: There's nothing to follow. You couldn't have put it any clearer.

RUSSELL: I haven't been to sleep, Alyce. Last night, after I left here, I started walking. Walked all the way to the Golden Gate. Then I walked back and got into my car. It was quite a walk, and I did a lot of thinking. And it all figures, kid. I figure I'm really ripe. Overdue. You see, if a man is really honest with himself, what he wants is an innocent, simple, mediocre woman. I'm being honest now, Alyce. You fit all of the required specifications.

ALYCE: I don't consider myself a mediocre, simple-minded woman.

RUSSELL: I said simple, not simple-minded. You're almost perfect, Alyce; you have all of the great womanly virtues, and I love you.

ALYCE: No, you don't. You're just giving me a line of some kind.

RUSSELL: No, I'm not giving you any line. But in any case, plan your defense, because I've planned my attack—

ALYCE: Please. Don't be mean to me, Russell. You've got me all confused—

RUSSELL: (*Rising angrily*) I'm not being mean! Do you know how much money I make a week, on the average? More than two hundred and fifty bucks. And that's every single week, except when I make more. I never make less. My pad alone costs me two hundred a month rent. And what do I see when I open the front door at night? Dust balls. Dust balls bigger than my head, rolling all over the floor in search of adherence. Can't you see that I need a woman like you to come home to instead of a bunch of fluffy dust balls?

ALYCE: Please, Russell. Don't say any more.

RUSSELL: Okay. If that's the way you want it. We'll work up to it gradually. But you haven't got a chance. Let's play some records; what do you say?

ALYCE: I've got some new ones—there was a sale at Walgreen's last week, and I got a half-dozen of them. Only ninety-nine cents apiece.

(*Russell crosses to record player, Alyce trailing him. Russell goes through them slowly, examining each title before passing the record to Alyce. He squats down, almost on his heels.*)

RUSSELL: It's a good selection of Mickey music, but I haven't found any jazz yet.

ALYCE: I like Guy Lombardo.

RUSSELL: That figures; you were bound to like Lombardo.
  (Enter Blackie. He shuffles forward like a boxer, chin down on his chest, hands up. With a straight left he pushes, rather than hits, Russell on the shoulder. Russell falls to a sitting position. He looks up, supporting himself with his arms behind him.)
What the hell is this?

BLACKIE: You leave my television set alone!
  (Blackie dances around in the center of the room, his dukes up, snuffling through his nose.)

RUSSELL: Television set? I haven't been close to any television set.
  (Russell rises, reaches into his coat pocket, and brings out a switchblade knife. He pushes the button, and the blade springs out. He holds the knife expertly, easily, the blade flat with the floor.)
Who is this comedian, Alyce?

ALYCE: Stop it, Blackie! This is Blackie Victor. Mr Haxby. Blackie, say hello to Mr Haxby.

BLACKIE: You leave my television set alone!

ALYCE: Shh! Nobody's touched your television set, Blackie. Behave! Why aren't you at the movies?

BLACKIE: *(Calms down, but still breathing hard through his nose, glowers at Russell.)* I don't like nobody to touch my television set.

ALYCE: Answer me. Why did you come home?

RUSSELL: Yeah? And another good question: why do you live here?
  (Russell closes the knife and returns it to his pocket.)

BLACKIE: *(Sullenly)* I got hungry.

ALYCE: Why didn't you buy some popcorn in the lobby?

BLACKIE: I don't want no popcorn. I want something good to eat. I want you to fix me something good.

ALYCE: *(Crosses to her purse, takes out a bill and hands it to Blackie.)*
Here. Go down to the corner. Chang's is open today, and get a pound of hamburger. You'd better get two onions, too.

BLACKIE: And a pie?

ALYCE: If you want one, get a frozen apple pie, and I'll bake it for you.

RUSSELL: *(Blackie turns to go, and Russell stops him.)* Just a minute.
  (He hands Blackie a coin.)
Here's a quarter. Pick me up a small box of aspirin.

BLACKIE: *(Smiling from doorway)* Goodbye!
  (He waves, and then exits.)

ALYCE: *(After a long pause)* Well . . . ?

RUSSELL: *(Lights cigarette, shrugs.)* Do you want me to ask you who he is, or do you want to volunteer and tell me?

ALYCE: I think the best thing all around would be for you to just leave, Russell.

ALYCE: *(Shakes his head)* No. I don't think so. Not only do a good many interesting things happen when I'm in your company, but I have an interest staked out here besides. To refresh your memory, I committed myself. I said I was in love with you, and you let me say it.

ALYCE: But you weren't serious.

RUSSELL: I wasn't? Then why did I say it?

ALYCE: I don't know! I don't know why you say anything. And I don't understand half of the things you say. Why don't you just go? It would be easier for both of us.

RUSSELL: There isn't any easy way for me. Who is this Blackie? Who is he?

ALYCE: *(Turning away)* My husband.

RUSSELL: I had it figured, but I wanted to hear you say it. Do you know what? A man can get killed bringing another man's wife home at two in the morning. And he can get killed at two-thirty in the afternoon playing with another man's television set.

ALYCE: I'm sorry, Russell. But I sent him to a double-feature this afternoon.

RUSSELL: And what about last night? Did you send him to an all-night movie? No wonder he got tired of popcorn . . .

ALYCE: He was here last night. But he was in his room asleep.

RUSSELL: I see. That's why you didn't want me to play the music so loud—

ALYCE: For once in my life—just once—I tried to get away with something. And I didn't. I am sorry, Russell, really and truly sorry. But Blackie wouldn't hurt you. He's a sick man, a very sick man.

RUSSELL: So am I. Sick to my stomach.

ALYCE: Mine doesn't feel so good either. Believe me.

RUSSELL: Why didn't you tell me about him?

ALYCE: If you think back a minute, you'll remember who he is. He was Blackie Victor, the middleweight, ten years ago.

RUSSELL: You mean he's *that* Blackie Victor? Jesus, I remember him all right, although I never saw him fight. He was a leading contender for awhile, and sometime middleweight champ of California, wasn't he?

ALYCE: That's right. And he made a lot of money, too. He had a bad head injury after he fought Diego Ramirez, and the doctors told him he couldn't fight anymore. That was when they were cracking down on the physical exams, and all. But he had money saved, and he opened a seafood restaurant on Fisherman's Wharf. Blackie's Place—maybe you remember it?

RUSSELL: Of course. I've eaten there—but that was a long time ago.

ALYCE: Well, one day Blackie came home from work and sat down in that chair. And he continued to sit there for twenty-four hours without moving. I called a doctor, and he said that Blackie needed rest and a lot of it. I took him to the hospital, and he got worse. He wouldn't eat or talk to anybody. And he had a terrific headache all the time.

RUSSELL: Punchy from too many hard ones to the head, I suppose.

ALYCE: That's what they told me. There had been signs, warning signals, but I hadn't noticed them. I could make a long and bitter story out of it, but there's no point to it. He used to get angry for no reason whatsoever. He'd go into the restaurant and get mad at one employee and then fire everybody, for example. You can't run a business that way. And after I sent him to the sanitarium I lost the business in hardly any time at all. I didn't know how to run a restaurant, and you know how fierce the competition is on the wharf.

RUSSELL: Sure. And you don't speak Italian, I suppose.

ALYCE: When I look back on that period, I still don't know that I could have handled things any better; once you get into something like that, there's no way out of it. The money, I mean. There was about ten thousand in the bank, and that went the first year. Doctors, examinations, treatments. The sanitarium was expensive—impossibly so. All of the doctors I took him to advised me to commit him to the state hospital, but I couldn't do it. I simply couldn't stand up in a courtroom and say that my husband was insane. Because he isn't; I know he isn't. For the first few months Mother and I used to visit him every Sunday. Then I brought him home. Mother was still alive, and she helped me a lot. Then she died—but Blackie was better, much better. Well, he can work now, and the money helps. He's beginning to pick out a few words in the newspaper . . .

RUSSELL: It's been a rough go, hasn't it?

ALYCE: It was at first, because I was so stupid. I tried to get a job, and I didn't know how to do anything. I've got a good job now, though—

RUSSELL: When did your mother die?

ALYCE: Fourteen months ago. She always used to say to me, "Alyce, go out. Don't stay at home now. Get something out of life." Mother worried about me all the time. She was afraid all this might ruin my life. And maybe it has—I don't know . . .

RUSSELL: Don't worry, baby. I'll work something out for you.

ALYCE: No, Russell. There isn't anything to work out. It's hopeless now, and only time can work out anything. When I told you I hadn't gone out with anyone—on a date or anything—it was god's truth. And Blackie is the reason why. Down at the parking garage where I work, not even the boss knows that I'm married—and I've been asked for dates plenty of times. A cashier is supposed to be fair game, I guess. But everybody down there thinks that I'm just an old maid who's afraid of men. I can't bring anyone home, because of Blackie, and even if one of the other girls asks me to dinner or something I can't go because I can't return the invitation.

RUSSELL: What's your reluctance to send him to a state institution? That's what they're for—and besides, it isn't up to you, is it? The judge commits him, not you personally.

ALYCE: No. I won't send him back. He didn't like the expensive private sanitarium, and it was a beautiful place. He'd die if I sent him to the state hospital. And he is getting better. Up there he'd only get worse. Blackie needs a home. Security. A place where he feels wanted.

RUSSELL: You aren't a doctor. What can you do?

ALYCE: He's much better, Russell. Honestly. (*She laughs.*) You should've seen him when I first brought him home! He was like a wild man around here. If he keeps on improving, maybe I can get him a nice outdoor job on a farm or a ranch. He likes to work with his hands; it's like training for him.

RUSSELL: Are you so much in love with him, then? Do you really love this old-timer so much?

ALYCE: (*Bitterly*) Love him? I hate him! I never did like him, and now I detest him!

RUSSELL: Really? Why'd you marry him, then? There must have been something. He must be at least twenty years older than you!

ALYCE: More than that. He was a friend of my father's. There isn't anything unusual about what happened; it happens all the time. When my father was alive Blackie used to visit us, and the two of them would sit around drinking beer and talking about Stanley Ketchel. My father thought Blackie was a better fighter than Ketchel. After Father died, Blackie came around and visited Mother. He got her an apartment house to manage, and we got our apartment rent-free. He was just a—what you'd call a friend of the family, I guess. But what he was really doing—and Mother didn't realize it either—was waiting for me to grow up. Father didn't leave much insurance, and Mother was busy trying to learn how to manage the apartment house. Blackie brought me presents everytime he called. He let me drive his car. And then he started to give me money, small sums at first—and I took it without telling Mother. Then he gave me more money; he would take me downtown and let me buy clothes—anything I wanted. So when he asked me to marry him, about a week after I finished high school, I was in debt to him. There was no way out.

RUSSELL: That's an awful story, Alyce. I consider myself as a pretty keen observer, but I never dreamed that you were married. I mean, the way you act and everything—you and Blackie . . . and wifely duties . . .

ALYCE: You're getting very personal now . . .

RUSSELL: I'm the personable type.

 (Lights cigarette, examines the tip.)

Mr Haxby wanted to know; Mr Haxby found out. Best taste yet—in a filter cigarette.

ALYCE: All right—I've gone this far—I might as well tell you the rest. I don't expect to see you again, anyway. So if you must know, Blackie sleeps in a small bedroom beyond mine. After he goes to sleep at night, I lock his door. I am always the first one up in the morning, and then I unlock his door. That's all there is to it.

RUSSELL: And how long has this been going on?

ALYCE: Several years. We haven't . . . slept together since before he got sick . . . some time before.

RUSSELL: How did you get him to agree to that kind of an arrangement?

ALYCE: I—I don't know; it sort of arranged itself, in a way. I'm not very proud of myself; I know what a wife is supposed to do. But I didn't know anything when I got married, not a thing. I was only eighteen, and I just thought it meant having a man living in the house—like Daddy being home again. Only Blackie would be my husband instead of Mother's. I couldn't understand why Blackie didn't want Mother to come along when we drove to Reno to get married . . . And then, after we got married, and I found out what Blackie wanted to do to me I got hysterical. He had to get the hotel doctor to come up to the room and give me a shot.

RUSSELL: *(Grinning)* That must've been some honeymoon.

ALYCE: Don't laugh at me; it was terrible, that's all, as all ignorance is terrible. We drove back the next morning, and then I had a long talk with Mother. She told me then what she should've told me before I got married.

RUSSELL: I can't understand such innocence—not in a city like San

Francisco. Didn't you ever have any girlfriends in school to discuss such things with?

ALYCE: No. Mother always took me to school and then picked me up afterwards. And after Daddy died and she had the apartment house to manage I had to help her. So I didn't go out or anything. I never had a date with a boy my own age. I was awfully fat in school, and that had something to do with my not having dates, I guess. Can't we talk about something else?

RUSSELL: Yeah. How'd you work things out with Blackie after your talk with your mother?

ALYCE: I married him because I was indebted to him, and I had to pay off my debts, that's all. You wouldn't be interested, but I worked out a schedule for him, that's all.

RUSSELL: A schedule! And you think I wouldn't be interested! Why that's the most marvelous thing I've ever heard. It's not only logical, it's a continuation of the All-American Way of Life. A man is scheduled for school, scheduled by IBM cards for college, married on-schedule—some time between twenty-one and twenty-five—and follows a schedule on his job. And then through promotion schedules he attains a terminal sinecure and retirement. So why not schedule his sex life as well? How did you work it out? Tuesdays and Thursdays? And what about Sundays and holidays? What a fool I've been to stay single all these years. I could've had a lovely, well-regulated sex life; and instead, I drive all over San Francisco in my Continental without knowing where or when my next piece is coming from—

ALYCE: Now you're being vulgar . . . and cruel, besides . . .

RUSSELL: Sure, I'm cruel, but you're kindly Alyce, aren't you? You bring home stray tomcats and keep them nicely penned—well-fed, well-petted, and you give them plenty of water. And poor old Blackie. Scheduled love, up to a point—so long as you feel indebted, and then you cut him off. When he's sick, you send him to the hospital like your little dog—Spiky, the cripple with two front feet missing. Did the idea ever occur to you that part of Blackie's so-called sickness is your fault?

ALYCE: I think you'd better go.

RUSSELL: I'm not going anywhere.

(He paces the floor.)

Last night I walked into a public dance hall with nothing on my mind except to kill an hour or so. And there you were—smiling at me. Eve. The most sophisticated woman in the world. In your tailored suit you stood out like—well, you didn't belong there. Every other woman there looked common—just because you were there. And I said to myself, "That's for me." Now I'm involved in the most complicated affair in the City of St. Francis—

ALYCE: You aren't involved in anything. You can walk out the door, and it's all over. But I can't walk out.

RUSSELL: No, I'm staying. I like it here. I believe in you, Alyce. And, as I said before, I'm in love with you.

ALYCE: There isn't any solution. There's nothing you can do.

RUSSELL: Thinking back, though, I'm a little surprised at your mother. It seems to me that she—

ALYCE: Don't say anything about my mother! She was a saint!

RUSSELL: Sure. I guess she was at that. Now let's talk about Blackie; he's something of a saint himself.

ALYCE: I shouldn't have told you anything! I shouldn't have asked you in last night, and I shouldn't have asked you to come back today. Please, Russell, don't ever say anything to anybody about Blackie.

RUSSELL: Say anything? What do you mean?

ALYCE: Don't say anything to anybody; that's what I mean. If my boss ever found out I was married I'd lose my job. He doesn't hire married women.

RUSSELL: You really are confused, kid. I'm not going to say anything, baby. Don't you trust me? I'm probably the nicest guy you've ever met.

ALYCE: I—I—I don't know . . . I'm all mixed up. I was lonesome, so lonesome . . . I liked you, and . . .

(She begins to sob.)

RUSSELL: *(He pulls her down to the couch, puts his arm about her shoulder.)* Don't. For god's sake, don't cry.

(He kisses her gently on the cheek, on her lips, and strokes her leg. Alyce begins to respond.)

I told you I'd work something out. Now stop crying.

BLACKIE: *(Enters. Stands in doorway watching as Russell and Alyce kiss. Alyce dabs at her eyes, and breaks away.)*

I put the hamburger in the kitchen.

(Russell gets to his feet, puts his hand in the pocket that contains knife, and leaves it there. Alyce stands, addresses Blackie.)

ALYCE: Did you remember to get the onions?

BLACKIE: They're in the kitchen, too. *(Exit Blackie)*

ALYCE: He's hungry; I'd better fix him something to eat.

RUSSELL: And I'd better go.

ALYCE: You don't have to rush off. Stay and eat something. It won't take long to fry some hamburgers.

RUSSELL: But what about—?

(*He jerks his thumb toward the doorway.*)

ALYCE: Oh, don't worry about him. He forgets right away. It's like hearing a dirty word on the radio. You don't remember it because you don't really believe you heard it.

RUSSELL: (*Puts on his hat, rubs his jaw.*) Just a second. (*Excitedly*) I've got an idea. You said that Blackie likes to work outside, in the open. Right?

ALYCE: Yes. Even now he sometimes talks about road camp, and how he used to chop wood and run eight miles every morning . . .

RUSSELL: I've got the solution, then. I've got an aunt in Sausalito who has a rooming house. It's a big place with lots of lawn to mow, and there's even a big garden out back. She's always telling me how hard it is to get help. I'll drive over there this afternoon and talk to her. She'd be happy to have a husky guy like Blackie around to do all the heavy work and all. She'll give him a room of his own, and a job. He can putter around outside all day, and maybe he can even learn how to make beds, or clean windows and so on—

ALYCE: No, no. That wouldn't work, Russell. Blackie wouldn't want to leave home, and—

RUSSELL: That's too damned bad about him—what he wants and doesn't want to do. You just leave things to Old Russell Haxby from now on, d'you hear? I'll drive over right now.

(*Crosses to doorway.*)

ALYCE: No, Russell! Wait! You can't rush anything this important. Any change has to have a careful preparation. Blackie has to be adjusted gradually to changes of any kind.

RUSSELL: (*From the doorway*) Don't worry about it, Baby. I said I'd take care of things and I will. So long for now; I'll call you tomorrow. Have him packed and ready to go!

(*He throws a kiss. Exit Russell.*)

ALYCE: (*She runs after him*) Wait, Russell, wait!

(*Quick curtain.*)

ACT III

SCENE 1

SCENE: *Same as Act I.*
TIME: *2 a.m., one week later.*

(As the curtain rises, Alyce, Ruthie, Blackie, and a Police Officer are discovered onstage. The policeman perches on the edge of a chair balancing a cap and saucer on his knee. His black slicker, still wet, and his cup and nightstick make a small pile by the side of his chair. Ruthie sits next to him in another chair, wearing bathrobe and slippers. Blackie sits in his red womb chair, and he is so wet he looks as if he had just climbed out of the bay. His shirt is soaking, and his long wet hair hangs down over his forehead. He doesn't move his head or eyes; his eyes are fixed on the wall, and there is a blank but sullen expression on his face. In his lap, Blackie holds—clutches—his television set grimly, and it is covered with his black leather workman's jacket. Alyce stands by the window, looking out, wearing a robe and slippers. She turns and walks to Blackie's chair. The tone of her voice is weary; she has asked the same questions before.)

ALYCE: Blackie ... Blackie ... Why don't you go to your room and change your clothes? You'll get a cold if you don't. Blackie, do you hear me, Blackie?

(Blackie does not look at her or respond to her presence. She returns to her place beside the window, and looks out again.)

I wish Russell would hurry up and get here.

RUTHIE: *(Reassuringly)* Give him time.

ALYCE: He said he'd be right over.

RUTHIE: The poor man has to get dressed. Men don't move very fast when they first get out of bed at two in the morning, believe me.

ALYCE: *(To Policeman)* You don't have to wait, Officer. My friend will be along any minute now.

POLICEMAN: Oh, that's quite all right, Ma'am. I don't mind staying, it's all a part of the job. And I wouldn't feel right about leaving when there isn't a man around. Begging your pardon and all, but your husband gave us a conniption fit when we tried to take his television set away from him. In fact, we couldn't manage it without hurting him, so we let him ride with it in his lap. He's as strong as an ox.

ALYCE: Blackie wouldn't hurt a fly.

POLICEMAN: Yes, Ma'am. But I'll stay awhile if you don't mind. (*To Ruthie*) You know, at first I thought he was drunk or something. But when I looked in his wallet and found out that he was Blackie Victor, I brought him home instead of taking him down and booking him.

RUTHIE: We're grateful for that, Officer. Blackie doesn't drink; I doubt if he's ever had more than a beer or two in his whole life, if that. He was in the ring so long, he's a little . . . (*She gestures with a forefinger.*)

POLICEMAN: I understand. I used to do a little boxing. And I've seen Blackie fight; a wonderful left he used to have.

RUTHIE: Would you like some more coffee?

POLICEMAN: I don't mind. This is pretty good coffee, even if it is instant. If you make instant right, it tastes as good as fresh perked.

(*Ruthie fills his cup from the pot on coffee table.*)

I'll bet my partner's sore. (*He laughs*) He's down in the car listening for calls. But he can't say nothing about me staying up here because I'm senior to him, you see. And this is, after all, official police business.

RUTHIE: How long have you been on the force, Officer?

POLICEMAN: Me? Ever since right after the Korean War. I was in the M.P.'s—and now I'm up for sergeant.

RUTHIE: How wonderful.

POLICEMAN: Oh, I don't know. (*Shrugs*) All you gotta do is keep your nose clean.

ALYCE: (*Crosses to Blackie's chair*) Why won't you go into your bedroom and change your clothes, Blackie?

(*Blackie turns his head away from her, and stares fixedly at the wall.*)

What happened in Sausalito? Tell me. Why did you run away? Was Mr Haxby's aunt mean to you in any way? If you don't change clothes you're liable to get pneumonia. You know that, don't you?

RUTHIE: Can't you see that you're wasting your time, honey? The dummy isn't going to tell you anything. You'd get more sense out of talking to his TV set.

ALYCE: We have to do something; we can't let him sit there all night in those wet clothes!

POLICEMAN: *(Reluctantly)* If you want me to, Ma'am, I'll try to put him to bed. But I don't relish trying to rassle that TV set away from him. When both me and my partner couldn't do it, I—

RUTHIE: That's quite all right, Officer. We'll manage. We'll just wait for Mr Haxby; he'll take care of things for us.

(With a grateful sigh, the policeman sits back and drinks more of his coffee.)

ALYCE: I can't imagine any reason in the world why Blackie would walk all the way across the Golden Gate Bridge in the driving rain. What do you suppose happened, Ruthie?

RUTHIE: Maybe his reception wasn't so good over in Sausalito—I mean his TV reception.

ALYCE: Russell will simply have to call his aunt and find out. I don't want to call her this early in the morning. She might not even know he's gone.

(She shudders.)

It's cold in here. Pour me a cup, will you please, Ruthie?

(Ruthie pours a cup of coffee for Alyce. Doorbell rings.)

That's Russell!

(Exit Alyce, running. The policeman stands, puts on his hat and raincoat.)

RUTHIE: *(Holding a cup of freshly poured coffee. To Blackie.)*

How about you, Blackie? Would you like a cup of nice hot coffee?

POLICEMAN: I don't believe he can hear you, Ma'am.

RUTHIE: Oh, he can hear me all right. He's just being stubborn, that's all. Alyce may give him sympathy, but I won't.

RUSSELL: *(Enter Russell and Alyce. Russell is wearing a damp trenchcoat and a rain-spotted gray hat. He does not remove them throughout the scene. He stops in front of the policeman.)*

It was very nice of you to wait, Officer, and I appreciate it.

(He takes out a money clip, removes a five dollar bill, and tries to hand it to the policeman.)

Here. Buy yourself some cigars.

(Policeman will not take the money.)

POLICEMAN: No, thank you, Sir. I was merely doing my duty.

RUSSELL: Buy yourself a drink.

POLICEMAN: *(Crosses to doorway, turns, and ignores Russell.)*

I'll be cruising around the neighborhood. If you need any help with Mr Victor, just call the precinct . . .

(Exit Policeman. Russell returns bill to his money clip.)

RUSSELL: *(To Ruthie)* All right, Ruthie. What's the story?

RUTHIE: Do you want a cup of coffee?

RUSSELL: No—perhaps later. What's the story?

ALYCE: It was about an hour ago and the police came and—

RUSSELL: Never mind. You're incoherent. Let Ruthie tell it.

RUTHIE: I really don't know what's behind it myself, Russell. As Alyce said, about an hour ago the police brought Blackie home, soaking wet, just as he is now. I guess he didn't like Sausalito, or else something happened over there. So he waited for a driving rainstorm, wrapped up his Little Caveman TV set in his leather jacket and walked across the Golden Gate Bridge. He got as far as the tollgate, and the tollgate man called the police. The policemen looked in his wallet, found his address, and brought him home. Luckily, they knew who he was; otherwise, we'd be down at the police station trying to get him out—apparently, he put up quite a struggle before they could get him into the police car.

RUSSELL: Why did he leave? Did he say?

RUTHIE: We haven't been able to pry a sound out of him.

RUSSELL: *(Crosses to Blackie.)* Okay, out with it. Why did you take off from Sausalito in the middle of the night? *(Pause)* Do you hear me?

> *(Blackie turns his head away.)*

Look at me when I talk, d'you hear me?

RUTHIE: *(Mocking)* Oh, so you won't talk, huh?

RUSSELL: *(Irritated, turns.)* All right, that's enough out of you. You can both leave the room. Right now!

ALYCE: We've got to get him out of those wet clothes, Russell.

RUSSELL: I'll take care of it. Go on, now. Out!

ALYCE: You be nice to him, Russell—

RUSSELL: What?

ALYCE: Don't be mean to him, or shout at him, or—

RUSSELL: I don't know what in the hell you're talking about! What kind of a bastard do you think I am, anyway?

ALYCE: I didn't mean anything—

RUTHIE: *(She shoos Alyce toward the door.)* Come on, sweetie.

> *(Exit Alyce and Ruthie. Ruthie slides the doors closed.)*

RUSSELL: *(Lights cigarette, looks sardonically at Blackie.)*

So Blackie Victor didn't like Sausalito; the San Francisco bedroom for lawyers, yachtsmen, account executives, and unlonely women with substantial alimony . . . Well, I can't say I blame you a helluva lot—are you listening to me?

(Blackie shakes his head vigorously. Without warning, Russell steps in close and slaps Blackie sharply across the face. Blackie releases his grip on the television set and covers his face with both hands. Russell rips the jacket off the set and sails it across the room. He removes the set from Blackie's lap and puts it in its regular place above the radio-phonograph console. Russell backs off, takes out his knife, flips it open.)

Now listen to me, Old Refugee from Sausalito. You are in hot water with good old, kind old, benevolent old Russell Haxby. I sent you to Sausalito to get rid of you—and it wasn't an easy matter to convince my sweet old Aunt Margaret to take you in, either. But I didn't send you because you were off your rocker, because you aren't. I know. I can tell. When a nut gets wise to himself, he's halfway out of the shell. And you are wise; and you have been for a long time. But I don't play hunches, not until I've backed them up with concrete evidence. I had a long talk with your foreman, Mr Harvey Swettmann—with a name like that, he was born to be a foreman, wasn't he?—and he told me that you were one of his best workers, no punchier than any of the others down at the shipyard. Surprised? Didn't think I'd check on you, did you?

(Blackie spreads his fingers, and watches Russell play with the knife as it is shifted from hand to hand.)

No, you may not be exactly crazy, my friend, but the point is that I can prove you are. You've left me with two choices. One. Back to the institution!

(Russell points with the knife.)

Do you want to go back up there—that is, to the state funny farm?

(Blackie puts his hands in his lap, and shakes his head.)

Then how about Number Two? The window.

(Russell crosses to window, and looks down at the street.)

About a thirty-six foot drop, I'd say. It would do very nicely. One little leap from you and all of your troubles would be over. No Sausalito. No state institution. No nothing. Nada, my friend, nada. Oblivion. Blackness. How does it sound?

(Blackie shakes his head vigorously.)

Then I guess it's the institution, Old Fighter. You'll like it there, after you get used to it. They'll teach you how to play dominoes, weave baskets. Only they call it O.T., Occupational Therapy. You see, Blackie, I've got you pegged, all the way down. You've been fooling simple-minded Alyce for a long time, but you can't fool me. That's *my* business. I sell dreams to fools in the form of used automobiles. When you discovered that Alyce wouldn't ever grow up, you tried to get younger. But it didn't work out, did it? But I can see your logic—it's rational enough. Maternal love is better than no love at all—so you became a child again. A child needing constant protection—love—affection—attention—eternal supervision. Love is another word for Mother. I will always wonder now how far back you were willing to go in order to win her back completely. It doesn't matter. I think your best bet is the window, after all. Because Russell Haxby wants Alyce for himself, and Russell Haxby doesn't share!

(Slowly, very slowly, as Russell watches with an amused expression, Blackie slides out of the chair and onto his knees. He rolls over on his side, and curls into a ball, raising his knees, and pulling his elbows and arms in tightly. He lowers his head and shuts his eyes. His position is foetus-like.)

I see. You're willing to go all the way back.

(Russell laughs.)

You know, Blackie, that's a pretty good imitation of a catatonic position; you must've been reading Ruthie's medical books on the sly. *(Sternly.)* Come off it, Blackie! It won't work. It's either the institution or jump! And you can make up your mind to which it'll be right now!

(Russell turns toward the window. Blackie uncurls, jumps to his feet and, in a boxer's crouch, leaps toward Russell. Russell turns, jumps back out of reach, and, as Blackie throws a long left jab, Russell calmly sticks his knife into Blackie's hand.)

I didn't say jump for me. *(A short angry laugh.)* I said jump for the window.

(Defeated, Blackie yelps, clutches his wounded hand with his right hand and returns to his chair. He hugs his hands to his chest and stares at the floor.)

Okay, Blackie. The institution it is.

(Russell walks to the window and kicks. There is a crashing of glass.)

Alyce! Ruthie! Come here!

(Enter Ruthie and Alyce. Ruthie crosses to Russell, Alyce to Blackie's chair. Ruthie looks at the broken "window.")

RUTHIE: What happened, Russell?

RUSSELL: The damned fool tried to jump out the window. *(Modestly.)* I caught him just in time.

ALYCE: *(Examining Blackie's hand.)* He's cut himself.

RUSSELL: Good thing I managed to grab him; he might have killed himself.

(Doorbell rings.)

ALYCE: Who can that be? I'll get it. Will you get a bandage and some iodine, Ruthie?

(Exit Alyce.)

RUTHIE: What are we going to do, Russell? Alyce and I can't go on like this. He's disrupting our entire lives!

RUSSELL: The answer's obvious. *(Shrugs.)* There's only one thing you can do. You've got to commit him, that's all. And I mean tomorrow, or as soon as possible. He should be under the care of a doctor. I stuck my neck out when I took him over to my Aunt Margaret's place—and I won't do it again.

RUTHIE: I know you did—but Alyce won't go into court—

RUSSELL: *(Quickly)* She doesn't have to! You're a relative by marriage, and I'll testify—and so will the policeman who picked him up tonight—

(Enter Alyce and Policeman.)

ALYCE: You haven't got the bandage—?

RUTHIE: I didn't have time.

RUSSELL: Never mind. They can fix his hand at the hospital. You girls take him into the bedroom and get him changed into dry clothes. And pack his pyjamas and razor while you're at it.

(Russell crosses to Blackie, helps him to his feet. Blackie is docile, and Russell pats him gently on the shoulder.)

Now you go along with Ruthie and Alyce, Old Timer. They'll take care of you.

(Ruthie and Alyce take Blackie out of the room.)

He tried to kill himself, Officer. Poor devil. I caught him just in time. He's a very unhappy man.

POLICEMAN: He came pretty close to being middleweight champion of the world for awhile there.

RUSSELL: A great fighter. He was as light on his feet as a featherweight. But he hung on too long; those poor guys get beat to death.

POLICEMAN: It's a damned shame. They ought to have rules or something, making them quit before they get their heads beat in.

RUSSELL: They do have regulations. But you know how it is. They get a taste of the big money, and—they keep on fighting, and . . . well, look what happens. Oh, can you call an ambulance?

POLICEMAN: Yes, sir.

RUSSELL: You'd better call one then. And tell them they'd better put him in a locked ward to keep him from hurting himself. I'd feel pretty damned bad if anything happened to old Blackie Victor. But it isn't safe to leave him alone here with those girls. There's a phone on the hall table—

POLICEMAN: I'll call on the radio. I'll have to make a report on the whole thing now. I wasn't going to before—being it was Blackie Victor, and all—but I can't cover up any suicide attempt—

RUSSELL: No reason why you should. In fact, it will help Mrs Victor if you put in everything that happened tonight. Resisting arrest, and all. When she commits him, it'll help the judge make his decision.

POLICEMAN: Yes, sir. I'd better call the ambulance.

(*Exit Policeman. Russell lights cigarette. Enter Alyce.*)

RUSSELL: How is he?

ALYCE: He'll be all right in the morning. He's just tired, that's all.

RUSSELL: The ambulance will be along in a few minutes.

ALYCE: That won't be necessary. The cut on his hand isn't serious. Ruthie and I can take care of it.

RUSSELL: (*Patiently*) You don't understand, baby. Blackie tried to commit suicide. That's against the law, and the cop has to make out a report. And that means the hospital and a psychiatric evaluation.

ALYCE: How long will it take? Blackie should go to sleep—he shouldn't run around all night—

RUSSELL: You might as well face it, Alyce. Blackie isn't going to get well. The time has come when Blackie can no longer take care of himself. Don't you realize that by now?

ALYCE: Oh, I think he'll get better.

RUSSELL: No he won't. Why do you kid yourself? You've got a shelf full of medical books that say he won't—why not read some of them?

ALYCE: I have read them.

RUSSELL: All right, then.

ALYCE: Until you took him to your aunt's, he was coming along fine—

RUSSELL: Are you going to suddenly blame me because Blackie Victor had a hundred and eighty some odd professional fights?

ALYCE: I'm sorry, Russell, I didn't mean it was your fault. It's just that I'm upset and—

RUSSELL: I'll say this slowly. Blackie was *not* getting better. You were simply getting used to him, and it isn't the same thing. I'm not going to argue about it. I am telling you. He has to be sent to an institution; that's where he belongs; that's the only place he can get the care he needs.

ALYCE: I just can't, Russell. I—

RUSSELL: Then Ruthie'll have to do it for you. Good night, Alyce. It's late. I'll call you first thing in the morning.(*He kisses Alyce quickly, pats her on the shoulder. Exit Russell.*)

ALYCE: Wait, Russell, wait!
   (*She starts to follow, changes her mind, and sits in Blackie's chair as the
   curtain falls slowly.*)

ACT III

SCENE 2

SCENE: *Same as ACT I.*
TIME: *2 p.m., one week later.*
 (The curtain rises on an empty stage. Enter Russell, Ruthie, Alyce, and Stanley. They are all dressed for the street, but in dark clothes. Stanley wears a black mourning band on his left sleeve. The two women are wearing hats, with dark off-the-face veils. Russell removes his hat, and tosses it onto a chair. Alyce and Ruthie hesitate just inside the doorway.)

ALYCE: Would you boys like some coffee?
RUSSELL: Coffee, no. But I could stand a drink.
RUTHIE: How about sandwiches?
RUSSELL: Anything.
STANLEY: Coffee's fine with me.
ALYCE: I'm sorry, Russell, but there isn't anything to drink.
RUSSELL: *(Shrugs)* All right. Coffee, then. Half a cup, the rest hot water.
 (Russell crosses to window, and looks out.)
Your wife had a damned nice funeral, Stanley.
STANLEY: Thanks. Them undertakers sure did a fine job. I didn't know my wife could ever look so good.
RUSSELL: She certainly did look life-like, all right. Of course I never knew her . . .
STANLEY: *(After pause)* She looked even better, I think. Now it's all over—I'm glad it's all over. It was tough on me, you know: her being an invalid so long.
RUSSELL: *(Raising his eyebrows, although Stanley can't see his face.)* I'll bet it was, Stanley.
STANLEY: I don't want you to get me wrong, now. I don't mean I'm

sorry she's dead; I don't mean that at all. She's a lot better off where she is now, even so. It was no good her layin' there like that, month after month, not raisin' a finger hardly. She's better off now, but that don't mean I'm glad she's dead.

RUSSELL: Of course she's better off. And so, of course, are you, my friend.

STANLEY: Well, now, when you put it that way, I've got to admit it. I guess I am.

RUSSELL: How do you like the new used car, by the way? Giving you any trouble?

STANLEY: No, no, I like it just fine.

RUSSELL: I got you a damned good buy, all right. I'll bet that's the best running Edsel in San Francisco.

STANLEY: It works all right; I ain't complaining. It ain't as good as your car, but then it didn't cost so much, either.

RUSSELL: *(Quickly)* That isn't my car—the Lincoln convertible. I don't own a car, Stanley, and I've never owned a car in my life. Driving that Lincoln is just one more advantage of selling used cars. When I need a car I just take one off the lot. I don't believe in owning anything you can't squeeze into an ostrich-skin wallet.

STANLEY: I thought it was your car. You drive it all the time.

RUSSELL: A Lincoln suits my mood these days, that's all. But if you have any trouble with that Edsel, let me know. I know a mechanic who'll take good care of you.

STANLEY: *(Worriedly.)* Do you think I'll have any trouble?

RUSSELL: No. But if you do, let me know. There aren't many expert Edsel men around these days.

STANLEY: *(Hesitantly)* Tell me, Mr Haxby. I've been meanin' to ask you before. How come Blackie left Sausalito and walked home in all that rain? I been wonderin' about it . . .

RUSSELL: Why?

STANLEY: Just curious.

RUSSELL: He was homesick, Stanley, that's all. My Aunt Margaret couldn't understand it either, but that's what we both decided it was. Blackie was a mighty sick man, Stanley. And he needed to be in a hospital where they could look after him.

STANLEY: No doubt of that. I was just wonderin' was all.

RUSSELL: There was nothing mysterious about it.

RUTHIE: *(Enter Ruthie with a tray holding cheese and crackers. She sets it on the* *coffee table beside Stanley.)* This is all I could find; the old larder is bare these days. Life has been so hectic around here lately there's nothing in the refrigerator—not even eggs. But cheese and crackers will hold you till dinner.

STANLEY: Suits me.

(Stanley makes a cracker and cheese sandwich.)

RUTHIE: Coffee'll be along in a minute.

(She slices a piece of cheese, and nibbles on it.)

RUSSELL: What are your plans these days, Ruthie?

RUTHIE: Plans?

RUSSELL: That's right. Plans. With Blackie in the hospital, you and Alyce aren't going to need this expensive three-bedroom apartment.

RUTHIE: We might . . . and there's a lease—

RUSSELL: You mean that you and Stanley are getting married right away?

STANLEY: *(Caught with a mouthful of crackers—splutters.)*

Oh, no! We can't get married right away! My wife's relatives would raise hell, and—

RUTHIE: What do I care what your ex-wife's relatives say?

STANLEY: Not only that. There's the will, yet. It's gotta go through probate, and—

RUTHIE: A formality. She left everything to you, didn't she? This is a community property state.

STANLEY: Oh, yes. No trouble there. But it just wouldn't look right. I leave it to you, Russell. What about it? How would it look?

RUSSELL: *(Shrugs.)* I wouldn't know.

RUTHIE: Listen to me, Old Man of the Sea. We're getting married in the very immediate future. By next month at the latest, if not before!

STANLEY: There isn't time. I've got to settle the property first. And I've got to give the relatives something—some of the household furniture, maybe. Otherwise, they might try to tie up everything in court. They never liked me, you know.

RUTHIE: You aren't going to give her relatives anything! When we're married I'll be the closest relative you have; and if you want to give anything away you can give it to me!

STANLEY: Let's leave it to Russell. How would it look to the Probate Court, Russell? Me married again only a week or so after I bury my wife, and her not good and cold yet in the ground? How about it, Russell?

RUSSELL: *(Shrugs)* I wouldn't know, Stanley.

RUTHIE: Never mind for now. We'll discuss it later, Stanley. Have some more cheese and crackers.

STANLEY: I ain't hungry.

RUSSELL: What will you do with your house, Stanley?

STANLEY: I don't know yet. Sell it, I suppose.

RUTHIE: Over my dead body! We aren't selling it; we're going to live in it.

STANLEY: *(Shaking his head)* No, I can't do that. That house has got too many sad memories for me.

RUTHIE: And so has this damned apartment for me!

RUSSELL: *(Nodding sagely)* In other words, Ruthie, you plan on an early marriage?

RUTHIE: Yes, and the sooner the better.

ALYCE: *(Enters, with coffee and cups, etc.)* Here we are. And I've poured yours, Russell, just the way you like it.

RUSSELL: *(Taking cup, and retreating toward the window.)*

Have you heard the news, Alyce? Stanley and Ruthie are getting married next week.

STANLEY: *(Once again, Stanley is caught with a mouthful of crackers—and splutters them out.)* Now wait a minute!

ALYCE: Next week, Ruthie?

RUTHIE: *(Ignoring Stanley)* That's right.

ALYCE: Oh, I'm so happy for you!

(The two women embrace.)

STANLEY: I can't see how we can—not next week! We're going to have to wait a while . . . a couple of months, a month, maybe . . .

RUTHIE: *(Pours two cups; hands one to Stanley, takes one herself.)* Let's go into my bedroom, Stanley. We've got a lot of things to talk about.

STANLEY: You going to rush me down to City Hall before I finish my coffee?

RUTHIE: Come on. You can drink it in the bedroom.

(Exit Ruthie and Stanley. Stanley glares malevolently at Russell as he leaves.)

RUSSELL: *(Cheerfully)* Well, it looks as if everything has worked out all right for Ruthie and Stanley.

ALYCE: For Ruthie, anyway.

RUSSELL: And for you too, Alyce.

ALYCE: For me? I'm still married to Blackie Victor—or have you forgotten?

RUSSELL: Right now you are, sure. But not forever.

ALYCE: What about us, Russell? How do we get married?

RUSSELL: *(Genuinely surprised)* Married? I've never said anything to you about marriage. Do I look like Stanley Sinkiewicz? He's the type that gets married—not me.

ALYCE: I don't understand . . . I thought you said you loved me, and—

RUSSELL: I *do* love you, Alyce. Good god, I straightened out your life for you once. Do you want to get yourself in another mess already?

ALYCE: I don't think that every marriage is a mess.

RUSSELL: Baby; I love you very much. Don't you love me?

ALYCE: Yes. I love you, Russell. You know I do.

RUSSELL: Then we won't spoil our love by getting married. You see, I'm not any Blackie Victor, nor am I a Stanley Sinkiewicz. I'm a man. You've got a lot to learn about love, and I'll be very patient with you.

ALYCE: In other words, what you're really saying is, you aren't Stanley, but I am. Is that it?

RUSSELL: Don't get me wrong, baby.

ALYCE: How *am* I supposed to get you, then?

ALYCE: Just as I said. Nothing is permanent in this life, baby. And love least of all. Let me tell you something. A few ritualistic vows muttered in ignorance don't make a happy marriage. To build families, for example, you have to have a foundation to build on. And love is air. Nothing but air. Love is light, a frothy mixture of soft golden clouds and sunlight; that's what love is. Marriage is a pretty concept, but it doesn't last. A young couple—and we're no longer *that* young—marries a dream, and the dream disappears the day they start using the same bathroom.

ALYCE: I see what you mean, Russell. You want me as a cheap pickup, a girl you found on the streets. No, thanks. Oh, I love you all right, but not your way. I want a good marriage, a normal marriage, a home . . . and maybe even babies some day. But I won't go to you under your terms. Never!

RUSSELL: Is that the way you want it? Because if it is, I'll walk out that door and I won't be back.

ALYCE: That's the best idea you've had yet. Just leave, and don't come back.

RUSSELL: *(Puts on his hat. Alyce turns away from him, and balls her fists.)* All right. I'm leaving.

(He turns at the door, and pushes his hat back.)

Did you ever read Dostoyevsky, Alyce? Probably not. I forget the name of his book, but it doesn't matter. This character, though, got to thinking about the eternal verities of death. And he came to the conclusion that eternity itelf wasn't a very large place. No vastnesses, no enormity, no unlimited vistas stretching into infinity. He figured that eternity was just a little room, a tiny little room, about the size of a clothes closet. And in that room there were nothing but spiders. Millions, billions of spiders, all shapes and sizes. Nothing but spiders.

I think he was right, Alyce. And you've got the same thing right here. Blackie's gone, and Ruthie soon will be. But you won't be gone. You'll rattle around in this apartment like a pebble in an empty gas tank. But you won't be all alone—not quite. You'll have your tomcats and a crippled dog for company. And spiders. The spiders of doubt, the spiders of memory. You have no friends, and you don't know how to make any. You've never even been a woman, Alyce.

(*Alyce covers her face with her hands.*)

And what do you expect me to do, Alyce? The French Foreign Legion has been disbanded—

ALYCE: I don't care what you do.

RUSSELL: Goodbye, Alyce.

ALYCE: Goodbye.

(*Exit Russell; he softly closes the double doors. Alyce wipes her eyes, and turns toward the "window."*)

(*In a high anguished voice*) Oh, Russell!

RUSSELL: (*The doors slide open with a bang. Russell enters, throws his hat on a chair.*) Nobody ever takes the name of Russell Haxby in vain!

ALYCE: You came back!

RUSSELL: I've never been away.

ALYCE: (*She rushes into his arms, clasping him tight around the waist.*) You do love me, don't you, Russell?

RUSSELL: Of course I do; you know I do.

(*He closes double doors, turns the key to lock them. He returns to Alyce, who now stands in the center of the room. He removes her jacket. He unbuttons her blouse, and puts it on the chair. He unzips her skirt, and it falls to her feet. She closes her eyes, and clenches her fists, waiting, looking ridiculous in her pillbox hat, as Russell continues to methodically undress her . . . The curtain falls.*)

THE END

CHARLES WILLEFORD
WILD WIVES

RE/SEARCH PUBLICATIONS/SAN FRANCISCO

"She wasn't wearing much beneath the skirt. In an instant it was all over. Fiercely and abruptly."

In the darkest hard-boiled tradition Charles Willeford mixes sex, brutality, deception, and crime in his classic amoral novels, *High Priest of California* and *Wild Wives,* written in 1953. Deep characterizations of near-psychopaths and their victims, caught in complex webs of fantasy and futility. Brilliant, sardonic writing, full of vile surprises. By the author of the recently acclaimed *Miami Blues,* soon to be a movie.

"—No one writes a better crime novel."
—*Elmore Leonard*

"Mr. Willeford never puts a foot wrong, and this is truly an entertainment to relish."—*The New Yorker*

**TURN THIS BOOK OVER FOR
SECOND COMPLETE NOVEL**

Publishers/Editors:	Andrea Juno and V. Vale
Production Editor:	Catherine Reuther
Managing Editor:	Francisco de Oliveira Mattos
Photographers:	Bobby Neel Adams, Ana Barrado
Typesetting:	Caroline Ewing, Susan Becker, Leslie Pollock
Photo Session Models:	Christine Alicino, Susan Arick, Clara Bellino, Luther Blue, Michael Dingle, Madeleine Gavin, Annette Kerns, Francoise Remy de Cournon, Jeff Sand, Elliott Shannonhouse
Layout:	Mary Sheppard, Deborah Valentine, Ed Wojciechowski
Book Design:	Andrea Juno

Paperback: ISBN 0-940642-11-5
Hardback: ISBN 0-940642-12-3

Library of Congress Card Catalog Number: 87-061283

BOOKSTORE DISTRIBUTION: Subco, PO Box 10233,
  Eugene OR 97440 (503) 343-6324
U.K. DISTRIBUTION: Airlift, 14 Baltic St, London EC1 Y0TB,
  U.K. (01) 251-8608

SUBSCRIPTIONS: $35 for 3 issues ($45 air overseas/$50 for Australia/
  Asia). Write for catalog.

RE/SEARCH PUBLICATIONS, 20 Romolo #B, San Francisco CA 94133
  (415) 362-1465

For permission to reproduce this play, contact Jim Trupin, Jet Literary
Associates Inc, 124 E. 84th St Suite 4-A, NYC NY 10028.

Printed in Hong Kong

All photos: Bobby Neel Adams, except for portrait of Charles Willeford
  by Ana Barrado
Cover photos: Bobby Neel Adams

RE/SEARCH PUBLICATIONS
20 Romolo #B, San Francisco, CA 94133

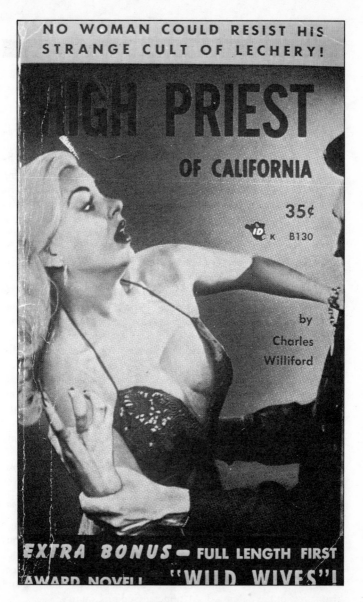

NO WOMAN COULD RESIST HIS
STRANGE CULT OF LECHERY!

HIGH PRIEST

OF CALIFORNIA

35¢

K   B130

by
Charles
Williford

EXTRA BONUS — FULL LENGTH FIRST
AWARD NOVEL   "WILD WIVES"!

Original cover of WILD WIVES, 1956 Beacon Book paperback.

America is rediscovering, on a massive scale, the cynical, hard-boiled novels (Jim Thompson, David Goodis, Charles Willeford, and others) that were a product of the fifties/early sixties—the last transitional decade before television saturated language. At a time when millions of relatively ordinary folk still *read,* these books satisfied the universal craving for adventure, romance, psychological understanding and linguistic surprise, at their best providing a wealth of blunt street-*poetic* dialogue amidst sudden, unexpected acts and counter-acts.

While masculine and feminine characterizations were often ludicrously polarized, nevertheless a harsh, deeply realistic unsentimentality prevailed, occasionally veering toward dark, psychotic depths. The doomsday mentality engendered by the post-nuclear age Cold War lent an edge of despair to the ruthless greed and desire manifested by the power-hungry characters starring in these black thrillers. A type of hero without ideals, possibly even mentally unbalanced, was asserting itself.

In contrast to the bland, homogenized speech and entertainment purveyed by today's mass media, this fiction was strong and colorful, etching vivid pictures in the reader's mind. The power of this language yet survives to speak to new generations of readers dissatisfied with the superficial, predictable quality of experience commonly accepted as adult entertainment.

Charles Willeford's 1953 first novel, *The High Priest of California,* offers a rare treat: the opportunity to see the world through the eyes of a ruthless, misogynistic near-psychopath, used-car salesman Russell Haxby, *without moral comment* on his acts. This radical approach is in direct counterpoint to most hard-boiled writers of the time. Usually such a character is presented from the outside, with a pious commentary. Or the work will be propped up with some moral justification system, like a Mickey Spillane novel in which the hero, under the patina of "right"-ness, excuses numerous immoral and brutal acts in the defense of Manliness, God or Country.

By using the structure of a first-person narrative, Willeford makes the reader identify and empathize with the hero. Then repul-

sion intrudes when early on the author offers a stunning clue to the hero's nature: for no *good* reason he knees a parking attendant in the groin and judo-chops him to the ground, away from where his date can see. The first-person narration makes very little of it, yet this act of casual brutality is a shocker, an irrational act and a harbinger of more to come.

What makes *High Priest* exceptional is that here the hero's basic misogyny is *isolated,* undisguised by missions for patriotism, crime-solving or other reasons. The only mission in this book is to conquer a woman. Further, the hero's characterization is deep and *complex*— Russell Haxby, who listens to Bartok and tries to translate James Joyce's *Ulysses,* defies facile categorization as a villain. Even though his persona is pure hypocrisy and opportunism (he's even willing to murder if he can get away with it), he also has far more wit, sardonicism and style than anyone else. And the first person narrative forces the reader to confront the character's unconscionable twists of evil lurking in one's own self.

In the hard-boiled tradition, Willeford's second 1953 novel, *Wild Wives,* stars Jake Blake, an amoral detective whose nemesis is the beautiful, insane young wife of a socially prominent, elderly San Francisco architect. Initially hired to shake off two goons who've been paid to follow her, Blake becomes entangled in a web of deception, intrigue and murder in which he ends up the fall guy. This work is completely contemporary in its homosexual character-izations and sexual morality, presenting some very colorful players and scenarios.

Genuinely creative writing functions as *antidote* to the mediocri-tizing language (mostly from television and newspapers) inundating us today. All of Charles Willeford's writing is marked by the unusual: devious plots, dialogue rich in innuendo, eccentric detailing of even the smallest roles, wry touches of perversity, sardonicism, plus an overall no-nonsense truth to character. Multiple levels of meaning and mystery, as well as authentic poetic inventiveness, are there to perform the vital function of renewing and refreshing our perceptions and reinvigorating our thought. Good writing, like the works reprinted here, can cut across time to find its own audience and assume new life on its own.

—V. Vale and Andrea Juno, San Francisco, 1987

CHARLES RAY WILLEFORD III
PARTIAL BIOGRAPHY

(pseud. Will Charles)

1-2-1919	Born Little Rock, Ark., son of Charles Ray II and Aileen (Lowey) Willeford.
1936-1956	U.S. Army, retired as Master Sergeant. USA, Philippines, Europe, etc. Military Awards: Silver Star, Bronze Star, Purple Heart, Luxembourg Croix de Guerre.
7-1-1951	Married Mary Jo Norton, an English professor.
1956	Beacon Fiction award for *Pick-Up*.
1960	Palm Beach Jr. College: A.A.
1962	University of Miami, B.A. (magna cum laude)
1964	M.A. Associate editor, *Alfred Hitchcock Mystery Magazine*.
1964-1967	Coral Gables, Fla: University of Miami, instructor in humanities.
1967-1985	Miami, Fla: Miami-Dade Junior College, taught English and philosophy (asso. professor, etc).
1973	Mark Twain Award for *Cockfighter*.
1974	*Cockfighter* made into movie starring Warren Oates, etc.
10-1976	divorced
1987	*Miami Blues* optioned for movie.
Other:	[source: *Contemporary Authors,* New Revision Series, Vol. 15] Columnist for *Village Post, Miami Herald, Mystery Scene* (3840 Clark Rd SE, Cedar Rapids IA 52403, sample issue $6), articles in *Books Abroad, Saturday Review, Playboy, Writer's Digest, Sports Illustrated, Air Force, Publishers Weekly, Armchair Detective* (129 West 56th St, NYC 10019, sample issue $8). Biographical articles in *Harpers, The Face, Spin,* etc. Dennis McMillan publishes obscure Willeford titles; write 1995 Calais Dr #3, Miami Beach, FL 33141 for info. Member: Authors League of America, Mystery Writers of America, Vorpal Blades. Quotation: "I had a hunch that madness was a predominant theme and a normal condition for Americans living in the second half of this century. The publication of *The Machine in Ward Eleven* (1963) and its reception by readers confirmed what I had only heretofore suspected."

BIBLIOGRAPHY

POETRY:

The Outcast Poets (1947) portfolio of Willeford & 4 other poets gathered in an envelope; #8 in the Alicat Book Shop Press "Outcast" Chapbook Series

Proletarian Laughter (1948) Alicat #12, 1000 copy press run

Poontang (1967) New Athenaeum Press, Crescent City, FL, 500 copy press run

NOVELS:

High Priest of California (1953), Royal Giant Editions pb; bound with *Full Moon,* a novel by Talbot Mundy

Pick-Up (1954), Beacon Book pb #109; repr. 1967 Softcover Library pb; repr. 1987 Black Lizard Books pb

Wild Wives (1956) Beacon Book pb, bound with *High Priest of California* (orig title of *Wild Wives: Until I Am Dead*)

Honey Gal (1957) Beacon Book pb (orig title: *The Black Mass of Brother Springer*)

Lust Is A Woman (1957) Beacon Book pb (orig title: *Made In Miami*) Reprinted 1967 Softcover Library pb

The Woman Chaser (1960) Newstand Library pb (orig title: *The Director*)

Understudy for Love (1961) Newstand Library pb

No Experience Necessary (1962) Newstand pb

The Burnt Orange Heresy (1971) Crown hb. Reprinted 1987 by Black Lizard Books.

The Hombre from Sonora (1971) Lenox Hill Press (Crown) hb under pseudonym "Will Charles" (orig title: *The Difference*). Reprinted 1973 by Robert Hale, London in hb.

Cockfighter (1972) Chicago Paperback House B-120. Reprinted 1974 as Avon pb Reprinted 1987 by Black Lizard Books

Off the Wall (1980) Pegasus Rex Press, fictionalized hb biography of the "Son of Sam" (David Berkowitz)

Miami Blues (1984) St Martin's Press hb. Reprinted 1985 in Ballantine pb

New Hope for the Dead (1985) St Martin's Press hb

Sideswipe (1987) St Martin's Press hb

Kiss Your Ass Goodbye (Oct 1987) Dennis McMillan, 1995 Calais Dr #3, Miami Beach FL 33141 ($43 ppd; signed & numbered edition of 400 copies)

SHORT STORY COLLECTION:

The Machine in Ward Eleven (1963) Belmont pb; repr. 1964 by Consul Bks, U.K.

NON-FICTION:

A Guide for the Underhemmorrhoided (1977) privately printed, 1000 copies

Something About A Soldier (1986) Random House hb

I Was Looking for a Street (unpublished, ms completed)

Jim Tully: The Underworld Years (in preparation, a bio)

New Forms of Ugly (critical study of modern literature), Dennis McMillan Pubs

She leaned well over the desk, reached behind her and lifted her plaid skirt, exposing pink panties and a firm, beautifully rounded bottom.

"Go ahead," she said calmly. "Spank me. I deserve it."

Chapter One

The rain hit hard at my window. It slowed down to a whisper, then hit hard again. All afternoon the rain had been doing this while I sat behind my desk with my feet up, doing nothing. I looked around the ratty little office and wondered vaguely what time it was.

It wasn't much of an office. The four walls were painted a sickly lime-green, and the only bright spot in the room was the famous Marilyn Monroe calendar with its flame-red background. Two ladder-backed straight chairs, a two-drawer file cabinet, a cheap combination typing-and-writing desk and a swivel-chair completed the furnishings. The rugless floor was laid with brown and yellow linoleum blocks. As I sat facing the door, looking over my feet at the milk-glass pane, I could see in reverse the lettering of my name:

JACOB C. BLAKE
PRIVATE INVESTIGATIONS

Behind me was my single window with its excellent view of the air shaft. The office was on the mezzanine of the King Edward Hotel and it was probably the worst location for a private investigator in San Francisco. But I hung onto it for two reasons. One: I lived in the hotel.

Two: It was cheap.

I lit a cigarette and tried my best to blow smoke rings. After several tries I blew a good one. While I watched it disintegrate the door opened and a girl entered. She was young and she held a pistol in her hand. I left my feet on the desk and raised my arms in the air as high as I could reach.

"Stick 'em up!" the girl said, out of the corner of her mouth.

"They are up." My voice came out higher than I'd ever heard it before. My body felt suddenly cold and damp. The girl came around to the side of my desk, shoved the pistol into my face and pulled the trigger. A jet of lukewarm water splashed on my forehead and dribbled into my eyes. The girl made a noise; a foolish, school-girl giggle.

My fear had become unreasoning anger. I jerked the black water pistol out of her hand and broke it in two. I threw the shattered plastic into the wastebasket, twisted my hands into the lapels of the girl's gabardine raincoat and started shaking her. I shook her so hard her head whipped back and forth like a marionette's. When she started to cry I cooled off. I shoved her into a chair and sat down again in my own. My hands were trembling from the combination of fear, anger, and now sudden remorse for ill-treating the girl. I took a calmer look at her.

She seemed about fifteen years old. A mop of auburn poodle-cut curls topped a pretty, innocent, delicate face. She carried a small, black patent-leather handbag and her shoes were single-strap Mary Janes. She took a tiny handkerchief out of her purse and dabbed at her blue eyes.

"You hurt me." Her voice was a bubbling, light soprano.

"You scared me."

"I was just having a little fun."

"It wasn't funny!"

She giggled. "You should have seen your face!"

"What were you trying to prove, anyway?" I smiled in spite of myself.

"I'm waiting for my brother," she explained.

"I see. You thought I was your brother."

"No! Freddy's visiting Mr Davis in his room and he told me to wait for him in the lobby."

"This is the mezzanine."

"I know that! But I've been waiting for over an hour, and I've been exploring sort of, to kill time. I saw your office, and I wondered what a private detective would do if someone tried to stick him up, and then I remembered I had my little brother's water pistol with me—"

"The brother Freddy, visiting Mr Davis—"

"No! My *little* brother's water pistol! Freddy's my big brother. He's eighteen years old!"

"He won't let you use his water pistol?"

"My goodness! He doesn't even have one! That was my little brother's water pistol you broke up, and I'll have to get him a new one."

"What's his name?"

"Melvin. Melvin Allen."

"And what's your name?"

"Barbara Ann. They call me Bobby, but I hate it. Don't you?"

"Is your last name Allen too?"

"Of course it is, and my big brother Freddy, the one upstairs visiting Mr Davis—his name is Allen too!"

"Then it isn't Freddy?"

"Yes! Freddy Allen."

"The one upstairs. The one who doesn't own a

water pistol."

"That's right. My, you sure do have a hard time understanding things!"

"I think I'll give you a spanking." I was having a lot of fun
with the girl. Barbara Ann had put some life into a dull,
dreary day. Her eyes widened, and for a moment, she stared
at me with a scared expression on her innocent face. Then
the corners of her mouth turned up slightly and formed a
knowing, truly feminine smile. Without a word she got up
from her chair, removed her raincoat, folded it, and put it
on the seat. She leaned well over the desk, reached behind
her and lifted her plaid skirt, exposing pink panties and a
firm, beautifully rounded bottom.

"Go ahead," she said calmly. "Spank me. I deserve it."

This was my second surprise of the afternoon. And I
would have enjoyed giving a spanking to her. But my native
intelligence came to my rescue. I reached over and pulled
her skirt down, resisting my strong desire to pat her nicely
rounded buttocks.

"I didn't *think* you'd do it," she said scornfully, tossing her
curls. She put her raincoat back on.

"You knew I wouldn't," I said, "but you'd better watch
out for that cute little rear end of yours. Next time, you
might not be so lucky. And now, with that fatherly advice,
you can leave. Beat it."

I put my feet back up on the desk. Barbara Ann pulled a
chair up close and sat down. She was prim and business-like.
Her hands were folded neatly in her lap and there was a set,
serious glint in her blue eyes.

"Mr Blake," she began earnestly, "I proved something
when I came in here with that toy pistol. I showed you how
alert I was, and how nervy a younger girl can be. Why, no

one would ever suspect a girl like me of being a private detective, and I could get away with almost anything . . ."

"Go on."

"Well, I'm still going to high school, but I don't go on Saturdays, and I can stay out real late at night, and Daddy never says anything. Many times I come in as late as eleven o'clock and still he doesn't say anything. So how about giving me a part-time job working for you?" She sat back in the chair.

"How old are you, Barbara?"

"I'm going on sixteen, but I look a lot older."

"I can see how old you look." I shook my head. "That's too young. I'd lose my license. But even if you were older I couldn't give you a job, kid. I don't have enough business to keep myself busy."

"Oh, you don't have to pay me, Mr Blake! I'll work for the experience—"

"I'm sorry, Barbara. I can read your mind. You think that being a private detective is a glamorous, exciting job— well, it isn't. It's a boring, underpaid profession. Doors slammed in your face, creditors after you all the time; soliciting work from cheap loan outfits, and you end up nine times out of ten with the dirty end of the stick. You don't want any part of it."

"But I do! And I'm going to sit right here until you give me an assignment." She set her pretty lips in a tight line.

"All right." I owed her something for the dirty trick she had played on me with the water pistol. "I'll give you an assignment. Without pay, of course."

"I told you, I don't care about that!"

"Listen carefully, then." I made up a lie. "Do you know where the big 'E' department store is?"

"The Emporium? Of course."

"Well, tomorrow, Saturday, they're having a sale on women's ostrich-skin pocketbooks. These are very expensive, you know. Now, I've heard something through my sources in the underworld, which I can't divulge to anyone—you understand that?"

"Of course. You can't expose your stoolies."

"Right. There's a notorious shoplifter who's coming up from Los Angeles expressly for that one sale. My job is to get her. But, unfortunately, she knows me and that's where the trouble comes in. If she spots me, she won't steal any pocketbooks, and unless I can catch her red-handed, we can't prove anything. Do you follow me?"

"Oh, yes!" Barbara's eyes were round with excitement. "But she doesn't know me and I can watch for her instead of you!"

"That's the idea. Here's what you do. I'll check with my sources tonight, and if she comes to town, I'll open my office door tomorrow morning and wave a handkerchief at exactly 8:30. If she doesn't come I won't open my door, and I can call you later if I find a suitable assignment. Okay?"

"I get it. I'll watch your office door from the lobby in the morning and if the shoplifter is in town you'll wave a handkerchief. Then what do I do?"

"Go down to the big 'E' and hang around the counter where the ostrich-skin handbags are. When you spot her lifting one, arrest her and turn her over to the manager."

"Aren't you going to be there?"

"I told you already. She knows me."

"What does she look like?"

"I don't know," I said truthfully. "I've never seen her."

"You can depend on me, Mr Blake. I won't let you

down." Barbara stood up. I shook hands with her gravely.

"Until tomorrow then."

"Right. 8:30 sharp." She left the office, her cheeks glowing with excitement. I felt a slight tinge of remorse, but I shrugged it away. The hell with it. Do her good. At the time I didn't know that I was making a terrible mistake by playing a practical joke on Barbara Ann Allen. It seemed like an amusing idea, a way to get rid of the kid, but no man can see into the future, and even now, I have no regrets.

I smoked a cigarette with enjoyment. It's the little surprises in life that go to make a good day. When nothing ever happens, the day is a lousy one. My whole outlook was changed by Barbara's visit. I decided to do a little work. I cracked the telephone book to the yellow section to look up addresses of loan companies, intending to solicit a few skip-tracing jobs by correspondence . . . but again my door opened and I looked up.

No teenager this time. This was a woman. She was about twenty-six or -seven, with sparkling drops of rain dotting a thick mass of dark, almost blue-black hair. Her face was very pale. This made her eyes, which were the color of freshly washed blackberries, appear even darker than they were. She had plenty upstairs, but her posture was erect and her body slim, with narrow hips. She closed the door and stood with her back against it, smiling at me with a set of little white teeth. The teeth weren't perfect; they slanted toward the center slightly.

"Are you Mr Blake?" she asked, raising her dark eyebrows.

"Yes, I am. Won't you sit down?" I pointed to the chair vacated by Barbara Ann.

She removed a slick raincoat, exposing a tailored suit of

heavy ochre tweed. I could see the sticks and twigs in the material. It was at least a two-hundred-dollar suit.

She removed her yellow gloves and tossed them on the desk. She sat down and crossed her legs and we waited each other out.

"Do you know who I am?" she asked.

"Am I supposed to know? This is a good-sized city." I smiled.

"My name is Florence Weintraub." Her voice was flat, toneless.

"Yes?"

"My father is Milton Weintraub."

"I've heard of him. He's the architect who built those city projects."

"That's right. He's my father."

"And what can I do for you?"

"I'll show you. Open your door a crack and take a look around the lobby."

I got up, moved to the door, opened it and scanned the lobby. In addition to the lobby regulars and the easily spotted tourists, I saw two men who didn't belong there. Both were the bruiser type, big enough to wrestle for TV. One was standing by the entrance pretending to read a newspaper and the other was lolling near the short staircase leading to the mezzanine. As I watched they exchanged glances, and the man with the newspaper shrugged.

"See what I mean?" Miss Weintraub was at my shoulder and I got a whiff of the perfume in her hair.

"Yeah, I dig them." We backed into the office.

"Those two men are holding me prisoner."

"Why?" I didn't doubt it. They were rugged enough to do it.

"They've been hired by my father. They follow me everywhere I go; except the bathroom. In fact, they think I'm in the ladies' room now."

"I see. But you don't know why your father hired them?"

"Certainly I know," she said bitterly. "He's afraid I'll get into some kind of trouble. If I enter a bar they follow me in, take me by the arm and lead me outside again. If I start an innocent conversation with anybody, they get right on me, both of them. 'Oh, here you are, Florence!' they say, and off we go. After I've been removed from whoever it was I happened to talk to, they let me go again and fall in behind me. How would you like it?"

"I wouldn't like it, Miss Weintraub."

Her purplish eyes were angry and her breathing was quick. She was beautiful this way, very much so, and yet there was something about her that put me on my guard.

"How old are you, Miss Weintraub?"

"Twenty-six," she said without hesitating. "Certainly old enough to dispense with nursemaids."

"I agree. What do you want me to do? Lose them for you?"

"Can you?"

"For a while. They can pick up your trail again easily enough. That can be done by returning to where they first lost you, or to your home, or by checking your regular hangouts—many ways. But if you want to lose them for an hour or so, it can be done."

"I'd like to lose them permanently."

"The only way to do that is have your father call them off. Want me to talk to him for you?"

"Oh, no! That wouldn't do any good."

"Without more thought on it, then, that's all I can

suggest."

"Could we lose them for two hours, Mr Blake?"

"Sure."

She took a checkbook out of her purse, raised her eyebrows.

"Twenty-five bucks a day and expenses," I said, and I sat back, waiting for an argument.

She filled in a check and handed it to me. It was for fifty dollars. I folded the check, put it in my wallet and got to my feet. I opened the second drawer of my file cabinet and got my slicker and hat. I put them on.

"Have you a watch?" I asked. She nodded. "All right. Give me eight minutes, then walk through the lobby to the door, turn left up Powell, and when I come by in a cab, I'll whistle. Make for the cab on the run and we'll leave them stranded at the curb. Okay?"

"Eight minutes."

"Right."

I opened the door and closed it softly behind me.

Chapter Two

As I walked through the lobby I took a better look at the two bruisers. The larger, standing by the staircase, had a face as roughly textured as a second-hand football. He wore a gray suit. The other man, while not as tall, was almost as wide through the shoulders as the back of a Greyhound bus. Someone had sold him a Harris tweed (ugh!) double-breasted suit.

I climbed into a cab at the hack stand on the corner and told the driver to go around the block. The traffic was heavy, and it took almost four minutes to complete the circuit. As I had suspected, Miss Weintraub was already outside and standing on the sidewalk. She looked nervously up and down the block. There isn't a woman in the world who can follow instructions and I'd counted on this fact when I had told her to wait eight minutes.

"Stop here," I told the driver. He slammed on the brakes and I whistled. Miss Weintraub ran blindly across the street, narrowly avoiding an up-dragging cable car, and got in beside me. I pulled the door shut.

"Drive down to Market," I instructed the driver, "and turn right to Van Ness. Take another right at Geary and when you hit the Union Square Garage, pull inside."

Miss Weintraub looked out of the window and bit her thumbnail. The hackie moved the heavy vehicle out with a

jerk and I settled back in the seat.

"Relax," I told her. "We'll get rid of them."

"I've tried cabs before." She shook her head. "I think there's too much traffic to get away."

We were on Market Street, and I couldn't see anyone behind us. The driver barked over his shoulder: "I just thought of something. I can't make no left turn into the Union Square Garage. There's a sign."

"Don't worry about it," I said. "You make the turn anyway. It'll only take a minute and you can dodge out the other side. If you get a ticket, I'll take care of you."

"I'll try it—"

We turned right at Geary and the driver made good time to the Square. Ignoring the NO LEFT TURN sign he angled his wheels hard and skidded to a stop inside the garage. We got out of the cab and I handed him three bucks. I took Miss Weintraub by the arm and led her into the tunnel.

"Where does this go?"

"To the lobby of the Saint Francis," I said.

"I never knew this tunnel was here."

"I'm hoping your friends don't know about it either."

As soon as we gained the lavish lobby I took a short breather, reaching for a cigarette. Then I remembered they were still on my desk, and with the girl holding my arm, I headed for the cigar counter. The man in the gray suit was smoking a cigar and leaning against the counter. His leathery face wore a wide grin. He lifted the brim of his hat, pulled it down again.

"Oh, there you are, Miss Weingraub."

"Where's your friend?" I asked pleasantly, hiding my chagrin.

"He's outside waiting in the car, but we aren't taking you along. I'd like to, but it's a private party. Some other time, maybe."

He was cocky, well pleased with himself. Miss Weintraub's face was pale except for her cheeks. They had turned a mottled red. She gave me a helpless look, and that did it. I stretched my arms out; my left above my head, my right almost to my knee, and yawned as if I were bored. I brought my right fist up from my knee and caught the man in the belly, an inch above his belt buckle. His lungs were full of cigar smoke and the smoke belched out of his mouth with a loud whoof. His knees sagged and he dropped to the floor in a praying position.

"Let's go!" I said. We walked briskly through the lobby toward the Powell Street entrance, ignoring the looks passed our way. A cab was waiting in the white zone and the doorman opened the door for us. We climbed inside, and he closed the door.

"Golden Gate Park," I said. The driver bluffed his way into the traffic stream. "I still haven't got a cigarette."

"Here," Miss Weintraub said, taking a pack of Marlboros out of her purse. "Oh, that was simply wonderful! The look of surprise on his face was marvelous. I didn't expect you to hit him!"

"Neither did he."

When we reached the park I had the driver circle through the grounds for five minutes before I was satisfied no one was following us. It was almost dark and the rain was coming down as hard as ever.

"We've lost them," I said. "Where do you want to go now?"

"My car is parked in the lot at Eighth and Market."

"Do they know it?"

"I don't think so. I had some work done on it yesterday and I told the mechanic to park it there for me. I gave him a five dollar tip . . ."

"Drive to the parking lot at Eighth and Market," I told the driver. I leaned back on the seat and closed my eyes. Tomorrow I could expect two visitors. Perhaps I should wear my gun. The man in the gray suit surely would be looking for a little revenge for the belt in the belly. I sighed. Sometimes twenty-five bucks a day didn't seem to be enough money for what I had to go through to earn it. Then I smelled perfume. Soft lips covered mine and an arm curled around my neck. I opened my eyes. Miss Weintraub's firm, insistent tongue pried my teeth apart and I responded gallantly. The kiss lasted a long time. She was the first to break away, not me. She folded her hands self-consciously in her lap.

"That was for being so brave. And if that isn't good enough for an excuse, I'll think of another."

"If you can't think of another one, ask me," I said.

We got her blue Roadmaster out of the parking lot and she drove through town to the cut-over for the Golden Gate Bridge.

"There's a place in Sausalito that you'll like, Jake." With only one kiss, we were now on a first-name relationship. "We can have dinner, and maybe dance afterward. I haven't been out in a long time."

"Suits me, Florence. After a day like today I could stand a drink and a steak."

I watched her as she drove. She was expert enough, although I thought she took too many chances darting in and out of traffic. She concentrated on what she was doing,

however, and kept the big Roadmaster under perfect control. After we crossed the bridge we dropped down the narrow winding two-lane highway that led to Sausalito. When the road leveled she made a left turn up an unpaved cliff road, dropped to low-drive, and we twisted and turned for two miles before we reached the top of the cliff and swerved into a gravel parking lot. A blue neon sign flashed intermittently from the roof of a long, low red-brick building:

THE KNOCKOUT CLUB

"Ever been to this place, Jake?"
"I didn't know it was here. I don't have a car."
"You'll like it."
She parked as close to the building as she could and we dashed for it through the wet. I checked our raincoats and my hat while she went into the ladies' room. The bored headwaiter raised his chin and lowered his eyelids the way they do and I held up two fingers. He nodded and I got a pack of Camels out of the machine next to the checkroom. I smoked one and a half cigarettes while I waited for Florence. The wait was worth every minute of it. When she appeared, Florence had undergone a complete transformation. She looked as if she had spent the entire afternoon in a beauty parlor. Her fine dark hair was piled high on top of her head and held in place with two plain silver combs. She had added the faintest blush to her cheeks and colored her full lips a coral red.

We were early and there were only a few other couples on hand. The room was large, dark, and lighted solely by the electric candles on the occupied tables. I told the waiter

to bring us two Martinis while we looked over the menu.

"You'll like the trio, Jake." Florence smiled. "They're nervous."

"Fine. I like nervous trios. What do you want to eat?"

"You order. Men are so much better at ordering than women are."

I ordered two rare sirloins and while we waited we drank our second Martini. She didn't ask for my olive and I liked her for this one non-feminine trait.

We didn't talk to each other, because we both had the same thing on our minds, and talking wasn't necessary. How long would we have, and would there be enough time to do what we wanted to do before her father's bodyguards caught up with us? After the kiss in the cab I could easily see why Milton Weintraub kept a guard on his daughter. She wasn't the type who is hard-to-get; she was *anxious*-to-get!

The steaks arrived, swimming in mushroom gravy, and with their appearance the curtain behind the ridiculously small dance floor swept upward and revealed the imprisoned trio on the raised stand. It was a colored trio consisting of guitar, accordion and bongo drums. They wore tuxedo trousers and red dinner jackets. White ties. They started off right with a mambo arrangement of *Tangerine,* and the bongo thumper did things with the beat that I didn't know were possible.

"Let's dance," I said, and I took a large bite of steak to hold me over for a while.

"Do you know what they call themselves?" We picked our way through the empty tables to the dance floor.

"No," I said, chewing.

"The Knockout Drops."

We started to dance. Florence was remarkably good. She

clung to me like jello to a moulding tin, following my lead as though we'd practiced the mambo at Arthur Murray's for ten years. When the music stopped we walked over to the stand. The leader smiled widely and hit three questioning chords on his guitar.

"Please play, *I Got It Bad*—"

"And *that* ain't good!" He finished for me.

"Play it." I opened my wallet. The smallest I had was a ten-dollar bill. I gave it to him. "Play it ten times."

"Yes, *sir!*" He slammed his foot down and they went into it. The first time through they played it slow, not sickening slow but danceable. After the third chorus some of the other dancers threw hard looks at the trio. The bongo bumper sang the fourth chorus and he was so good nobody minded the repetition of the song. Perfect enunciation, and yet you didn't exactly follow the words. Just the meaning. Before he finished the chorus I led Florence across the room to the side double-doors leading outside. We closed the doors behind us and we were standing on a narrow three-foot ledge that overlooked the parking lot. The night was inky black and it was still raining. We were partly protected by a striped awning, but now and then the wind would whip the rain in on us and it would get to our legs. Through the white-curtained double-door I could see a man and a woman eating at a table less than three feet away from us. This lent an extra excitement to my ardor, along with the knowledge that any car entering the parking lot with its lights on would pick us out against the building. I pulled Florence hard against me and kissed her.

"Here?" I asked.

"Oh, yes! Here! Now!"

I gathered the heavy tweed of her skirt in my fingers,

and lifted. The heat of her body reached out for my hands. The flesh of her was firm and yet oddly relaxed. She wasn't wearing much beneath the skirt. In an instant it was all over. Fiercely and abruptly. Florence arranged herself, opened the door and walked calmly across the dining room to the ladies' room. I had to light and take several drags on a cigarette before my hands stopped shaking enough for me to go back inside. When I did go in the man eating by the door looked at my face and gave me a wide grin. I wiped my face and mouth with my handkerchief and got rid of the lipstick.

The trio was still playing *I Got It Bad.* I laughed out loud on my way to the men's room. Florence would hardly be satisfied with the rapidity of my attack; we'd have to do better than that . . .

Florence still hadn't returned to our table when I got back from the men's room, so I crossed to the trio stand and talked with the leader.

"That was real low down," I complimented him. "Very nice."

"That's the way we play it," he said seriously. "We're *spelaen* specialists. Real spelunkers. All the *way* down!" He grinned happily.

"Play it ten more times." I took a ten-dollar bill out of my wallet.

"Man, I can't do it," he said, shaking his head from side to side, his eyes on the bill in my hand. "You want me to get fired?"

"Okay. Take it anyway."

"Thank you, sir!" He jammed the bill into his pocket.

Florence still hadn't returned, but I started in on my steak. It was cold, but it tasted wonderful. Florence

appeared, and I held her chair for her. Her eyes were very bright.

"Our two hours are up," she said unhappily.

"Don't worry about it. Eat your steak. You'll need it."

She wasn't wearing much beneath the skirt. In an instant it was all over. Fiercely and abruptly.

this expense thing too far, Jake."

"You're the one who put it on a business basis. If you want to work things out my way, all you have to do is say so."

"What's your way?"

"Let me talk to your old man. After all, this is a ridiculous situation. Bodyguards, home by ten, sneaking around—"

"We'll do it my way, Jake. Don't go near my father! Do you understand?"

"I won't. Don't get excited."

We rode in silence the rest of the way. Florence lived in the old Nob Hill section of the city in a venerable house set well back from the street. The grounds surrounding the house still contained grass, trees and gravel paths. This was a bit unusual for this section of the city. The other houses in the same neighborhood were jammed against each other. She parked at the curb instead of taking the sweeping driveway leading into the deep front lawn and fronting the entrance to the house.

"I'll walk from here," she said. "You take the car and I'll call you some time tomorrow and tell you where to meet me."

"Fine. Just call the hotel. My phone's on an extension from the switchboard. It saves paying a telephone answering service—"

"Do you always think of money?"

"Only when I don't have any."

"From now on, lover boy, money will be the least of your worries."

She pushed my hat off my head, put her arms around my neck and kissed me. I felt the blood stir in me where it felt

the most sensitive. I did my own kissing after that. I clutched Florence by the hair and pulled her head and face in tight against mine. She pulled away from me.

"No, Jake," she said hoarsely. "Not here in front of the house. I'll call you in the morning, just as soon as I can." She opened the door and got out of the car. I scrunched across the nylon seat covers to the driver's side and pushed the button that slid the window down.

"Goodnight," I said.

"Goodnight," she whispered. She ran through the open gate and up the graveled path. I was out of breath. I felt as if I had been running. I shoved the dash-lighter in and took a cigarette out of my pack. The lighter clicked out and the car door jerked open at the same time. A hand clutched the collar of my raincoat and another caught my left wrist and twisted it up behind my back as I was dragged out of the car. I tried to break away, but the hand that held my collar had shifted to my neck. Two thick fingers were jabbed deep into my throat. With a sudden movement I jerked forward and the sharp pressure on my twisted arm caused me to yell out. A hard wrist now held me under the throat and if I remained as still as possible I was merely in agony. Any movement at all was more painful than I could possibly bear. Through a film I could see the tall man in the gray suit standing in front of me with a wide grin on his face. That meant that Double-breasted was the one holding me. The tall man was talking and I did the best I could to listen.

"I told you it was a private party, Mr Blake, but you wouldn't listen to me." His voice was very pleasant, like a waiter recommending pressed duck. "You mustn't butt in when you're not invited."

He drew his fist back. I saw it coming but I didn't feel it.

It was a sure-shot solar plexus blow and the film turned a dirty black, interspersed with shooting stars . . .

There was a drip-drop, drip-drop sound. The back of my head was wet and my first thought was that I was lying in a pool of blood. I sat up and blinked my eyes several times to get them in focus. I was on a well-kept lawn under an apple tree. The dripping noise was the water dribbling through the leaves of the tree and dropping into several shallow pools. My head had been in one of them. It was raining again, and hard, but under the tree it only filtered through. My hat was out in the rain, partially filled with water. I got to my feet and instantly bent double again with the pain in my stomach. I straightened up slowly, retrieved my hat and dumped the water out of it. I coud see the outline of Florence's house through the other trees. There was a light in one of the upstairs windows. The rest of the house was dark. Bending over slightly to ease the pain in the pit of my stomach I staggered across the grounds to the wrought iron gate.

The Buick was gone.

I stumbled down the hill for five blocks before I hit a street with traffic. Sitting on a fire hydrant, I waited for ten minutes before a cab came along. On the ride to my hotel I seriously considered dropping the business with Florence Weintraub. But there was money to be made out of the screwy situation, I figured. Maybe a whole lot of money, and besides, Florence had something that I'd never run into before in my entire life. During the many years I had spent in the army, I'd met women in Paris, Berlin, Manila and Tokyo, but never, never one like her before. The mundane domestic variety I'd clashed with in the States I didn't count at all—

I decided to stick it out for awhile to see what would happen.

Certainly I was more clever than the two men who had worked me over . . . I ought to be able to protect myself from such.

But why had her father hired them, anyway?

My mind was too foggy to think. When I got to my room I undressed and got under the shower. I let the hot water beat down on my head and body until I relaxed enough to sprawl across my bed and go to sleep.

Chapter Four

I awoke the next morning at six; a nasty habit carried over from the army and one that I couldn't break. I was very sore. There was a large blue bruise on my stomach and two more bruises on my left side. I must have been kicked in the ribs after I had lost consciousness. I showered, shaved and dressed hurriedly. I detested the ascetic bareness of my hotel room. Although I'd lived in Room 720 for more than a year, I had added nothing of my own to its bareness. It was merely an ordinary hotel room, furnished with the minimum, ordinary furnishings familiar to guests of all second-rate hotels. It was still a place meant for transients. My suitcase, the suits hanging in the closet, and the fresh laundry in a brown-paper package on the dresser were the only evidences of my occupancy.

Every drawer except the bottom drawer of the dresser was empty. It was my practice to keep my dirty laundry in the bottom drawer, and to use my clean laundry from my returned bundle as I needed it. I kept the fresh bundle on top of the dresser; partly to see how I stood on clean laundry and partly to cover up the lower part of the mirror, which was distorted by ripples.

Carrying my hat and raincoat, I rode the self-operated elevator down to the mezzanine and entered my office. I put the slicker and hat into the empty file drawer, ordered

my usual breakfast on the extension phone, and lit my first cigarette of the day. I smoked two before my breakfast arrived.

Old Timmy, the ancient bellboy, entered the office and put the tray on my desk.

"Thanks, Timmy. Put it on the bill."

"Yes, sir, Mr Blake." He hesitated.

"That's all."

"Yes, sir. This isn't me, Mr Blake. This is the man, but he said your bill is mighty high to keep on ordering meals without paying what you owes already . . ." He trailed off nervously.

"Who said that?"

"Mr Saunders in the coffee shop—"

"I'll tell you what to tell Mr Saunders," I said angrily. "You tell him that I don't want him to discuss my bills with the help. Do you understand that?"

"Yes, sir, Mr Blake."

"If he's got anything to say, he can say it to me! Now get the hell out of here."

"Yes, sir. I sure will tell him. I sure will." He sidled out, gently closing the door behind him.

My breakfast consisted of a double-shot of gin, a glass of orange juice and a pot of black coffee. I drank some of the orange juice, poured the gin in the space I'd made, and finished the glass. By the time I'd finished my coffee, the pains in my stomach and side were gone. I didn't feel like sitting behind my desk. I left the office and ran down the short flight of stairs to the lobby. I bought a newspaper at the cigar stand and turned to Earl Wilson's column. E.J. Stewart, the desk clerk, poked me in the shoulder with his forefinger and said:

"Do you know Mr Davis, Mr Blake? Jefferson Davis?"

"Not personally. He was a little before my time, E.J."

This E.J. Stewart was the oldest of the three desk clerks, and the friendliest, although I was on good enough terms with all three of them. Actually, none of them was named E.J. Stewart, but there was a beautifully carved, ornate, walnut nameplate on the desk labeled "E.J. Stewart," who long since had gone. It was too nice to throw away and none of the clerks had their own nameplates so, as a consequence, all of them were called "E.J." or "Mr Stewart" when they were on duty.

"No," the old man said nervously, "not that Jefferson Davis. I mean Mr Davis, the art dealer; the man who lives here in the hotel in 624."

"I don't know him either. Did you read Earl Wilson this—"

"That's him over there." He pointed rather guardedly to an overstuffed couch where a man in gray spats and an Oxford gray suit sat reading a copy of *Art Digest*. His necktie was a blue-and-red paisley, and a black homburg was pushed well back from his forehead and partly covered steel-gray hair badly in need of cutting. He looked dignified despite the horsy length of his face and his outcropping of buck teeth.

"Yeah, E.J. I've seen him around the lobby several times, but I don't know him. What about it?"

"He said he wanted to meet you."

"I'm in my office all day. Why doesn't he come in, then?"

"He mentioned it casually the other day when he got his key. That's all I know."

I folded the newspaper, put it under my arm and walked

over to the overstuffed couch.

"Mr Davis?" I asked politely.

He nodded, closed his magazine and got to his feet. "You're the detective chap, and I've been intending to visit you," he said. His upper teeth were well exposed when he smiled. "You are Mr Blake, are you not?"

"That's right. Can I help you in any way?"

"Well, no, not exactly." He laughed pleasantly. "I thought I might be able to help you. I reside in this dismal hotel myself, for the security, you know, and I understand that you too are a permanent resident."

"Yes. Unfortunately."

"I have an art gallery on Polk Street. Do you know where it is, Mr·Blake?"

"Not exactly. But I've seen it. I'm aware of it."

"Well, my room here was pretty much the way yours is now—that is, if you haven't had your room decorated?"

"I haven't."

"I have, you see. It's completely changed, and I've put my entire collection of Paul Klees on the walls. Makes a difference. I thought you might like to see it some time with a view to doing something with your room to make it more attractive."

"I don't spend much time in my room, Mr Davis. And I certainly can't afford any Paul Klee art."

"Prints aren't so awfully expensive, and Klee isn't the only painter—he is for me, but I sell other things too. And whether you're interested or not, drop in some evening, have a drink, take a look at my collection. Tonight, perhaps."

"What do you want to see me about?" I asked him bluntly.

He colored slightly. "It's rather delicate . . ."

"All right, Mr Davis." I stuck my hand out and we shook hands. "I'll drop in this evening. I'd like to see your collection."

I returned to the desk and looked in my box. The mail wasn't in yet. I opened my newspaper to the sports page and E.J. poked me in the shoulder.

"What did you think of him?" He displayed great interest.

"Seemed like a nice old fellow. Why?"

"He's as gay as a bird dog!" The clerk laughed in a dirty way. "As gay as a bird dog!" He turned to answer the ringing telephone and I left the desk. As I walked across the lobby toward the staircase I looked sideways at Mr Davis. The clerk was merely guessing, I thought. Davis certainly didn't talk or act like the gay type to me. I climbed the stairs and entered my office where I could read my newspaper without interruption.

After I finished the paper I threw it into the wastebasket. As I sat idly behind my desk I suddenly remembered Barbara Ann. It was 8:27. I opened the door slightly and took a peek into the lobby. Barbara Ann was standing just inside the entrance and staring at my door. She was wearing dark glasses and a heavy, dark-brown overcoat. Her head was covered with a black beret. For a second I considered getting her upstairs and calling off the joke, but I knew she would only pester me for something else to do, and I didn't want to bother with her. I waved my handkerchief two or three times from the doorway and she turned abruptly and scuttled through the door like a woman rushing to a sale. I wondered vaguely if there were such things as ostrich-skin handbags. I knew there were wallets made out of ostrich

skin, but I couldn't remember seeing women's handbags made out of the expensive leather. I shrugged and sat down behind my desk.

At nine, old Timmy brought my mail in, and put it on my desk.

"Did you tell Mr Saunders what I told you, Timmy?"

"Yes, sir, Mr Blake, I told him."

"What did he say?"

"He didn't say nothing, Mr Blake. Nothing at all."

"It's a good thing he didn't."

"Yes, sir, Mr Blake. It sure is a good thing." He left the office.

There was a letter from a woman in Mill Valley asking me how much I charged for handling divorce cases. I answered her letter with a postcard telling her I didn't handle divorce cases. If her husband happened to get the mail before she did, there would be an interesting argument between them, I speculated. There were two bills; one for a scarf I'd charged at the May Company, and another from Saul Bennet, the tailor. Bennet's had a rather bitter note attached, requesting at least a partial payment on the last suit I'd had made. I endorsed the fifty-dollar check Florence had given me and put it in an envelope which I addressed to Saul Bennet. I mailed the letter and postcard at the mail chute and returned to my office.

I waited until noon, and still no call from Florence. After deliberating whether to call her instead, I thought better of it and went out for lunch. I ate the special hot roast beef sandwich at Moar's cafeteria and returned to the hotel. When I opened my office door, Barbara Ann got up from the chair she was sitting on, flew across the room and did her best to claw me with her fingernails. I caught her wrists

in time and held onto them, turning sideways to avoid being hit in the crotch by her pumping knee.

"Hold on," I said to her. "What's the idea?" I was holding her so that she couldn't do anything, but it didn't prevent her from spitting in my face until she ran out of saliva. I shoved her roughly into a chair and wiped my face with my handkerchief.

"You liar, you!" she shrilled at me. "You big, big, big, big fibber, you!"

"What's the matter? What are you talking about?"

"Ostrich-skin handbags!" she shouted. "That's what I'm talking about! There isn't any such thing at the Emporium. I looked all over the store. Everywhere. Finally, I talked to the assistant manager, and he told me he'd never heard of ostrich-skin handbags. You made it all up just to get even with me for shooting you with the water pistol. Didn't you? And there probably isn't any shoplifter, either!"

"What store did you go to, anyway?"

"The big 'E.' Just like you said."

"I didn't say the big 'E', I said the May Company. You're confused, that's what's the matter with you. You've failed me on your first assignment. The shoplifter's come and gone by now . . ."

"You did so say the big 'E'!" I could detect the small doubt in her voice. I pressed my advantage.

"No, I couldn't have told you that." I shook my head sadly. "The May Company is where the sale is, so why would I tell you the Emporium?"

"I don't know, but that's what you said."

"No, Barbara, I didn't. You made a mistake and then you try to blame it on me. I suppose now I'll have to do the job myself, as I should have done in the first place."

"I'm sorry, Mr Blake," Barbara said contritely. "Really I am, but I've got an awful temper and—"

"You'll never make a detective if you can't control your emotions any better than that. I'll give you one more chance. Go on over to the May Company and look through the store. You might catch the shoplifter stealing something else. Maybe it wasn't ostrich-skin handbags after all. Maybe it was plastic handbags—"

"They're too cheap to steal."

"You might be right. My stoolies may have been wrong. But go ahead and see what gives at the May Company. I'm giving you another chance."

"Yes, sir," she said happily. Barbara got up from the chair and kissed me. I pushed her away from me.

"Where did you learn to kiss like that?"

"We girls practice kissing at school sometimes. Why? Don't you like it?" She smiled mischievously.

"Beat it." She left the office, first putting her dark glasses over her eyes. Whew! I sat down behind my desk and lit a cigarette.

At 2:30 I had a telephone call. It was Florence.

"Did you think I wasn't going to call, Jake?"

"I was beginning to wonder."

"Can you pick me up at the Paramount Theatre on Market at six?"

"I haven't got your car anymore. Your two impetuous friends caught me with it last night and worked me over."

"They did?"

"They did."

"Where's the car now?"

"I don't know."

"Are you hurt bad?"

"Not that bad."

"Oh. Well, how about the Seal House, at the beach. I'll get away somehow and meet you there for dinner at six."

"Fine." She racked her phone.

There was no reason to hang around the office any longer. I had only waited for her telephone call. I took my hat and raincoat out of the file cabinet and put them on. The door opened and Florence's two bodyguards walked in.

"Going somewhere, Mr Blake?" The tall man asked the question. He was wearing blue serge instead of gray today. Double-breasted was still wearing his double-breasted. However, there was a pistol in his right hand. A large one. He handled it carelessly, pointing it in the general direction of my stomach. He smiled out of the side of his mouth.

"No. I wasn't going any place in particular," I said.

"Then we'll take you with us, if you don't mind. Mr Weintraub wants to talk to you. He wasn't happy about Florence going out to dinner with you last night, Blake."

"And I didn't like it either." Double-breasted put in his two cents.

"What are you goinxg to do with that automatic?" I asked. "Shoot me, for Christ's sake?"

"Oh, no, nothing like that," the tall man said. "Would we, Melvin?"

Melvin shook his head. He was the one in the double-breasted.

"He didn't say to shoot him. He said to bring him in."

"Come on, Blake," the tall man said, all business now, "let's go. And don't try anything. Melvin wouldn't want to shoot you, but sometimes he gets nervous."

I preceded them out of the office and down the stairs. There was something odd about this. Weintraub must place

a high value on his daughter to guard her into her twenty-sixth year. I walked slowly across the lobby trying to think of a way to get out of going along with the two gorillas. After all, there are limits to how many times a man should be worked over for one mistake. I didn't relish the prospect of another beating—I looked toward the entrance and a brief happy laugh escaped me. An old acquaintance of mine was coming through the door.

Detective Sergeant Ernest Tone.

Chapter Five

Sergeant Tone stopped inside the doorway, looked us over, and rubbed his chin with his left hand. After he eyed Melvin and the tall man suspiciously, he looked at me.

"What are you doing with these two creeps, Blake?"

"I was walking them to the door. I wanted to make sure they didn't steal anything on their way out."

"When did you get out, Ferguson?" Sergeant Tone asked the tall man.

"I've never been in, and you know it," Ferguson said defensively.

"When are you getting in, then?"

"I'm not. Let's go, Melvin." Ferguson and Melvin hurried out of the lobby and I remained with Tone. He was a little guy, not much more than 5'5", but he was a tough policeman. He rubbed his chin, cocked his head to the right like a bird.

"They wanted you for something, Blake. Something was up, and I could smell it."

"They were taking me somewhere to work me over, I believe. And then you appeared and they changed their mind."

"I'd like to pick them up—"

"Melvin's got a gun on him. Is that a reason?"

"I wish it was, Blake, but it ain't. He's got a license for it."

"That hood's got a license?"

"That's right, and don't ask me how he got it."

"Okay. What are you doing at the King Edward? Slumming?"

"In a way. I'm taking you in." Tone grinned.

"What for?"

"Ever heard of the Child Labor Act?"

"Yeah, what about it?"

"Come on." I followed him outside. A uniformed cop was sitting at the wheel of a police car by the curb and we climbed into the back seat. I was puzzled, but it was useless to pry any information out of Tone. If he wanted to tell me, he would; if not—and that was more likely—I could wait until we reached headquarters. I settled back comfortably in the seat.

"What's the story, Blake, on Melvin and Ferguson?"

"It's a case I'm on. Nothing confidential, I suppose. I'm working for Florence Weintraub—"

"Don't tell me you're mixed up with her!"

"Do you know the girl?"

"No, thank God!"

"Why? What's the matter with her?"

"Don't you know?"

"Well, I—"

"Everybody else does," he said grimly and tightened his thin lips.

"I've got an idea, maybe, but business is lousy, Tone. I need the dough."

"That's your concern. I'm not giving advice to private investigators. Right now, you'd better worry about your

license, anyway."

"What's this all about, for Christ's sake?"

"I'll let Lieutenant Pulaski tell you about it. He thinks he's got your license this time, Blake. And maybe he has."

Nothing more was said. At the station we ducked under the stairs, entered the basement and walked down the hollow-sounding corridor to Lieutenant Stanley Pulaski's office. Pulaski was the Number Three man on the detective force, and was gradually working his way up to the Number One spot. He didn't like me very much. The newspapers had given me the credit instead of him on an attempted kidnap case about eight months before. I had done the go-between work and deserved the credit, but he didn't think so. Some people are that way . . .

Pulaski grinned at me when we entered his office. He was more than a little paunchy and liked to sit behind a desk. His desk was covered with various objects with which he fiddled as he talked. There was an ivory paperweight carved into the shape of a lion. There was an old-fashioned pen-and-ink stand in brass, with a container of sand, which he used instead of blotting paper. And there were several pictures of his wife and five children, each framed in heavy leather, and lined up across the desk like football linemen. The dark walnut desk was oversized, but Pulaski was large enough himself to overpower it and the many ornaments. His dew-lapped, blotchy face was happy as he pointed to a chair.

"Sit down, Blake," he said cordially. "I've been expecting you."

I sat down in the indicated chair. Sergeant Tone leaned against the wall and concentrated on stripping a wooden match into splinters. Slowly, maddeningly slow, Pulaski

took a cigar out of his desk drawer and removed it from its glass tube. He sniffed the cigar with enjoyment, rolled it back and forth between his enormous hands, then very carefully cut the end off with a pair of tiny scissors. He lighted the cigar with a kitchen match, rolling it around in his mouth to insure an even light. He inhaled deeply, expelled the smoke with sensual satisfaction.

"Your business hasn't been too good lately, has it, Blake?"

"So-so," I said.

"More business than you can handle by yourself?"

"No. Not that much."

"Then why did you hire a teen-aged girl to work for you?" He shot this question angrily and the blotches on his face joined forces, making his face completely red.

"I didn't," I replied calmly.

"Bring her in, Tone," Pulaski ordered sharply. Sergeant Tone left the office and returned in less than a minute with Barbara Ann Allen. She was still wearing her brown coat and beret, but she had taken off her dark glasses. She was visibly frightened.

"All right, dear," the lieutenant croaked pleasantly, "tell us again about your assignment."

"Yes, sir." Barbara Ann looked to me for encouragement, but I kept a deadpan. "Mr Blake hired me, without pay—just for the experience, he said—to watch for a shoplifter in the May Company. Well, I didn't know exactly what department to look for her in and I didn't know what she looked like, but I thought to myself that the best place to look was where there were little things around that a woman could put in her purse or coat pocket. So . . ." She hesitated.

"Go on, dear," the lieutenant encouraged her.

"I've told you this before."

"Please tell it once more."

"Well, first I looked in the book department. I don't know why, but books are small, and people *might* want to steal a book, and there were a lot of people in that section of the store. I was standing by the counter where they sign people up for the Book-of-the-Month Club and I saw this woman slip a copy of *The Robe* under her coat. She pushed it up under her arm—inside her coat, and I could tell she was stealing it because it wasn't wrapped. So I grabbed her around the neck and called for help. The floorwalker came running over and I told him I saw her take the book. The woman was screaming like everything, but the floorwalker acted real nice and polite and took both of us into the little office in the back. I told him again that I saw her take the book. The woman said she didn't steal it. She claimed she was looking for a salesgirl. It was a lie, but when she paid for the book they let her go. But he kept me there and called the police . . ." Barbara Ann was almost in tears, but she shook her head and bravely continued. "I told you already that I was hired by Mr Blake, and you've kept me here ever since. I was just doing my duty and you're trying to make it look like I'm the one who's in the wrong!" She turned to me. "Tell them to let me go, Mr Blake!"

"Well, Blake," the lieutenant said pleasantly, "what about it? Shall we turn your operative loose?"

I grinned. "What are you trying to pull, Lieutenant? I've never seen this girl before in my life."

Barbara Ann's eyebrows raised with amazement. "Why, you liar, you! You great big fibber, you! You did so tell me to go to May's and look for a shoplifter!"

"Not only do I don't know what you and the lieutenant are trying to pull," I said, "but I don't even know what you're talking about."

Barbara Ann made for me with her fists clenched. Sergeant Tone reached out quickly and caught her by the wrist. "Take it easy, kid," he said quietly.

"You're lying, Blake," the lieutenant said. "A story like Barbara's can't be made up successfully, and you know it. It's screwy enough to be the truth."

"Okay," I said, shrugging, "charge me with it. See how far you get."

Pulaski thought it over. He looked sharply at Tone and Tone shook his head and shrugged. Holding his cigar like a dagger, Pulaski smashed it out in the ashtray on his desk.

"All right, Tone," he said, "get 'em out of here! Drive the girl home. You're a rotten bastard, Blake! I can't figure out what your purpose was, but I do know it was a cheap trick. I'd like to kick your teeth in!"

"Go ahead and hit me, Lieutenant," I said quietly. "I'll have you suspended."

Sergeant Tone opened the door for Barbara Ann, but she didn't budge. She stood motionless, both feet planted, still staring at me with amazement and anger.

"You'd better keep away from this man, Barbara," Pulaski told her with a kindness in his tone that was surprising. "We'll take care of him for you. Go on with the sergeant."

Tone and Barbara Ann left the office. I stood up, fished a cigarette out of my package and lighted it with one of the kitchen matches on the detective's desk.

"You're going to have to dream up a better frame than that to get my license, Pulaski," I said, putting as much

disgust into my voice as I could under the circumstances. "You aren't even trying hard."

I left the office, slamming the door on my way out.

Sergeant Tone was leaning against the guardrail outside, puffing on a handmade brown cigarette. He raised his chin as I climbed the stairs and reached the sidewalk.

"What is the story, Blake?" he asked, hooking his short arms over the railing.

"There is no story," I replied. "Where's Bobby?"

"I sent her home in a police car. How did you know her name was Bobby if you've never seen her before?"

I laughed. "She's a teen-ager, isn't she? Bobby-soxer? Bobby is short for bobby-soxer."

"Pulaski wants your license pretty bad, Blake. I've got a hunch he's going to get it one of these days." Tone threw his cigarette into the street, turned away from me and ducked down the stairs into the basement.

At the next corner I caught a cab for the hotel.

Suddenly, from behind, a heavy blow struck me between the shoulder blades. I saw that I had been hit with a large fire extinguisher . . .

Chapter Six

rode the elevator up to my room, removed my clothes and got under a shower as hot as I could stand it. A visit to a police station makes me feel dirty all over. After I looked at my face in the bathroom mirror I decided I could get by without shaving again. I dressed carefully, selecting a shirt with a Mister "B" collar, and my one-button-roll, blue gabardine suit. I pulled on a pair of white clock sox and my gray suede shoes. It was hard to select a necktie. My wine-colored bow didn't look so good so I exchanged it for a cream-colored knitted tie. More contrast. I looked in the mirror admiringly for quite awhile. I really looked sharp.

As I started out of the room, the telephone rang. It was Jefferson Davis.

"My, I'm glad to catch you in, Mr Blake," he said. "I thought you might like to come down for a drink."

"What time is it now?"

"Oh, a little after four."

"What's your room number?"

"Six-twenty-four."

"All right, I'll be right down. I want to see those Klee paintings." I hung up.

Without waiting for the elevator, I took the corner stairway down one flight to the sixth floor. It was quicker. I

knocked on the door and it opened immediately, as though Davis had been standing inside with his hand on the knob.

"What can I fix you, Mr Blake?" he asked pleasantly.

"Something with gin in it." I gulped. I could hardly talk. The sight of his room had done something to my voice. It was a riotous blaze of varied color. His room was no longer than mine, but it seemed so; it did not have my dull, cocoa walls. Every available space contained a picture by Paul Klee, either an original or a print. It was similar to being caught up in the midst of a child's nightmare. The colors were breathlessly hot.

The room was furnished with new, modern furniture, and instead of a large double bed there was a two-seat, hide-a-bed sofa pushed up against the wall. It helped make the room look larger than mine, but the pictures closed the gap by appearing to leap out from the walls. Davis was fixing drinks on the coffee table and there was an amused smile on his face.

"How do you like them?" he asked, handing me a glass of orange juice and gin. He wore a wine-colored smoking jacket, gray slacks and red leather slippers. Somehow, without a hat, his long grayish hair looked natural. To cut it would have been a shame—in this exotic setting.

"Frankly, Mr Davis, I've never seen anything like it before. You said you had a few Klee's, but I didn't expect to see a room covered with them."

"He's my favorite painter," he replied, sipping his drink.

"He must be." I tasted mine. Cold and good.

"Sit down, sit down, Mr Blake." Davis graciously waved me to the sofa. I sat down, looking at the walls with my mouth partly open. The pictures must have cost him a fortune.

"What did you want to see me about?"

"Well, I didn't ask you here just to look at my art, I'll admit . . ." He sat beside me on the sofa, although there was a comfortable armchair directly across from me.

"Get to the point, Mr Davis. I can't stay too long."

"Now, now, don't rush me." He put his hand on my knee and squeezed gently. "You must spend the night with me sometime, Mr Blake." He smiled horsily.

"I've got my own room, Davis." I laughed. "And I'm too old for that sort of thing. I'm in my thirties. What you need is a youngster." I laughed again, and poured more gin into my glass.

Davis' smile was a trifle annoyed. "That's the crux of my problem, Mr Blake. I've got a youngster and I'm trying to get rid of him. I haven't actually thought things out yet—but, I suppose, that's one of the reasons I wanted to cultivate your friendship."

"We don't have to be friends," I grinned. "I charge twenty-five bucks a day and expenses."

"You wouldn't be interested in . . . ?"

"No. But I might be able to help you, after I find out what you want to do. I'm smarter than I look. I know, for instance, that your young boyfriend is Freddy Allen." I let that sink in. I had remembered Barbara Ann telling me she was waiting for her brother who was visiting Mr Davis.

Davis was startled. "Don't tell me we've been that obvious?"

"How old is Freddy now?" I asked the question casually, as though I knew Freddy Allen well, but couldn't remember his age.

"Twenty," he lied. "And I have no control over him whatsoever." He sighed. "You know Freddy, then?"

"I know of him. And although I'm not certain, I've heard that he was spreading the word around about your relationship . . ."

Davis jumped up from the sofa and paced the floor several times.

"Are you sure?" he asked worriedly.

"No. But then if I know, there might be others."

"I can't afford to let anything like that get around, Mr Blake. Not in my position. I know he's jealous as hell, and he might not stop at anything."

"You haven't been true to him, then?" I thoughtfully pursed my lips.

"Of course not! Why should I be?" He spoke bitterly.

"Maybe he's true to you and he expects the same kind of treatment."

"He's nothing but a spoiled brat!" It was odd to hear Davis speak that way. His voice was a rolling bass, and somehow, a voice like that is never associated with a homosexual. I didn't laugh, however. I was as grave about the situation as a young priest hearing his first confession.

"Do you think he wants to marry you?" I asked seriously.

"My God! I wonder if something like that is in the back of his mind! It's never come up, but such things are done, as you know . . ."

"He's only eighteen, actually, so that might be it." I said. "And you should have it out with him, at any rate." I finished my drink and made another. I enjoyed the conversation and I'd given the old boy something to think about. It was asinine to me, but it was very serious to Jefferson Davis.

"I thought I knew Freddy," Davis said softly, "but maybe I don't know him at all. I've given him money, clothes, and only last week I gave him an early Picasso drawing for his

. . . our anniversary. He was the one, now that I think of it, who remembered the anniversary of our, ah, relationship, and he surprised me with a gift of my favorite English preserves. Gooseberry, imported from England, you know. In my surprise, I retaliated with the drawing. He appeared pleased, and I know he was, although we had a terrible scene before the evening was over—"

"What was it about?"

Davis blushed; his crimson face was as bright as the pictures on the walls. "It was nothing of interest to you, I assure you. Just a foolish argument."

I got up from the sofa, finished my second drink on my feet, and placed the empty glass on the low table.

"To sum up, Mr Davis, you have a problem. You've got a jealous lover and you want to get rid of him. He's cramping your style, or rather, he's limiting your time. You'd like to get rid of him and you don't know how. Am I right or wrong?"

"You're right, that is, in a way, but I'm not so sure I want to get rid of Freddy. I'm rather fond of him, you know."

"Then I'll be running along. Thanks for the drinks, and I'd like to look at your paintings again some time. I don't know much about modern art and maybe you could explain some of it to me."

"I'd be glad to. Come in again, later tonight if you like." He squeezed my arm affectionately.

"Do you make a pitch for every man you meet?" I laughed. "I can see right now why Freddy's so jealous."

"I'm just trying to be friendly, Mr Blake," he said sternly. I had hurt his feelings.

"Thanks again for the drinks," I said. I opened the door and left the room. I felt greatly relieved to be free of him.

Davis closed the door quickly and bolted it with the chain lock.

I walked down the carpeted hallway to the elevator and pushed the button. I waited patiently, watching the moving loops of cable through the glass of the door. Suddenly, from behind, a heavy blow struck me between the shoulder blades, and the force of the blow threw me against the door of the elevator. The wind was knocked out of me and I was partially paralyzed. I saw that I had been hit with a large fire extinguisher, and the nozzle of its rubber hose was spewing forth a frothy mixture over me as I lay on the floor. It was a brew of water, sulphuric acid and soda and it was ruining my blue gabardine suit. But until I could catch my breath I couldn't do anything about it.

A blond, chubby-faced young man, wearing gray slacks and a yellow sweater, was standing against the wall across the hallway. There was a sullen, righteous, frightened look on his fat face. His arms were spread, and the palms of his fleshy hands pushed hard against the wall behind him.

Chapter Seven

My wind came back to me all at once and I took a deep grateful breath. With an effort I got to my feet and a sharp fiery pain seared my back. The handsome, chubby young man against the wall didn't attempt to run, but he didn't try to attack me again either. I approached him slowly, reached out quickly, and grabbed a handful of his yellow sweater with my left hand.

"You're Freddy Allen, aren't you?" I asked him, twisting the sweater a little more to get a better grip.

He nodded his head, once, and then, without warning, tears overflowed his pale blue eyes and rolled down his baby-fat, dimpled cheeks.

"You've taken him away from me!" He blubbered through his tears. "He doesn't love me anymore and it's your fault!"

Now, I don't really object to homosexuals. It's a big world and there is room for everybody. The way some men prefer to make love is their business, not mine, but it seemed to me that I was being used as a short blunt apex for a crazy triangle. I didn't like it and I didn't like Freddy. Davis was one type of homosexual and Freddy was another . . . Davis, at least, earned his own living, and he spread a certain amount of beauty in the world by selling art, explaining it, and enjoying it himself. But Freddy was nothing. He was a

filthy leech. He had attached himself to Davis so firmly that the older man was desperate to break away. As I held Freddy against the wall and watched the juicy tears boil out of his eyes through his girlishly long lashes I was filled with loathing and aversion. And in addition to being an overly pretty, petty-minded kept boy, he had ruined my suit with a fire extinguisher . . .

I smashed my right fist into his face. His nose crushed noisily and blood spattered and smeared against his skin. His nose would never be termed aristocratic again. I hit him again in the face several times. After each blow he tried to scream, but before he could get it out I would hit him again. I didn't try to knock him out. I wanted him conscious; I wanted him to feel it. He covered his face, or tried to, with his left hand. I hit him again and the bones of his hand splintered. He dropped his hurt hand, screamed shrilly, and I loosened my grip on his sweater. He slumped weakly to the floor, cuddled his broken hand against his chest, and whimpered like a kicked dog, interspersing short, sharp yelps of pain between the whimpers. Without letting up any on his weird noises he put his right hand into his pocket, pulled out a knife with a spring button, pressed it, and the blade flipped out. He was fast with his leap to his feet. His legs had been gathered beneath him and he came up off the floor like a cat. The point of the long blade narrowly missed my throat. This was the excuse I needed to really clobber him.

Freddy whirled quickly after the missed thrust, crouched, and held his knife low at his side, looking for an opening. Patiently, flat-footed, I waited for him to make up his mind. He jumped forward, bringing the knife up awkwardly. I sidestepped his rush and chopped down on his

wrist with the side of my right hand. The knife dropped to the rug and his rush carried him across the hallway. Following him up, I jerked his broken hand away from his chest and crushed it between both of mine. His whimpering ceased, the blood drained out of his face, and he turned white as a clown's makeup. He pitched forward to the floor. Unconscious.

I left Freddy lying in the hallway and ran up the stairs to the seventh floor instead of taking the elevator. I unlocked my door, entered, and undressed as quickly as I could. I didn't want to get burned by the sulphuric acid seeping through my suit. I showered again, using plenty of soap and hot water. As I toweled myself I examined my body carefully for red spots or burns. There weren't any, but there was a new blue bruise on my back where Freddy had hit me with the fire extinguisher.

If he had planned his attack with care I could have been seriously injured. In my life I'd been hit and nearly hit with a variety of weapons, but this was the first time anybody had ever used a fire extinguisher on me.

My blue gabardine was ruined. I felt more than a little unhappy about it. It was the first suit I'd bought when I got out of the army, and every time I wore it I was reminded of my freedom. I could never wear it again. I put on a white shirt, blue knitted tie, and my gray flannel suit. I wrapped the damp blue gabardine, pink shirt and cream necktie in a sheet of newspaper, put the bundle under my arm and left my room. I rode the elevator down to the lobby and left the hotel.

Walking up Powell Street, looking for a trash can, I was stopped by the red light at the corner. A maroon Ford was waiting for the light to change and I wedged the bundle

between the rear bumper and the body of the car. The Ford moved out with the light change and took my suit with it. At the hack stand I dropped wearily into the rear seat of a cab and told the driver to take me to the Seal House.

The Seal House is at the beach and it overlooks a pile of rocks in the ocean. Seals spend a lot of time on that particular pile of rocks. And people interested in seeing seals over rocks flock to the Seal House restaurant to eat, drink, and look at the seals. I got a table by the window, ordered a drink and looked at the seals. It was almost six and the sun had gone down behind San Francisco. It still reflected its light on the ocean and turned the water into a flaky, shifty mirror. The seals, sprawled carelessly on the rocks, moved listlessly from time to time. Music by Muzak played softly over the speakers set in the four corners of the large dining room. My gin concoction arrived and I ordered another before the waitress got away from the table.

I was draining the dregs of my second drink when Florence sat down across the table from me. She was breathing hard and it added freshness to her beauty. She was wearing a plain cobalt suit with two huge gunmetal buttons. She smiled, expelled a long breath, smiled again.

"I was looking for you in the bar," she said.

"When I come to the Seal House I watch the seals."

"Am I late?"

"I don't know. I haven't got a watch."

"Did you order dinner?"

"No. How do I know what you want to eat?"

"I always get the mixed seafood platter. Out of a mixture there's bound to be something good."

I ordered two mixed seafood plates, and two more drinks.

"Your father sent your bodyguards to see me today," I told her, to make conversation. "One of them said your old man wanted to talk to me."

Florence wore a puzzled expression. "He lied then. Father is in L.A. tonight. He flew down this afternoon to address a builders' association of some kind."

"Did you see him leave on the plane?"

"No, but I saw him leave the house. He left right before I called you at 2:30."

"It isn't the same. He might still be around. Of course, they might have lied as an excuse to take me somewhere and work me over again."

"Did they hurt you very much last night?" Florence asked solicitously.

"Not much. By the way, how did you get away? Or did you?" I looked over my shoulder with a mock terrified expression. Florence laughed, showing tiny sharp teeth.

"They're fired. After I told Daddy about you and I getting away last night he called them in and fired them."

"That may have been a blind . . ."

"No." She shook her head emphatically. "What good would it do?"

"I don't know." I grinned. "But if you aren't being followed anymore, I'm out of a job." I finished my drink.

"You've still got your job, Jake, if you insist on calling it that."

We both laughed. The seafood arrived and we let the conversation drop to pick around on the platters. The crab legs were good, but the sauce smelled like spoiled mayonnaise and olive oil. It tasted like spoiled mayonnaise and olive oil. I ordered coffee and lit a Camel.

"Want a dessert, Florence?"

"No." She lit one of my Camels with her Zippo lighter.
"I want to take you home with me. We can have dessert
there."

"Suits me." We left the Seal House, walked to the
parking lot, and climbed into her Buick.

"Where did you find your car?" I asked her.

"It was in the garage. I looked for it right after I called
you this afternoon."

She drove across town, driving expertly, squeezing the
big car in and out of places I didn't think it would fit in. I
admire a good driver. I'm not a good driver myself and I've
never owned a car. My sole driving experience has been
limited to driving cars belonging to others, and not too
much of that. When we reached her house she drove
through the wrought iron gate and stopped in front of the
entrance, putting the brakes on so hard the car skidded for
three feet in the gravel of the driveway.

"It's the power brakes I had put in the other day,"
Florence said self-consciously. "I'm not quite used to them
yet."

We entered the house. The living room was high-
ceilinged, and an enormous, cut-glass chandelier lighted the
farthest corner of the room like daylight. The room was of
no particular period or design. Provincial chairs were
mixed with mid-Victorian, and there was a low cocktail
table carved out of a granite block and fitted with a polished
marble top. It was about eight feet square and its legs were
carved into griffin's feet. A set of Noh masks were on one
wall, placed in imperfect alignment, and on another there
was a scattering of swords, dirks and cutlasses. A Degas
hung above the fieldstone mantel, depicting ballet girls in
blue chalk, and the far, remaining wall was completely

covered with a tapestry showing a crimson Roman army marching across a golden land.

It was an interesting room and I liked it. Florence mixed Martinis from a tray of bottles on the enormous stone table. I sat down on a seven-seat sofa that curved halfway around the table.

"I like your house, Florence."

"I hate it. It's too gloomy. Now, try this: I call it a Desert Wind. Nine-tenths gin, one-tenth vermouth. No olive. No onion. Nothing. Just a toothpick."

I sipped the Desert Wind. "It's fair," I said, smiling, "only next time, skip the toothpick. The wood absorbs too much of the gin."

She sat down beside me and I put my arm around her. I finished my drink, took her glass, and set both of the glasses on the table. I picked her up and put her on my lap. She put her arms around my neck and I kissed her. We held the kiss until it got sloppy. I pushed her away from me.

"I'll have another Desert Wind," I said. My voice was dry.

"Me too." Her voice was high and small.

She poured the cocktails and as I reached for mine, a man came through the doorway from the hall. He was in his fifties, with powdery white hair, and an enormous, beakish nose. His skin was tight over high cheekbones, but it gathered and fell in folds on his chin and beneath his neck. His eyebrows were black and very heavy, and beneath his eyes there were huge blue-black circles. His hands looked too delicate for his short, thickset body, and they were trembling. He wore a black tie, white shirt, and a white, linen suit. He resembled a giant panda bear in reversed shades of white and black.

"So you're the private detective, Jake Blake—" His voice was shaking with an anger that was barely under control.

"Yes, sir," I said carefully, and I got up from the couch. "You must be Mr Weintraub . . ." I stuck my hand out to shake hands, but he ignored it completely and turned to snarl at Florence.

"Go to your room!" He told her fiercely.

"Fuck yourself," she remarked quietly and wandered over to the fireplace.

"I wanted to take a look at you, Blake," he said, ignoring Florence's suggestion. "I made arrangements to see you this afternoon, but you squirmed out of it some way—"

"I was in my office," I said. "If you wanted to see me, why didn't you call for an appointment instead of sending two thugs after me?"

"You're an unscrupulous man, Blake. I've checked on you, and I know how to handle your kind."

"Money won't do everything, Weintraub. Your daughter's twenty-six years old. If you think you can keep her under lock and key forever, you're—" I broke off in midsentence. Florence was laughing with whooping peals of choking laughter, and clutching the mantel for support. Weintraub looked blankly at me for a moment, and then held up his hand. It had stopped trembling.

"Daughter?" he asked vaguely. "Did she say she was my daughter?"

Florence stopped her laughter abruptly and stared at us sullenly.

"Well," I said. "Isn't she?"

"No. It so happens that Florence is my wife!" He glared suspiciously at me, still undecided as to whether I knew or didn't know she was his better half.

"Oh," I said. There was one more Desert Wind remaining in the glass pitcher. I poured it into my glass and drank it down.

I kicked out with my right foot and caught the cat just right . . .
I don't like cats, anyway. Too independent.

Chapter Eight

remained as cool as I could, under the circumstances. Weintraub was watching me closely, looking for a reaction on my part that would prove me to be a liar. I set my empty glass on the table.

"Look, Mr Weintraub," I said feebly, "I didn't know she was your wife—"

Weintraub grimly set his lips and looked at Florence. She was standing in front of the fireplace; her arms were crossed beneath her considerable breasts, and her face bore a detached expression, as though she was thinking of something else.

"I believe you, Blake," Weintraub said with a trace of sadness in his voice. "A lot of her lovers didn't know she was married at first. But by the time they found out, she had them so completely—well, it's too late then. They don't want to give her up and I have to convince them that they'd better! It's all so—"

"Lies, lies. Lies, lies. Lies, lies. Lies, lies," Florence sing-songed.

"No, Blake, you're not the first of Florence's lovers by any means. And I really don't give a damn anymore what she does. If she had any discrimination, it wouldn't be so hard to take. But my wife doesn't draw the line," Weintraub said bitterly. "As far as she's concerned, there is no

line! I've been forced to have her watched all the time. But that hasn't been, what you might call, practical . . ."

"If I'm so bad," Florence commented, "why don't you give me a divorce?"

Weintraub shook his massive head. "No, I'll never divorce you—and you don't want a divorce, anyway! You and I made an agreement, and that agreement was marriage. I got what I wanted and you got what you wanted. Money for you, and for me," he smiled sardonically, "the best sex in San Francisco!" He turned to me. "And as far as I'm concerned, it's worth every cent it's cost me!"

Weintraub's face was an angry red; his cheeks puffed, and his eyes brightened as though a switch was clicked on inside his head.

"I intend to protect my investment, Blake." He faced Florence. "Marriage is no different from any other type of contract. I'll fight to the last moment of my life for anything and everything I own. And if you tried to get a divorce, I have enough evidence on you to have you laughed out of court. Any court. You wouldn't get a penny, not even in a California court!"

He crossed the room briskly and jabbed a finger into my chest.

"Do *you* want to marry her, Blake? Do you think *you* could support her?"

"I don't know," I said honestly. "I've never given it any thought."

He sneered. His face was quite red in the places it wasn't blue-black. "You couldn't pay her doctor bills! Her sani—"

Florence screamed and cut him off. It was a startling, awesome outcry. Starting low in her chest, like a police siren heard in the distance, it gathered force and momentum

and reached a terrifying crescendo. It stopped momentarily while she took another breath and then it started all over again. She exerted every muscle in her body to produce such a scream. Her eyes were closed and she stood with her feet apart and her fists clenched tightly; her elbows tight against her sides. It hurt my ears to listen to it. Taking Florence by the shoulders, I shook her back and forth as hard as I could. The hard shaking didn't even slow her down. I slapped her face three or four times.

"Stop it, Florence!" I had to yell at her to be heard.

I was knocked sideways across the room, hit from behind by Weintraub. I stumbled onto the stone table, banged my shin, and with luck, managed to remain on my feet. Weintraub had hit me just above my right kidney with a metal smoking stand. He swung the heavy stand again, but I evaded his clumsy swing by jumping backwards. The momentum of his charging swing whirled him around and I leaped forward with a looping right hand blow that caught him below the ear. He dropped the smoking stand and pitched forward to the floor. He didn't move.

"What's the matter with you, you crazy bastard!" I yelled. Florence had stopped screaming on Weintraub's fall, and my voice reverberated in the silent room. There was a sweet smile on Florence's face, and she wet her lips with the tip of her pink tongue.

"Do you think he's dead?" she asked excitedly.

"Of course not. What got into you, anyway?"

"I always scream when he starts to nag. It infuriates him and he usually goes away and leaves me alone." She rubbed her face ruefully. There was a large, red hand-mark on her face where I had slapped her. "You hurt me when you slapped me, but I don't mind."

"I thought you were hysterical, kid. Otherwise I wouldn't have done it."

"What difference does it make?" Florence shrugged comically. "As long as it's exciting." She sat down on the sofa, took a Marlboro out of the box on the table, and lit it with a table-lighter shaped like a miniature piece of Henry Moore's sculpture. "What about him, Jake?" she asked quietly, kicking her unconscious husband in the ribs with the point of her toe. "Is it worth the effort to bring him around?"

"I'll get some water. Where's the kitchen?"

"Through there." She pointed to the hallway and settled herself comfortably on the couch, puffing languidly on her cigarette.

I left the living room and wandered down the hall, holding my hand tightly against my sore side to ease the pain. Weintraub had hit me with only a glancing blow of the smoking stand. A square, solid blow and I'd have been the one unconscious on the floor instead of him. Marriage or no marriage, he was nuts to hang onto a woman like Florence. But that was his business, not mine. Under the circumstances, I was through. No more playing around with Florence for me. A man like Weintraub had a lot of influence in San Francisco, and if he wanted to push things, I'd be relieved of my private investigator's license in a hurry. I'd bring him out of it, try my best to explain things quietly, and then I'd push off. This was the second time in one day that I had been sucked into a triangle through no fault of my own. And I didn't like it. The fifth door I tried led into the kitchen.

I got an empty saucepan out of the cabinet beneath the sink and filled it with cold water from the tap. I plucked a

dish towel from the rack above the range and draped it over my arm. A cat meowed. There was a large charcoal-colored cat, with white feet, sitting on its haunches by the outside door. It meowed plaintively.

"Do you want out, Kitty?" I asked the cat. It meowed again. I put the pan of water down on the sideboard, crossed the kichen and opened the door to the backyard. The stupid cat sat where it was without moving. I shut the door and picked up the pan of water again. The cat meowed again. I set the pan down again, opened the door so it could get out, but the cat didn't make a move. I kicked out with my right foot and caught the cat just right. It sailed out of the door, missed the steps completely and landed running. It quickly disappeared into the darkness of the backyard. I slammed the door and left the kitchen with the pan of cold water. I don't like cats, anyway. Too independent. And even when you try to do them a favor they don't appreciate it.

Florence was idly leafing through a movie magazine when I returned to the living room. She tossed the magazine on the table and looked curiously at the pan of water when I set it down.

"What are you going to do, Jake?"

Weintraub was still inert upon the floor. He was stretched out, face down, with his arms spread. I turned him over on his back. It wasn't easy. He was heavier than he looked.

"I'm going to bring him to."

"Oh." Florence picked up her magazine again.

I wet the dishcloth and rubbed Weintraub's face with it. I slopped the cloth in water and wrung it out over his face. I slapped him lightly a couple of times. I dumped the entire panful of water over his face. There was a great deal of

water in the pan and it made a pool beneath his head. He didn't stir a muscle. I searched among the many folds of skin on his neck for quite a while before I found his jugular vein. I couldn't feel a heartbeat, so I wasn't sure whether I had the vein or not. Lifting his right eyelid with my left hand I jabbed my right forefinger into his eye. No reflex. Florence's purse was at the other end of the table where I couldn't reach it.

"Hand me your little mirror," I told her, pointing to her handbag.

"Why?"

"I said to give me your mirror!" I was a little excited by that time and I had raised my voice. Florence opened her purse and handed me her compact. For a moment I couldn't open it, and when I found the latch, I was holding the compact upside down and rose-colored face powder was scattered over Weintraub's set expression. I held the mirror part of the compact as close as I could to Weintraub's lips, and then I examined it. There was no moisture or fogginess on the mirror. Not a trace. I snapped the compact shut and tossed it into Florence's lap.

"Is something wrong, Jake?"

"Yeah," I said, getting off my knees. I poured a double shot of gin into an empty glass and poured it down my throat. I choked slightly and the raw gin brought tears to my eyes. I wiped them away. Florence had lost interest in the movie magazine and was sitting on the edge of the sofa with her eyes widened. Her mouth was partly open, her lips wet.

"Is he dead, Jake?"

"He couldn't be any deader."

Chapter Nine

"**D**o you want a drink, Florence?"

"A little one." She indicated the size by holding up a thumb and forefinger an inch apart.

I poured a jigger of gin into a glass and handed it to her. I sat down across from her in a soft leather chair. But I leaped up immediately. Now was no time to sit down and relax. I had to figure an angle, and the best way for me to think is on my feet. I paced up and down the room, turning the facts over in my mind and getting nowhere.

"What do we do now, Jake?" Florence asked, after she gulped her drink and put the glass on the table. I didn't know.

"I don't know. I don't know what to do."

I took a cigarette out of the box on the table and lit it with the table-lighter. My hands trembled, and the cigarette tasted as dry as fifty-year-old sherry. After two drags I crushed the cigarette out in an ashtray.

"I suppose the smart thing to do is call the police, kid. But when I do my name is Fall Guy. There's a lieutenant who's been after me for a long time, and if I don't end up in the gas chamber, I'll end up at Folsom crushing stones. Somehow, the prospect of prison doesn't encourage me to do my right and proper duty as a citizen ..."

"You and I both know it was an accident, Jake. But if I

told the truth, nobody would believe me. Milton and I have had some nasty arguments in our time, and his lawyer has some papers in his office that would—well, all I can say, is that this is very unfortunate."

"That's a good word for it. Unfortunate."

"I know what we can do, Jake. We can leave."

"Leave? Where would we go?"

"There are lots of places."

"Not anymore, there aren't. Twenty years ago a person could disappear, but not now. We might get away for awhile, but we'd be caught, and then it would be just that much tougher."

"What about me? I don't want to die . . ." Florence started to cry. I sat down beside her and tried to give her some comfort by putting my arms around her.

"Come on, Florence, crying isn't going to do you any good. The best thing to do is call the police. When they get here, we clam up, say absolutely nothing. Let them jump to a lot of wrong conclusions. Then, after we get a lawyer, we tell the exact truth and hope for the best—"

"No!" Florence pulled away from me and got to her feet. She glared down at me, and stood with her legs apart, arms akimbo. "Do you think I'm going to rot in prison over a son-of-a-bitch like him?" She kicked Weintraub's body viciously with her toe. "Take a good look at him! Go ahead! How'd you like to have something like that crawl into bed with you every night?" She turned away from me. "He was always sweating. Not a hot, decent sweat, the way a work-ing man sweats—oh, no, not him! It was a cold, clammy sweat, and his skin is just like a frog's. I put up with it, just the way he said I did; for the money, and I've got that money too. He thought he was so smart!" she said derisively. "He

never gave me any cash, you see, but he gave me charge accounts in every store and restaurant in town. So I figured out a system . . ."

She paused for breath, laughed wildly.

"It's a simple system, really. I'd buy a dress, or furs, something expensive—say a hundred dollars or so, and then I'd sell it back to the salesgirl for half price without taking it out of the store. The girl could sell it and make twice the profit for herself. See? I'd charge the hundred dollars and get fifty in cash from the salesgirl. Milton never complained about bills, and there was so much stuff I sent home anyway, besides the stuff I sold for cash, he never got wise to what I was doing. At least I don't think he did."

"How much money have you got?"

"Plenty."

"How much?"

"I don't know exactly."

"How much?"

"Five thousand dollars in the vault at the Desert Sands in Vegas. Another ten thousand in Mexico City, and five thousand in a safe deposit box in New York."

"That much?"

"That much, and maybe more."

It was enough money for me to think things over a little more carefully. In fact, twenty thousand dollars was a fabulous sum to a man like me. The most money I'd ever had in a lump sum was eight hundred dollars. That was my discharge pay when I got out of the army, and I hadn't hung onto it long enough to really get a good look at it. Maybe Florence and I could work things out, at that. If we picked up the five thousand in Vegas, it would be easy to get to Mexico City. Once in Mexico, we could live for a long time

on fifteen thousand dollars. At least long enough for the
hunt to die down. Then we could quietly move to New York
and lose ourselves in the masses. To stand trial and avoid
conviction was a thirty-to-one shot. A jury might take a
dim view of a so-called accident if it found out I was
sleeping with the wife. And as far as claiming self-defense,
a jury might figure Weintraub was entirely within his
rights to bounce a smoking stand off my ribs. After all, a
husband is justified in slugging a man who is fondling his
wife when he isn't supposed to be at home. One lousy,
indignant husband, or one church-going wife on the jury
could put me behind the bars on a second degree rap, if
nothing else. Ten years. Ten years in jail would raise my age
to forty-three instead of thirty-three. And I had already
wasted ten years of my life in the army. Florence was right.
It was best to leave quietly and hope for the best while we
were out of jail instead of in . . .

"Please, Jake," Florence said, putting her arms around
my waist and burying her face against my chest. "I'll make
it up to you. You'll see."

"I know you will, Florence. And I'll make it up to you for
putting the last punch in your meal ticket."

Florence blew her nose on a piece of Kleenex she took out
of her purse. She took a tiny brush and her lipstick and made
a new, coral mouth. I poured another shot of gin in my glass,
but I didn't drink it. If we were going to be on the run for
awhile, I thought it best to dispense with drinking.

"How long do you think we have, Florence?"

"What do you mean?"

"I mean servants! I know damned well you don't do the
housework in this place."

"We should have until Monday morning, at least. There's

a housekeeper, Mrs Watkins, and a maid, but I let them go for the weekend as soon as Milton left for the airport. The damned liar! I wanted us to have the place to ourselves."

I walked across the room to the large picture window, pulled the drapes aside slightly and looked outside. The circular driveway was empty except for Florence's Buick. There was a streetlight near the entrance to the grounds, but I didn't see anyone lurking about on the street or near the gate.

"What about those two clowns? Do you think he actually fired them? It's hard to tell."

"I think he did, Jake. As he said, what good were they?"

"I wish I knew for sure. They told me he wanted to talk to me when they tried to pick me up at the hotel. And he sort of admitted that he sent them for me. Of course, he could have fired them afterward."

"No. They were fired when I told you, all right. He must have asked them later to go on that one more errand."

"But they know all about us, baby. And if they tell the police the situation, we'd never prove to a jury that I hit Weintraub in self-defense."

"You don't have to convince me, Jake. I know I'm in this as deep as you are. I'm ready to go."

"I am too. I was thinking out loud. And I certainly don't want to be tailed on our way to Vegas."

"Let's skip Vegas and drive straight through to Mexico City."

"What about the dough in Vegas? I don't have enough money to get to Mexico. If we pick up the money in Vegas, we can charter a plane to drop us below the border."

"Whatever you say, Jake. You're the man, and it's up to you to decide."

"Then let's get going. Pack a bag with a few things, and the sooner we leave the better."

Florence kissed me quickly on the mouth and ran up the stairs. To make certain, I checked Weintraub again. He was dead all right. No mistake. He hadn't hit his head, so it must have been my right to the head that killed him. His face looked strange with the rose face powder sprinkled over it. It was like seeing again the first dead man I'd seen in Europe. He had been in the same position as Weintraub, only lying beside the road. The dust from the moving column had powdered his face almost the same shade of rose. Eyeballs and all. I shoved Weintraub's body under the table so that the head was out of sight. I didn't want to look at it.

It would be unwise to stop at a restaurant on the drive to Vegas, so I returned to the kitchen for a look inside the refrigerator. There was part of a ham, six tomatoes and an almost full jar of mayonnaise. I found a loaf of bread in the bread box and a table knife in a drawer beside the sink. I put this stuff in a paper sack and returned to the living room. We could make sandwiches on the road.

Florence came down the stairs with a small over-nighter in her hand. She was wearing a full-length mink coat over her suit. I took the small suitcase and she got her purse from the table. After I switched out the lights, we left the house and got into the Buick. I threw the over-nighter on the back seat and Florence drove through the gates. I kept my eyes open, but there was nobody on the street, and there were no cars parked near the house.

"Never mind stopping at my hotel, Florence. Head straight for the 101 bypass."

"I knew something like this would happen someday,"

Florence giggled. "Wasn't I smart to put some money away, here and there, just in case?"

"Yeah," I said. "Roll up your window. It's cold, and I'm not wearing a mink coat."

Chapter Ten

I have to give Florence some credit, but not much. She didn't start speeding until we cleared the traffic of the city and reached the wide four lanes of the 101 bypass. When we hit the bypass she floor-boarded the accelerator and passed everything in front of her. I found myself pressing the floorboard with my right foot as though I had a brake of my own. I was forced to say something to her.

"Listen, Florence. If we get picked up for speeding we'll be taken to the nearest jail. And once we're in jail we won't get very far on our trip to Mexico City."

"Nobody can catch us!" she exclaimed. "Nobody. Just let them try!"

"I don't want them to try. Now, slow down!"

Reluctantly she slowed to sixty miles an hour, and we coasted through the thirty-five mile zone of San Jose at this reduced speed. On the other side of this little city we were back to two-lane traffic and she was forced to keep the car at a reasonable speed. I was more relaxed and I'd stopped looking nervously out the rear window. I hadn't seen anybody following us anyway, and even if they had, they would have been lost long before we reached San Jose. I made two huge sandwiches from the ham, tomatoes, mayonnaise and bread. They hit the spot and we wolfed

them down hungrily, Florence driving with one hand.

"You were brilliant, Jake," Florence admitted, "to think of food. I never would have thought of it."

"A man should use his head. That's what it's for." I lit a cigarette from the dashboard lighter and settled back against the soft leather seat.

"Light me one," Florence said. I started to light another Camel from mine and she shook her head. "No, one of mine. They're in my purse." I opened her purse and found her Marlboros and lighted one of them. I was forced to dig for the cigarettes because she had so much junk in her purse: Kleenex, Midol tablets, book matches, compact, lipstick, keys, a chamois cloth full of jewelry, and a tiny, pearl-handled .25 caliber pistol. It was a semi-automatic, loaded with a magazine containing seven rounds.

"What's with the pistol?" I asked her.

"I thought it might come in handy so I brought it along."

"Do you know how to use it?"

"I've fired it a few times. Put it back."

I dropped the pistol back into her purse and zipped the zipper. I noticed a clock on the wall of a filling station as we whipped by. It was 10:30. The time had really passed in a hurry. It was hard to believe it was that late, and at the same time, so much had happened, it was hard to believe it was that early. We were well down 101, the other side of Salinas, and the big trucks crowded the highway. We pulled up behind a wide semi- and followed it for five full minutes at twenty miles an hour. The string of back lights on its right side blinked on and off several times and Florence stuck her head out the window.

"Don't worry! We won't!" she screamed at the top of her voice at the truck up ahead of us.

"What're you yelling about?" I asked.

"I was telling the driver we wouldn't try to pass him!" She was quite excited. "His signals," she explained. "When he blinks his lights like that he's telling us a car is coming and not to pass. See?" A car passed us going north. "That car was coming and he was telling us about it with his lights."

"But why did you scream at him? He can't hear you."

"He might be able to . . ."

"Never," I said.

She had calmed down. "I know all of the truck signals, every one. I used to know a truck driver and he explained them to me. They have signals for turns, slow down, speed up, police ahead, weighing ahead, all kinds of things."

"What kind of signal do they use when they want to pull off and take a leak?"

"What's that?" She looked at me sharply.

"Never mind. He's blinking again."

She blinked her lights back, we passed the truck, and as we passed the cab she blinked the headlights twice more. The truck driver blinked his headlights twice in return.

"I blinked 'thank you,'" she said proudly, "and he blinked 'that's all right.'"

"That's just fine," I said.

"It's common courtesy. If people used road courtesy the way truck drivers do, there wouldn't be any accidents. They are the noblemen of the highway."

"You must have been mighty impressed by the truck driver you knew," I said, bored by the subject.

"He was a gentleman in every respect," she said solemnly.

I hadn't realized it before, but Florence Weintraub was

just about as dumb as a woman could get. When it came to any thinking, I realized, I would have to do it all. At this time I thought about the license tags. As soon as the alarm went out, the tag numbers and description of the car would be teletyped to every city and county sheriff in the U.S. There were a lot of Buick Roadmasters, but only one license number to look for.

"Some time after midnight, Florence, we'd better exchange these license plates."

"How?"

"Trade them with another car. By the time they find out about the switch it'll be too late to do anything about it."

"If you trade with another car, the owner will know right away, won't he?"

"No." I grinned. "I'll trade with a parked car, a car on a used car lot. That way it won't be noticed until after the car is sold. See?"

"I never would have thought of that!" Florence said admiringly.

"Naturally," I said, reaching over and patting her on the leg. "We're going to beat this thing yet, kid. Just stick with me."

"I am sticking with you. I think you're wonderful and let's stop the car right now and take a little nap."

"It might be a good idea at that. We can spare an hour."

Florence dropped the speed down to thirty miles an hour. After about a mile I spotted a dirt road curving off the highway into a grove of young eucalyptus trees. The trees were not over ten or fifteen feet high, but they were planted close enough together to provide cover from the highway.

"Pull in there, baby," I ordered, pointing, and Florence turned onto the dirt road, twisted the wheels to the left

sharply, and we ploughed into the grove of young trees like a tank. We crushed trees down for thirty yards and then she cut the engine. All of a sudden it was very silent and very dark. A moment later the disturbed crickets began to rub their legs together noisily and I rubbed Florence's legs beneath her skirt.

"What do you think?" I asked her.

"I think it's a wonderful idea," she answered, shrugging out of her mink coat.

I found a clear spot near the car and spread the plaid lap robe on the grass. We undressed, shivering in the cold night air. We stretched out on the blanket and I pulled the mink coat over us. The blanket on the bottom kept the dampness of the grass away and we were warm in an instant. It wasn't a bit like the time on the porch of the nightclub. We had plenty of time and we took it. We both knew what we were doing and we tried several things before we decided on one we both liked best.

Afterward, I was warm and comfortable, and lay there smoking a cigarette, and Florence snuggled next to me with her head on my chest.

"Give me a drag on your cigarette."

I handed Florence my cigarette. I felt sorry for her. She was in trouble. What had her husband tried to tell me about doctor bills? Something about sanitation—sanity?

"Let's go!" I leaped to my feet, taking the mink coat with me.

"You're mean!" Florence laughed. We dressed hurriedly. I held her coat for her, folded the blanket, and we got back into the car. She backed slowly through the trees to the dirt road, forward to the highway and turned right. The Buick had a quick pick-up and we were soon driving south at

eighty miles an hour.

When we reached Santa Maria I told her to look for a used-car lot. There were a couple on the main drag, but there were still a few people on the street and I didn't want to take a chance removing a set of plates at either one of the well-lighted lots. She turned off the main street, which was also Highway 101, and we found a small used-car lot two blocks away. I found a pair of pliers in the trunk and slipped them into my pocket. Florence stayed in the car, parked at the curb, where she could act as lookout. I was on my knees, with the pliers in my hand, behind a 1934 Olds when Florence honked the horn. When I looked up quickly, a man in an O.D. watchman's uniform was standing less than three feet away from me. He was in his fifties, and his face was a kindly, weatherbeaten brown. He wore a red necktie with his uniform instead of a regulation black or blue.

"What're you doing, son?" he asked. He wasn't wearing a gun, but he idly swung a billy back and forth.

"How are you tonight, officer?" I asked him.

"I'm fine. What're you doing, son?"

"I sold this car to Mr Darstadt," I said. The name of the car lot was Jack Darstadt's Quick Deal Used Cars, and the name was painted in red on a blue background, on a sign that ran the length of the lot. "He only paid me eighty-five bucks, Officer, and I thought I'd drop around tonight to see how much he marked it up. You see, I wanted to see what kind of a deal he made me."

The watchman walked to the front of the car and I got off my knees and put the pliers back in my pocket. He looked curiously at the price marked on the windshield in whitewash.

"He's selling it for $135. Looks like you were took. What

were you doing with the pliers?"

"I don't like being took," I said ruefully. "I was planning on taking my spotlight back to sort of get even . . ."

The watchman shook his head and smiled. "I can't let you do that, son. I know just how you feel. These used-car salesmen'll take your eyeteeth if you let 'em. But tryin' to get back at 'em in the middle of the night ain't no way to do it. You got yourself a dirty deal maybe, and maybe you didn't. But it's best to forget about it. Now you go on and get in your car and move on along. There's a pretty girl waitin' on you, and you don't want to get her mixed up in no mess like this."

"Yes, sir. I was sore about the deal I got, that's all."

"Two wrongs don't make one right, son."

"Yes, sir. Well, thanks, Officer."

"Goodnight, son."

I climbed back into the Buick and shut the door. The watchman watched us from the car lot until we pulled away.

"We'll get the tags in Santa Barbara," I told Florence.

"What did he say to you?"

"He said to move along."

In Santa Barbara I exchanged the tags without any trouble at a car lot on lower State Street. Afterwards, we drove on, heading for Los Angeles. I was getting sleepy and I put my head back on the seat, trying to doze off. Florence jolted me awake.

"Jake, when we get to Vegas, let's get married."

"Why?" I said, sitting up straight.

"Because I love you, Jake, and that's the God's truth."

I lit cigarettes, a Marlboro for her and a Camel for me. I thought it over.

I really thought it over.

Chapter Eleven

The word I-D-E-A-L floated across the surface of my mind. I hadn't thought of that key word since I'd left the service. It was the key to the five-paragraph field order. If you followed it, nothing was left out; your thoughts were organized, and your orders to subordinates were clear, curt and complete. Maybe I could remember it . . .

I. *Information.* That was easy. Information of the enemy and friendly troops. My enemy was the law. All law and the personnel having anything to do with law enforcement. The enemy was Melvin and Ferguson, the two bodyguards who knew I was mixed up with Florence. The enemy was Milton Weintraub, even though he was dead. The enemy was the watchman in Santa Maria who might remember me and recognize me. There were other enemies back in San Francisco. Barbara Ann Allen and her fairy brother, Freddy. Police Lieutenant Pulaski. Who else? Myself. Sure. A man is always his own worst enemy. I'd have to be careful so I wouldn't give myself away. Enemy weapons? The Buick. This very comfortable big, blue car could give us away, even with its change of license tags. Florence. The money Florence had stashed away. I could count money and Florence among my friends. Until I could exchange Florence for the money, she was the only friend I had. Except

one. Myself. In addition to being my worst enemy I was also my best friend.

D. *Decision.* This was the decision of the commander or the overall picture of the situation. I was the commander as well as the troops. The big picture or idea was to get as far away as possible before the body was discovered. And en route, get the money. My objective was Mexico City with fifteen thousand bucks in my pocket. And perhaps a change of name. Jake Blake was a hard, harsh-sounding name. So far, I'd lived up to it. It would be best to change it. Jake Blake is too easy to remember.

E. I couldn't remember what E stood for. It meant the orders to be issued to subordinates after getting the Information of enemy and friendly troops, and the Decision of the commander. But the exact meaning of E escaped me. Expedient? Expedite? Entourage? What difference did it make? I'd issue my orders to myself anyway. Right now, my orders to myself were to go along with the gag . . .

A. *Ammunition.* In the fourth paragraph of the field order you were supposed to tell where the ammunition dump was, the weapons to be used, what kind of artillery support you could expect, and other backing. Well, Florence had a .25 caliber pistol. Mine was in my hotel room. If I took Florence's pistol away from her she might get suspicious. Let her keep it. She was my only friend. I'd keep it that way. As far as the support I could expect, there wasn't any. My wits, and that was all. Ammunition was money. When I got the money I'd have all the ammunition I'd need . . .

L. *Liaison.* Where the command post is located. How the messages are supposed to be transmitted. The police had a wire and telephone service that would stretch anyplace

they wanted it to reach. As long as we were in the U.S. we would be in danger. Even in the Vegas melting pot, where nobody checked on anybody, we would be in danger. But from there we could get a plane to Mexico. I didn't know how, but money talks, and money could charter us a plane. My contact was Florence. The smart thing to do was to keep the line tight. As tight as possible.

"Florence, baby," I said, keeping my voice fairly low so that it would sound husky with emotion and sincerity, "I fell in love with you the moment you walked through the door of my office. And everything I've done since has only increased my love for you. It makes me a little ashamed that you were the one to suggest marriage instead of me. I want you to be my wife more than anything else in the world. I love you, cherish you, and I'll try to make you happy for the rest of your life, no matter what happens." For an additional effect, I blew my nose.

Florence was crying softly. I passed her my handkerchief.

"Oh, Jake," she cried, wiping her eyes, "I don't know what I'd have done if you refused. I do love you so. I'll admit I married Milton for his money, and I haven't always been on the up and up with anybody else either. I never worked in a house and I never worked the street, but I was almost at that point when I met Milton. I was working as a B-girl in a bar on Howard Street. And . . . sometimes . . ." It was hard for Florence to make this confession. "I did it for money sometimes, but it was because I wanted to eat. That's the only reason."

"Sure, baby," I said, patting her on the shoulder. "I understand. What the hell, I've been around. What you did before doesn't make any difference to me. We're starting a new life together in another country, and

all that's past is past."

"I wanted you to know." She wasn't crying anymore. Now that her conscience was relieved she was happy.

"Don't even think about it. From now on it's us two and that's all. As soon as we reach Vegas, before we do anything else, we'll get married. Now I'm going to take a little nap. When you get tired of driving, wake me, and I'll take over."

"Put your head on my shoulder and go to sleep, Jake. Driving never makes me tired. I love it."

I put my head on her shoulder, stretched my legs out as far as I could, and I was asleep before I knew it.

■   ■   ■   ■   ■

I awoke at dawn and looked out the window. We were in the desert. The landscape looked like a crumpled winding sheet dotted with dead flies. The flies were the dark, scattered growths of cacti that were barely visible in the first light of morning. My mouth tasted like sour wine and my temples painfully throbbed. My neck was stiff and my legs were cramped. Both feet were asleep. I stamped them up and down on the floorboards to relieve the stinging sensation.

"Where are we?" I asked Florence.

"About fifty miles from Vegas." She smiled. Her eyes were red rimmed and sore looking.

"Why didn't you wake me so you could take a nap yourself?"

"I can't sleep in a moving car, so I just let you sleep. Believe me, you did all right!"

"How far are we from Vegas?" I asked again.

"About fifty miles."

I whistled. "You must have driven like mad!"

"It's easy to make good time on the desert."

"What's on the radio?" I switched it on and while it warmed up I lit a cigarette. The radio hummed into life and an announcer recommended a brand of dog food, finished his pitch and let a platter go for some music. I pushed a button for another station.

"What are you doing with the radio on?" Florence exclaimed.

"I want to hear the news, see if they discovered the body—"

"Turn it off!"

"Why? There might be some news—"

"I said turn it off!" Florence screamed at me. She leaned forward and turned the radio off herself. It made me sore.

"What's the matter with you?" I reached for the knob.

Florence bent down, keeping her left hand on the wheel, and removed her right slipper with her free hand. She banged the heel of her slipper against the face of the radio until the glass broke. She dropped her slipper, jerked the two knobs off the radio (the knobs for tune and volume) and tossed them out of the window. Her face was angry.

"When I tell you I don't want the radio on, Jake, I mean it!"

"I guess you do at that. But why?"

"I don't need a reason."

"And you don't have any either." She was a screwball in a lot of ways, no doubt about it. I sulked for awhile, then thought better of it. No use antagonizing the woman.

"I'm sorry, kid," I said. "There probably isn't any news anyway."

"I'm the one who's sorry, Jake. I'm tired, that's all, and I

didn't feel like listening to any yapping."

"Sure. I know how you feel. Forget it."

Once the sun comes up in the desert it rises fast. It hung on the horizon like a solid neon pumpkin, beaming through our windshield. It grew warmer all the time. The closer we got to Vegas, the more numerous the billboards. Every club, every gambling hall claimed to be better than the last one advertised. Each claimed to have better entertainment than the last. As I remember Vegas, it was a good town. I hadn't been there for several years, but I'd had a good time, even though I ended up by hitchhiking to Los Angeles to get away.

When we reached the outskirts, Florence slowed to forty miles an hour. I looked for a motel without a NO VACANCY sign.

"If we can find a vacancy we'd better grab it," I said. "We can get married afterwards."

"Do you think a motel is better than one of the hotels?"

"Certainly. You don't meet people in a lobby when there isn't any lobby. It's our best bet."

A car pulled out of a motel called the "Home Rest Motel" and headed east.

"Pull in there," I told Florence.

"There's a NO VACANCY sign—"

"I can see it. But that car's pulling out and we can get the cabin they vacated."

Florence turned sharply and skidded to a stop in the thick, white gravel that covered the patio of the motel. I got out of the car and pushed the night-bell by the side of the door at the cabin marked OFFICE. I waited. After awhile, a man so small he narrowly missed being a dwarf, opened the door and smiled up at me.

"I'm sorry, sir," he said pleasantly, "we don't have a vacancy." He turned away, scratching himself under his pajama top.

"A car just left. We'll take that cabin." I pointed to the empty garage at the end of the row next to Cabin Six.

"It isn't fixed up yet. Won't be ready till ten, anyway."

"We'll take it. We've got to get married first, so by the time we get back from the ceremony you can have it ready."

"That's different!" His wrinkled little face took on new interest. He opened the screen door for me and I signed the register *Mr John Smith and Wife.* He smiled and nodded his head up and down. He gave me four one dollar bills in exchange for a ten.

"Now, Mr Smith," he said, "have you made your arrangements for getting married?" He had a nice voice, very pleasant.

"No, but I understand it isn't much of a problem."

"Not if you know how to go about it. Suppose you and—?"

"Mary Brown."

"All right. Suppose you and Miss Brown come on into my little kitchen here and drink some coffee? I'll call up Luke's and take care of you, get things arranged."

"Who is Luke?"

"One of the best. He gives the nicest ceremony in Vegas."

"Friend of yours?"

"We throw a little business to each other now and then. His ceremony is very nice, though, and I know you and Miss Brown will like it. And as long as you're getting married anyway, might as well let Luke do it. He don't

charge no more than anybody else, and his connections cut
corners on the license. By the time you get there everything'll be set."

"Go ahead, Mr—"

"Anderson. Shorty Anderson."

"Call Luke, then." I returned to the car and Florence
raised her eyebrows.

"We're all set, Florence. Shorty's calling Luke to arrange
the wedding for us, and we've got the cabin."

"Who is Luke?"

"I don't know, but as long as he's authorized to give
weddings, I don't see what difference it makes."

We entered the office cabin and hesitated inside the door.
Shorty was talking on the telephone. He covered the
mouthpiece with his hand. "Go right into the kitchen. I
made that coffee on the stove fresh last night, so all you
gotta do is light a match under it."

I heated the coffee and Florence and I had a cup apiece
before the little man joined us in the kitchen. He smiled
admiringly at Florence, solemnly shook hands with both of
us.

"It's all arranged. And when you get back your cabin'll
be ready. It isn't every day I get newlyweds, but when I do
I'm just as pleased as punch. Planning to stay long?"

"Maybe a week," I said, pouring more coffee into my
cup.

"Well, that's just fine." He gave us directions to Luke's
and we left the motel.

On the drive through town to Luke's, Florence grew
suspicious of the little man. "Do you think he suspects
anything?"

"How could he? He's been asleep all night."

"It didn't help any for you to sign the register as John Smith."

"You're wrong. Nobody uses John Smith anymore because it's so common. The same with Mary Brown. You pick a fancy name to use and they know right away it's a phony."

"You're probably right. But John Smith, Mary Brown— *Jesus!*"

Luke was a middle-aged man with a pale complexion, a dark mustache and long, thin fingers. He was dressed for the ceremony in a dark blue silk suit with a red carnation in the buttonhole of the jacket. The papers were ready and we signed them, John Smith and Mary Brown, in the places he indicated. Luke led the way into the tiny chapel adjoining his living room and took his place behind a waist-high rostrum in front of a life-sized painting of Jesus Christ. The picture was amateurish, and the artist had painted the eyes so that they seemed to follow you no matter where you happened to be in the tiny chapel. Luke's wife, a heavy, buxom blonde, was seated at a Hammond electric organ, and as we entered the chapel she started to play *Rock of Ages.*

"Never mind the music," I told her. "Let's get on with it."

A man I hadn't noticed before was sleeping on the long bench that ran the width of the rear of the room. Luke apologized.

"I woke him up as soon as Shorty called, but he must have gone back to sleep again. I know he don't look so good, but lots of times I have to marry people in the middle of the night and a witness is a witness. You can give him a little gambling money after the ceremony if you want. That's the reason he sleeps here, just to get a little gambling money."

Luke woke the man by pulling his legs off the bench and standing him on his feet with one swift motion. He blinked his eyes and stumbled into his place at my right. Mrs Luke left the organ and stood at Florence's left. The witness reeked of gin and had a three-day stubble of beard on his face. I pushed him away from me.

"Don't stand so close," I told him.

Luke opened a small, white book and read the ceremony. It was very short, but as Shorty had said, it was nice. Luke read it rapidly in a deep, falsely emotional tone of voice, and parts of it were hard to follow.

He paused. "Do you have a ring?"

"I'm wearing it already," Florence said for me.

"Fine. I pronounce you man and wife." We shook hands all around and Mrs Luke kissed Florence on the cheek. I gave the gin-soaked witness a dollar bill and he left the chapel muttering under his breath.

The ceremony, including the license fee, cost me ten dollars, and I tipped Luke another five. Luke waved to us from the doorway as we climbed into the Buick. On the way back to the motel we stopped at a drive-in and ate breakfast at the inside counter. Florence complained about the wedding all during breakfast.

"It was the lousiest wedding I've ever seen," she grumbled.

"Don't let it bother you, Mrs Smith," I said, grinning. "You're lucky to get rid of a name like Brown in exchange for a nice one like Smith." I left the counter and lost four quarters in the slot machine by the cash register while Florence finished her coffee.

We returned to the motel.

Shorty was coming out of our cabin as Florence pulled

into the garage. I got her bag out of the backseat and Shorty took it out of my hand and led us into the cabin. He put the bag at the foot of the bed on the little stand, spread his arms wide.

"There you are, folks. I told you it wouldn't take long. Now, if you need anything, just holler. Your bed's been changed and there's plenty of extra towels in the bathroom. Congratulations, Mr Smith, and you too, Miss." We shook hands and he backed out of the door and closed it.

"What is he, a dwarf or what?" Florence asked.

"I don't know and I care less. All I want is sleep." I undressed and climbed into the big, soft double bed. Florence went into the bathroom for a shower and I was asleep before she came out. She woke me by nibbling on my ear with her sharp teeth.

"Cut it out," I said sleepily. "I'm too tired."

"Is that any way to treat your wife on your wedding day, Mr Smith?" She was naked and not quite dry from her shower. She pressed her damp body as close to me as she could get it.

"Now, look. I told you I'm tired and I mean it. Let's forget about it for now and take a little nap. After we're rested there will be plenty of time. Then we can pick up the five thousand at the Desert Sands; and tonight I'll see about getting us a plane out of here."

"What five thousand?" The surprise in her voice was genuine.

I was very tired. There was fatigue in every bone and muscle of my body, and I was in a deep, soft bed. But when I heard that tone of surprise I was suddenly wide-awake. Any and all thoughts of sleep were gone. I sat up in bed.

"The five thousand dollars you've got in the safe at the

Desert Sands." I said it slowly so there wouldn't be any misunderstanding.

"I don't have any money in Vegas. What are you talking about?"

"Easy now, baby. You told me definitely that you had five thousand at the Desert Sands Hotel, another ten in Mexico City, and five in a safe deposit box in New York. Now what about it?" I didn't raise my voice but there was a slight quaver in it.

"I didn't tell you that," she said indignantly.

"Yes, you did."

"No, I didn't either."

I didn't go on with it. I lit a cigarette and started dressing. All right. So she was crazy.

"Where are you going?" Florence asked worriedly.

"Out."

"Listen to me, Jake. I don't remember telling you anything like that. I've never even been here before, so why would I tell you a lie like that?"

"I don't know, but that's what you said."

"I *have* got ten thousand dollars in Mexico City!"

"You've never been to Mexico City."

"I was too! I was there all last summer with Milton. We stayed at the Casa del Oro Hotel. My money's in the safe there. If you don't believe me I'll send a wire and prove it to you!"

"Sure. And let the police know that the widow Weintraub is staying at the Home Rest Motel in Vegas under the name of Mrs John Smith."

"How else can I prove it to you?"

"I don't know. I don't think you can." I tied my necktie and slipped into my jacket.

"Where're you going? You're not going to leave me here?"

"No. I wouldn't do that. We're in this together, baby. But I'm going to get a drink and do a little thinking. Things are different now."

"I'll go with you." She threw the covers back and got out of bed.

"No. I don't want you with me. Get some sleep. You need it and I had some in the car. I want to do my thinking by myself."

I sat down in a chair and bent down and tied my shoes. When I looked up, Florence had her little pistol in her hand and she was pointing it in my face. Standing naked before me, she resembled a teenaged girl except for the black, coarse mat of hair between her legs that curled into a lopsided triangle halfway up her stomach. The ends of the long, white scars on her belly extended well down into the pubic hair. I raised my eyes to hers and stared at her for a full minute before I said anything.

"If you're going to shoot, go ahead."

The pistol wavered and she lowered her arm, dropped the pistol onto the carpet.

"You aren't going to leave me, are you, Jake?"

"I said I wasn't." I got up from the chair, put my arms around her and kissed her hard on the mouth. "Don't get excited, baby. I'll be back after awhile. I've got to think things out, that's all. Now get back into bed and go to sleep. Okay?"

"I wouldn't know what to do if you left me."

"I'm not going to leave you." I picked her up, dumped her on the bed and pulled the covers up to her chin. I kissed her again. "I'll be back in about an hour." She rolled over

and put her face into the pillow. I left the cabin, closing the door soundlessly behind me.

As I walked through the white gravel to the highway the full impact of my stupidity sank in. How dumb could a man get and still go on living?

Chapter Twelve

By the time I had crunched down the line of cabins and reached the highway I was almost sick to my stomach. I stopped for a moment and looked up and down the highway. A drink was what I needed. The Dry Bones Cabaret was the first joint down The Strip; two hundred yards away. I made for it, wiping the perspiration from my forehead with my handkerchief.

I had been played for a sucker and I didn't like it. Florence had what she wanted, although why she wanted to marry me was more than I could figure out. Of course, we were in it together, both equally guilty under the law, but just the same . . . then it hit me, and I laughed. Now that we were married neither one of us could testify against the other. That must have been the reason. I felt a little better. After all a rule like that worked both ways. Maybe she *did* have ten thousand dollars stashed away in Mexico City.

Well, I'll never know now.

I entered the Dry Bones Cabaret. It was plush. It had a wine-colored wall-to-wall carpet underfoot, a goldleaf bas-relief chase of cowboys and Indians circling the wall, and every form of gambling going on that you could think of except horse racing. The gambling room was jammed. There were women in shorts, slacks and evening dress, and there were men in shorts, slacks and evening dress. A few

conservatives like myself were wearing ordinary business suits. But everyone was gambling.

I headed straight for the bar and ordered a double Tom Collins. The air-conditioning helped some, but I was still hot from my short walk in the desert sun. I cooled off ten degrees merely by shaking the ice cubes in my tall drink. I downed it, ordered another. The tariff for the two drinks was cheap, much cheaper than I had thought it would be, and for a moment I was surprised. Then I remembered that the top entertainment and the reasonable drinks were all a part of shilling a gambler inside so he could be separated from his money. It was time for me to take a look inside my wallet. Why not? I had forty-seven dollars left. Not too bad, but not enough for a plane to Mexico. Florence may have had some money, but if she did, I didn't know how much. I decided to gamble with what I had anyway.

There were only six players at the nearest crap table. Not many for the size of the table. I got behind the dice and watched the play until it was my turn.

"Next shooter," the house-man intoned, snaking me the dice with his stick. I picked up the dice and laid a ten-spot on the line. Without shaking them I tossed the dice to the other end of the table. Three. I put another ten on the line, threw the dice. Two. Snake Eyes. I put another ten on the line and my last ten on the eleven. The eleven paid thirty-to-one if you hit it with the initial roll. I threw the dice and they bounced wildly when they hit the string in the middle of the table. Eleven. Letting it ride, all of it except the stack on the eleven, I tossed another eleven. I let the line ride. I rolled again. Seven. Again. Seven. Again. Four. I threw the dice five times, came out for a point, made it, then the four. I let it ride and tossed again. Eight. I made a side bet for hard

way, and found that I had to wait before I could toss the dice.

There had been six players at the table when I started and I had made the seventh. Now there were more than thirty people crowding the table, all of them trying to get on me before I could make my next roll. I tossed the dice. Eight. About this time I got cautious and I dragged most of the money from the line. I made four more passes and if I hadn't been so careful I would have made some real money. As it was, I walked away from the table with fourteen hundred dollars.

I had another drink at the bar and bought the bartender one. On my way out I dropped five silver dollars into the house-man's shirt pocket as I passed the crap table. Outside, I climbed into a cab and had him drive me to the nearest liquor store. I picked up a fifth of gin and had the driver take me back to the Home Rest Motel. I paid him off, watching him swing in a U through the gravel, and then I entered the cabin. Florence was asleep. I took the roll of bills out of my pocket and riffled them by her ear a few times. She awoke, turned over and faced me.

"Look." I riffled the bills again.

"It looks like a lot of money," she said sleepily.

"Better than fourteen hundred." I grinned at her dazed expression.

"Where'd you get it?" She sat up in bed, wide awake.

"I won it. Shooting craps. Crazy luck, that's all. But it's enough to get away on."

"Will it get us to Mexico City?"

"It should. I don't know. But once and for all, Florence, tell me the truth. Have you really got ten thousand bucks in Mexico City?"

"At the Casa del Oro Hotel." She looked me directly in

the eyes and I believed her. There was no other choice. I had to believe her.

"Then let's have a drink and I'll get the ball rolling."

I opened the gin, poured two fingers each into the glasses on the bedside stand, and handed one to Florence.

"Didn't you bring any mix?" she asked, staring distastefully at the straight gin in her glass.

"No. I didn't even think about it. Want some water in it?"

"I'd rather have mix."

"I'll get some Cokes out of the machine by the office."

"No. That's all right, Jake. I can drink it straight."

"It'll only take a minute."

I left the cabin, humming happily, and trotted through the gravel to the office. A red Coke machine was by the door. It took dimes. I looked through my pockets. No change. I had given all of my loose change to the cab driver. I pushed the night bell and Shorty Anderson was at the screen door in nothing flat.

"I need some change for Cokes," I told him.

He was back in a couple of minutes with change for a dollar.

"You get a free newspaper every morning, Mr Smith," he said, a slow smile on his face. "I'd have brought yours down when they came, but I didn't think you'd want to be bothered."

"I just wanted some Cokes," I said, dropping a dime into the machine.

"I'll get them for you. It's a trick machine. You gotta kick it after you put the dime in or it won't work. I've told Carl about it a dozen times. But every time he drops a dime in they come right out. Of course, he works for the company

and knows more about it than I do." He kicked the machine and a Coke dropped into the receiving slot. "How many you want, Mr Smith?"

"Four ought to do it." I handed him the change and looked at the newspaper he handed me. Nothing in the headlines. I turned the page and there was the item at the top of Page Two. It was headed:

S.F. ARCHITECT FOUND SMOTHERED

The "smothered" fooled me, and if "architect" hadn't been in the subhead, I'd have missed the item altogether. I hadn't smothered Weintraub, I'd clipped him on the jaw . . .

Weintraub had been found late Saturday night by Mrs Ronald Watkins, the housekeeper, who had returned home from a movie . . . The housekeeper lived in. That was something else Florence had neglected to tell me.

Mrs Milton Weintraub, who had recently been released from a mental institution on a trial visit, was being sought for questioning. That rocked me. Weintraub had been smothered to death, probably by a pillow, and police suspected foul play. The rest of the short item contained the usual malarkey, most of it supposition.

The only parts that interested me were the facts that Florence was an ex-inmate of a booby hatch and that I hadn't killed Weintraub with my sock to the jaw. I wadded the newspaper and threw it on the ground. As I started toward the cabin, Mr Anderson called me back.

"You're forgetting your Cokes," the little man said. I took the four unopened bottles, tucked them under my arm, and returned to the cabin. At the door I paused, made up a lie, and then I went inside.

Florence had fixed her face and a new coral mouth. She was still in bed, but she had put her slip on. I opened one of the Cokes and gave it to her. She poured the contents on top of her gin. We raised our glasses.

"To us," I said. I finished my drink and set the glass down on the bedside table. Florence patted the bed and I sat down beside her. I smiled. She smiled, finished her drink.

"Well, baby," I said. "We're really in luck."

"I'll say. Fourteen hundred dollars . . ."

"And now for Mexico. Know where San Berdoo is?"

"Of course."

"Well, I've got an old friend there, a pilot I knew in the army, and he owns his own plane. He owes me a favor and he'll take us to Mexico with no questions asked."

"Isn't it dangerous to go back to California?"

"For us, baby, it's dangerous anywhere. The sooner we get out of the country, the better."

"Don't you think we'd better wait until tonight?"

"The alarm might be out by then. We'd better leave right now."

"I wish you'd mentioned San Berdoo last night, before we drove—"

"If we hadn't come to Vegas, we wouldn't have been married, and I wouldn't have won fourteen hundred dollars. Now get dressed, and let's get the hell out of here." I smiled and it hurt my lips. I felt more like choking her.

While Florence dressed I had another drink. I sipped it slowly, thinking things out. The first thing to do was to get her back to California. And once we crossed the line I could turn in at the nearest police station. Hell, I had a fighting chance now. I had known already that Florence was a little screwy, but I hadn't suspected that she was actually crazy.

Not until I read the newspaper item. That gave me my chance. Florence must have killed Weintraub, not me. She must have smothered him while I was in the kitchen getting the pan of water to bring him around. No point in trying to run away now. I had enough of a chance to get off the hook and I was taking it. And to top it off, I had a nice little wad of dough. Enough for a fair, if not a good, lawyer.

"I'm ready, Jake," Florence said. "I sure hate to leave that bed," she added wistfully.

"We'll have all the time in the world in Mexico." I picked up the over-nighter, opened the door and shooed her outside. "Want me to drive for awhile, Florence?"

"No. I'm rested now. I'd better drive."

In a few minutes we had left The Strip behind and we were on the open highway. By the time we hit the mile-long stretch of dips she was doing better than eighty miles an hour. We passed a billboard and a moment later a siren screamed behind us. I looked out the rear window. A state patrolman was trailing us on a motorcycle and gradually closing the gap.

"Well, baby," I said angrily, "we won't get to California after all. But women nuts enough to smother their husbands are easily extradited!"

The look on her face made me laugh.

Chapter Thirteen

I didn't enjoy my laughter very long.

Florence's face, naturally pale, lost what little color it had. She wet her lips with the tip of her pink tongue. Her eyes lost their luster and turned a dull, dusty purplish color. Viciously, she jammed the accelerator to the floor. The Buick leaped forward with a burst of speed I hadn't suspected it possessed. I think, now, that Florence might have got away from the motorcycle, if it hadn't been for the dips. And the S curve that appeared for no good reason except the slight rise of ground . . .

The Buick squealed around the first curve on two wheels, but Florence was going much too fast to make the second curve. As she spun the wheel madly for the second half of the S we hit the dip and the car bounded the other way into the desert. It ploughed through loose sand for about forty yards, going slower and slower, and then like a tired elephant, it turned over and came to rest at a sharp angle against a low, loose pile of sand. I tried to open the door, but slid down the sloping seat into Florence. On my next attempt I held the handle down tightly and heaved hard against it with my shoulder. It flew open. I climbed out, dropped to the ground, and noticed that the right front wheel was still spinning.

"Are you all right, Florence?" I stood on the ground, reaching up to hold the door open with my left hand. Florence's head appeared, her left hand clutched the seat, and she was part way out. She looked at me as though I was an odd, overlarge insect pinned wiggling to a board. Her right hand cleared the top of the seat, and before I noticed the tiny pistol in her hand she fired quickly, without aiming. The bullet spanged into the metal edge of the door. I released the door in a hurry and started running across the desert toward the highway. The patrolman had stopped his motorcycle well past the second curve and was puffing on foot through the loose sand, a small gray first-aid kit clutched in his hand. He was a big man, built like a lamp, with narrow shoulders, an overhanging paunch, and an enormous rear end. I signaled to him.

"Follow me!" I shouted.

He halted, planted his feet, and looked first at me, then at the car. From the way he ducked, a bullet must have narrowly missed him. I looked over my shoulder and saw Florence drop to the ground and line up her pistol for another shot at the patrolman. He saw the pistol and started running again. Both of us reached the highway at the same time.

"Let's get behind the billboard," I said, pointing across the road. We ran across the highway and got behind the billboard, and lay down next to each other where we could look through the green lattice-work at the bottom of the sign. The patrolman puffed and panted, his red face dripping with perspiration.

"What's the matter with her?" he asked between gasps. "Is she crazy or something?"

"You can say that again," I answered. "It's Florence

Weintraub."

"Is that supposed to explain something?"

"I'm Jacob C. Blake."

"Oh. We're looking for you."

A bullet went through the sign about three feet above our heads.

"She's a little high," I said.

"She's trying to kill us!"

"Now you've got the general idea."

The patrolman was very frightened. His body quivered with fear. His large red hands trembled like a man with dengue fever. I felt contempt for the overgrown clown. I was afraid too, but at least I could control it.

"Listen, blubberbutt," I said. "That's Florence Weintraub over there. She's wanted in San Francisco for murdering her husband. Go and get her!"

"I'm not going no place!" He pushed his face into the sand and covered his head with his hands. I peeked through the criss-crossed laths, trying to see where Florence was hiding. All I could see was a lot of pink dirt, cacti, and three widely spaced Joshua trees.

It was up to me.

I would have preferred to have the patrolman shoot her. I liked Florence all right, even if she was nutty. But to remain behind the billboard would have been sheer stupidity. If this had been combat, and the patrolman had been in my squad, and if I'd told him to move out and he hadn't, I would have shot him then and there. But it wasn't combat . . . and he wasn't in my squad.

"Give me your gun," I ordered.

He reached down to his hip, unfastened the leather strap that held his pistol in its holster, and gave me the weapon.

"What are you going to do?" There was a thin ring of white around his mouth. His forehead and eyebrows were covered with sand from pressing his face against the ground.

"I'm going to kill her. She's wanted for murder. It's legal, isn't it, to kill a murderer?"

"Suppose you don't? I'll be here without my gun, and she'll be over here after me . . . and . . . and . . ."

"Don't cry, Sonny Boy." I was amazed at his abject fear. How do they train these guys, anyway? Surely there is more to law and order than passing out tickets for speeding. I could hardly keep the disgust out of my voice.

"Now listen to me," I said. "I'm going to crawl down the ditch there . . . to the dip. I'll cross the highway through the dip and she won't be able to see me. When I get close enough for a shot at her, it'll all be over. Meantime, to cover for me, you start talking to her to hold her attention. It's very simple. Hold and flank. Do you understand?"

"What do I say to her?" His lower lip trembled.

"Anything. Tell her to give up, throw her pistol into the road, things like that."

"What if she rushes me? And I don't have any—"

"All the better. I'll be behind her by that time and I can get a better shot."

He nodded, peered anxiously through the lattice-work, and worked his mouth several times.

"Give up, Mrs Weintraub!" he shouted. His voice was squeaky, a full octave higher than his speaking voice.

I crawled along the length of the sign toward the ditch. I squirmed along on my belly. A baby creeps and a snake crawls. I crawled, my head low to the ground. In a way, it was like being on a patrol. I was excited. There was a taste

of copper in my mouth and every sense was alive and tingling. This is why there is war. Men like this highly exalted feeling. Hunting animals is a poor substitute for the real thing. The only time a man is really alive is when he is close to death. I reached the ditch and rolled into it sideways, being careful with my feet so they wouldn't raise above the level of the rest of my body. I made better time in the ditch; it was almost three feet deep.

"Throw your pistol out in the road, Mrs Weintraub!" It was the patrolman again, with his high, womanish voice.

"The hell with you!" Florence answered for the first time. I grinned. "Send that sneaky, son-of-a-bitch out here!" Florence screamed. "After I kill him you can have this goddam pistol!"

Good. He had her talking, had her attention. I reached the dip and I hesitated. The dip gave me a bad moment. It wasn't as deep as I had thought it was. If a level was stretched across it, the bottom wouldn't have been more than a foot-and-a-half deep. But a car speeding down the highway wouldn't be able to see me crawling across it, because of the first half of the S curve. I had to take the chance. Both ways. If Florence spotted me, and I didn't know where she was, she'd pump four or five of those little .25 caliber bullets into me. Well . . .

I crawled across slowly, quietly, holding my speed down with all of the patience I could muster. If I made any noise, I'd be two hundred pounds of exposed body stretched flat on the asphalt highway. As I reached the other side of the road, a swiftly moving Merc convertible swung around the first curve, made the other one, and roared down the road. Lying flat on the ground I couldn't see the driver. The unseen driver must have seen the patrolman's motorcycle,

but that was no reason for him to stop. I lay there quietly until the sound of the powerful engine faded out of range.

The butt of the heavy .45 automatic was clutched tightly in my hand. I hadn't checked the weapon to see whether there was a round in the chamber or not. Silently, I cursed myself.

"Give up, Mrs Weintraub! You haven't got a chance!" the patrolman shouted.

Florence didn't answer.

I gripped the slide with my left hand and slid it back a quarter of an inch at a time until it was back all the way. I let it forward just as slowly and felt the first round leave the magazine and slide into the chamber. The safety was off. The hammer was at full cock. I inched my way across the sand to a small clump of cactus blooming with bristly red fruit. I got to my knees.

Florence was in plain sight, less than twenty yards away. She was crouched behind a Joshua tree like a movie cowboy. Her knees were bent, and she held her arm straight out in front of her, the pistol in her hand. Her eyes and head jerked back and forth warily, as she tried to watch both ends of the billboard at the same time. It was ludicrous, and at the same time, it was touching . . . in a way. I got to my feet slowly, taking my time. She didn't dream that I was to her left and slightly behind her.

I put my left hand in my hip pocket, did a half-right face, and aimed carefully. Over the V-sight, my bull's eye was her mop of dark, tousled hair. I squeezed the trigger. She hit the ground hard. The force of the heavy slug was like being hit with a locomotive. Her small, pearl-handled pistol flew through the air and fell to the ground.

I trudged through the sand and looked down at her body.

The lower half of her jaw was gone. Her jaw had deflected the bullet and it had pierced the roof of her mouth and entered her brain. Her upper teeth were all exposed in a cruel grin. Her eyes were the color of dusty blackberries without the slightest flicker of life. There was a run in her left stocking and the shoe was lost somewhere, probably back in the Buick. Tiny, black flies appeared from somewhere and bounced up and down on her bloody face like a handful of BBs dropped on the sidewalk. Overhead, a buzzard hung like a black kite in the sky. It banked tightly and then, head to the meager wind, anchored itself and waited.

I removed the magazine, jerked the slide back, and ejected the new round. I pulled the trigger of the empty pistol, replaced the magazine.

"All right, officer!" I called across the road. "You can come out now! The game is over."

Chapter Fourteen

The patrolman came out from behind the billboard and nervously crossed the road. I stood beside the Joshua tree, dangling his pistol by the trigger guard from my right forefinger.

"Is she dead?" he asked anxiously.

"Take a look." I jerked my head and handed him the pistol. I walked over to a crumble of boulders and sat down. I lit a cigarette and watched the patrolman with amusement. He took one hard look at Florence, stumbled away from her, dropped to his knees and tossed his lunch on the sand. He kept retching for quite a spell.

That's the way it is with guys who haven't seen it before. Violent death is a lot different from any other kind. Of course, he'd seen mangled bodies before. Every highway patrolman has. There are a great many wrecks on the highway in the course of a year. A murder, though, is something else again. It sort of adds to the shock. I didn't feel sorry for the cop. His should have been the life that was risked going after Florence. Not mine. The hell with him.

He got off his knees, and carefully averting his eyes from the body, sat down on a boulder next to me. I gave him a cigarette and a light. He looked a little better. The redness was back in his weather-beaten face. He took three deep drags on his cigarette in succession, inhaling

with calm deliberation.

"All right, Blake," he said, nice and friendly, "what's the story on this?"

"You don't know?"

"No, but I want it straight. It's between you and me."

"Okay. It's simple, and I'm clean. Without going into detail, I was at her house in San Francisco when her husband came in. We had a little argument and I slugged him. When I went into the kitchen to get some water to bring him out of it, she smothered him with a pillow. You can check this easy enough. It's in the Vegas paper."

"What else?"

"She told me I killed him. Well, not exactly. I assumed I'd killed him. I didn't know she had smothered him while I was out of the room. Anyway, we left town, and drove down to Vegas. I read the paper this morning and she didn't. I told her we could get a plane in San Berdoo for Mexico, and we were driving back to California when you got on our tail. I was going to turn in just as soon as I hit a California police station."

"Is that straight?"

"That's straight."

"What do you want to do now?"

"Get cleared."

"What about her?"

"She's dead."

"I know that. But . . ." His hand holding the cigarette was shaking. "Do you think it would help your case when it came out that you shot her?"

I thought this over.

"No."

"Well, then . . ." His face turned a brighter shade of red.

"Would you object to saying that it was me that shot her?" There was nothing ingratiating about the tone of his voice. He was direct about it. I have to give him that much credit.

"That would be a favor to me, for Christ's sake," I said.

"It would be a bigger favor to me."

I saw his point. It wouldn't look good for a uniformed officer of the law to hide behind a billboard while a civilian took his gun and shot an armed woman. And it would be to his credit if he shot a wanted murderer . . .

"You tell it anyway you want to, Officer. From now on I'm a clam, anyway. And I won't make any changes in your story."

"I appreciate this, Blake." We shook hands on it.

From then on, events moved fast. The patrolman called in on his radio, and in a few minutes a patrol car pulled up and took me back to the Vegas jail. The patrolman stayed with the body to await the sheriff, coroner and so on. I was glad to reach the air-conditioned jail and get away from the scene.

■　　■　　■　　■　　■

At the desk I played it innocent. I emptied my pockets and put my stuff on the desk, first counting my money, and making certain that the correct amount was written on the brown manila envelope before it was sealed.

"What's my connection with this Weintraub case, Sergeant?" I asked, smiling. "I don't get it."

"Neither do I. Nothing, as far as I know. But we'll find out when San Francisco tells us. Your name wasn't mentioned on the Weintraub all-points."

"Then what are you holding me for?"

"We've got a separate all-points on you." He grunted. "Let me see . . ." He dug through the stack of correspondence on the desk. "Here it is," he said, holding up a yellow flimsy. I had to wait while he put his glasses on. "'Wanted: Jacob C. Blake, Private Investigator.' You a private investigator?"

"Yes, sir."

"Well, what do you know about that! I've never met one before. "'Description: Height, five-ten.' You look taller than that."

"That's because I stand straight."

"I see. 'Weight: two hundred pounds. Eyes: blue. Hair: blond. Complexion: ruddy.' You don't have a ruddy complexion."

"They always say ruddy when the hair's blond," I said impatiently.

"You're right about that. I do myself. 'Identifying marks: three-inch scar, left buttock. One-inch scar, right calf. Eight-inch scar, chest, diagonal from left shoulder to left nipple. Missing: little finger, left hand. Tattoo: scroll and red roses, left forearm. Inscription: "Mother."'" Let me see that."

I removed my jacket, rolled up my sleeve and showed him the tattoo.

"How come it's so faded?" he asked curiously.

"I tried to have it taken off. Couldn't be done."

"I could have told you that. Once they're on there, that's it. Here it is: 'Wanted by San Francisco police for the murder of Jefferson Davis.'"

"Read that last sentence again, Sergeant."

"'Wanted by San Francisco police for the murder of

Jefferson Davis.' That's all it says, Blake."

"Thanks," I said.

They put me in a cell. I asked no more questions and I said nothing more about anything. I did make a statement about the death of Florence, adding an ironical last paragraph to the effect that Patrolman Burgess was one of the bravest men I'd ever seen in his fearless attack against the armed woman. But as to myself being on the scene, I said nothing. The Jefferson Davis deal was mystifying, and I believed the wisest course was to keep my mouth shut. Not that it made any difference in the long run . . .

■　■　■　■　■

The jail was all right. They let me spend my money and I had decent meals brought in from a restaurant down the street. I bought magazines to read, and the air-conditioning made me forget the desert heat. I passed three days in bodily comfort, at least.

On the third day, the sheriff brought a waiver for extradition to California to my cell. I signed it. Why not? They could get me back anyway. That afternoon I was leafing through a *Life* when the turnkey said something to me through the bars. I looked up.

"What's that?" I asked him.

"You've got some visitors. Want to see 'em?"

"Sure. Who are they?"

"San Francisco detective; a man named Allen, and his daughter."

It was Lieutenant Stanley Pulaski, Barbara Ann Allen, and the man was Barbara's father, not Freddy. Mr. Allen was prosperous-looking, with a rosy complexion and four

inches of side hair combed over a bald spot. He wore a yellow linen suit. Pulaski looked miserably hot in a heavy, blue serge suit. All three of them stared at me curiously for a minute or so, and then Pulaski put his big hand gently on Barbara's arm.

"Is this the man, Barbara?" Pulaski asked her.

"Yes, sir," she said.

"Are you sure, Bobby?" her father asked.

"I'm positive," she replied.

Pulaski grinned, and slowly removed a cigar from its glass tube. He cut the end off with a knife and lit it carefully.

"I don't get it," I said. "Somebody's up to something and I'd like to know the score. The last time I saw Mr Davis, he was very much alive. I didn't even know he was dead until the desk sergeant told me I was wanted in connection with his death."

Mr Allen laughed without humor and nudged Barbara Ann. She compressed her lips and glared at me.

"Oh, you dirty, dirty, dirty liar, you! I was in the lobby when you left the hotel! I saw you leave the hotel with the bundle under your arm!"

"Suppose you tell me how he was killed then? It's a mystery to me."

"You'd do better, Blake," Mr Allen said, "to save this innocent act for the courtroom. But it won't do you any good. My son, Freddy, saw you leave Davis' room right after you cut his throat. You might have thought that the vicious beating you gave my boy was enough to keep him quiet, but you were wrong! We Allens are made of sterner stuff than that. Freddy will be avenged for that beating—I swear, I swear!" His voice broke and tears rolled down his cheeks. He took a silk handkerchief out of his hip pocket

and blew his nose.

"Please, Daddy," Barbara Ann said, "let's go. This is the man . . . that's all you wanted to know."

They walked down the corridor, leaving Pulaski behind. Pulaski had a smug, self-satisfied look on his dew-lapped face. Sweat rolled down my back and I felt cold all over, with that strange feeling that a heated body feels under air-conditioning.

"Listen, Pulaski," I said desperately, "I didn't have anything to do with this. I swear it! I'll admit I worked Freddy over a little bit, but—"

"I guess you did, Blake. He's still in the hospital."

"The reason I hit Freddy a few times was because he hit me first. He ruined my suit with a damned fire extinguisher."

"What did you do with the suit, Blake?"

"I put it on the bumper of a passing car."

"Because it had blood on it?"

"No, there wasn't any blood on the suit. It had that acid and soda mixture all over it, from the fire extinguisher."

"Do you expect me to believe that?"

"Yes!"

"Well, I don't. You're going to the gas chamber, Blake. You're guilty and for once you can't claim a frame. Freddy even found your knife that you left behind, and he turned it in . . ."

"That's his knife!"

"I suppose you claim that Freddy killed Davis?" Pulaski snorted.

"It must have been him. I didn't do it!"

"The desk clerk said that you and Davis were talking together in the lobby . . ."

"What of it? I just met the man and we were talking about his pictures—!"

"I'm going to tell you something, Blake. I don't like you and I never have, but if I thought you were innocent I'd go to bat for you. You're as guilty as hell. We've got the knife you used; we know that you got rid of the clothes you wore because they had blood on them, and we've got a sworn statement from Freddy Allen that you beat him up in an attempt to make him keep his mouth shut. To top that, the hotel switchboard has a record of a call that Davis made to you in your room. We don't need any more, Blake. And Barbara Ann, who was waiting for her brother, saw you cross the lobby with a bundle under your arm . . ."

"That doesn't prove anything."

"The jury'll decide that."

"How about a deal, Lieutenant? I'll admit I was mixed up in the Weintraub case, and that I hit—"

"No soap. We're holding that up, just in case. Your prints were all over the room, but we won't need that case. The one we've got is better. I'll see you in court, Blake."

He turned heavily and clomped down the corridor.

There isn't any use to tell about the trial. It was in all the papers. The only defense I had was the fact that I was a good soldier during the war. My lawyer passed my medals around the jury box, and they were closely examined.

They didn't help a bit.

The End

Chapter Three

After we finished our beef I ordered two B&B's, bypassing the dessert. Florence got moody on me and smoked a Marlboro in an ivory holder, sulking like a young girl deprived unjustly of her weekly allowance. I took my notebook out of my breast pocket and added up the expenses. When I finished my figuring, I grinned at Florence across the table.

"The fifty you gave me won't cover the expenses. Counting tips to the band, you owe me another twenty for today's work."

"Do I get any credit for the assistance I gave you on the porch?" She jerked her head toward the window.

"I'm not charging you for that," I said solemnly.

Florence's head tilted back and she laughed heartily, with her mouth open. "You drive a hard bargain, Jake Blake, but I've had a good time. When do we do this again?"

"It's up to you."

"I've got to go home now. Daddy'll be angry if I don't get in early. But if I go home as though nothing has happened, and don't admit that I purposely evaded the guards, I'm sure they won't tell him they lost me for the evening. He pays them well, you see. In a way, we play a kind of game— grown-up hide-and-seek. I'm sick of it, but I've been going along with it for several weeks."

"What, exactly, did you do to make father put a body-guard on you?"

"You wouldn't believe me if I told you."

"I might and then I might not."

"Do you have to know?"

"No, I don't have to know."

"Then let's skip it. We'd better go."

I paid and tipped the waiter, redeemed our coats at the checkroom and we left the club. The rain had stopped and a smoke-thick fog had taken its place. Florence eased the car down the steep cliff road in low-drive. When we reached Highway 101 she opened the vehicle up and we crossed the Golden Gate Bridge at eighty miles an hour. This type of speed on a foggy night made me a trifle nervous, but I didn't say anything. It was her car, and if she wanted to wreck it, the hell with her.

"Where do you live, Jake?"

"Room 720 at the King Edward."

"That's nice. You can ride the elevator down to work."

"True. That's one of the reasons I took the mezzanine office. But it's a lousy location. I rarely have any walk-in business. There's not much I can do about it now, though. I signed a two-year lease."

"And you don't have a car?"

"I don't need one. It's easier to ride a cab or cable car. A car's a nuisance in San Francisco."

"You keep the Buick then. If you're going to work for me, and you seem to think it's work, you'll need a car. I'll drive home and I'll call you as soon as I get an opportunity."

"All right, I'll keep the car, but you'll have to pay for the gas and oil."

Her laugh wasn't so free and easy this time. "Don't carry

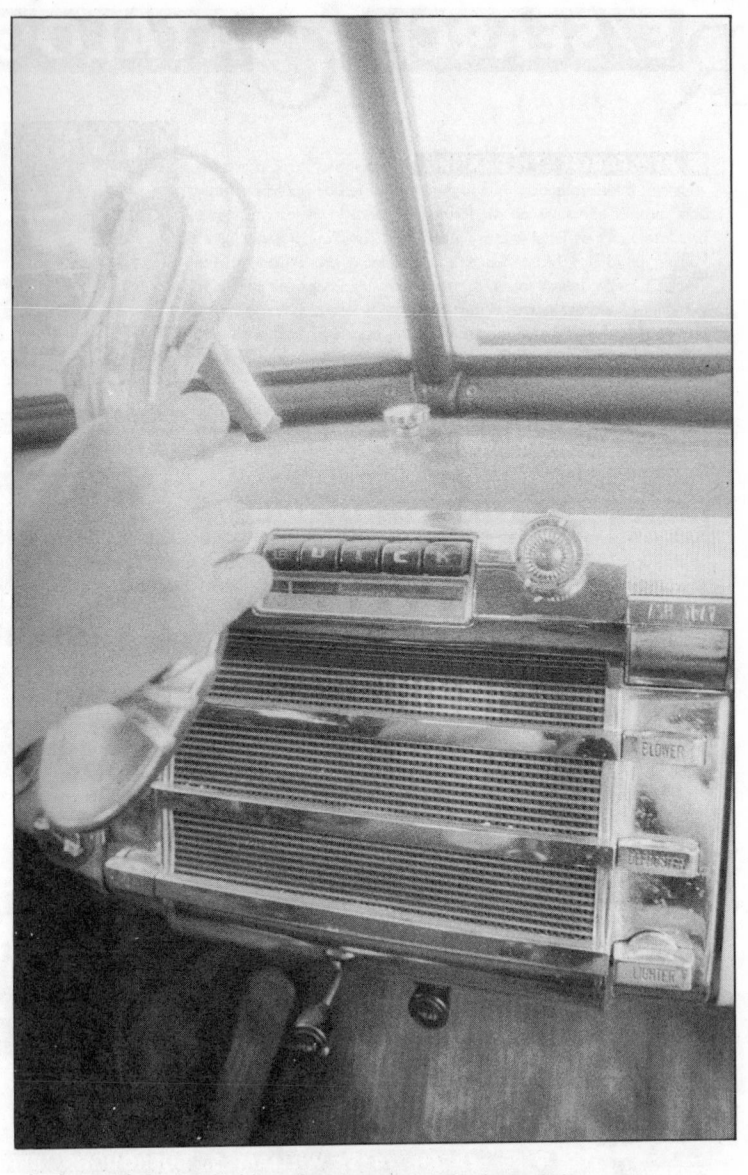

She banged the heel of her slipper against the face of the radio until the glass broke . . . "When I tell you I don't want the radio on, Jake, I mean it!"

RE/SEARCH CATALOG

■ **RE/SEARCH #11: PRANKS.** A prank is a "trick, a mischievous act, a ludicrous act." Although not regarded as poetic or artistic acts, pranks constitute an art form and genre in themselves. Here pranksters such as Timothy Leary, Abbie Hoffman, Paul Krassner, Mark Pauline, Boyd Rice, Monte Cazazza, Jello Biafra, Bruce Conner, SubGenius Church, John Waters, & Henry Rollins challenge the sovereign authority of words, images & behavioral convention. Some tales are bizarre, as when Boyd Rice presented the First Lady with a skinned sheep's head on a platter. Interviews, plus essays, & photos. 224 pp, 8½x11", **$17** ppd; **$18** seamail (**$24** air overseas).

■ **Charles Willeford TRILOGY: HIGH PRIEST OF CALIFORNIA (novel & play); WILD WIVES (novel).** 304pp, 5½x8½". Paperback **$12** (**$17** air overseas); signed hardbound (collector's item; edition of 250) **$42** (air **$47**).

■ **RE/SEARCH #10: INCREDIBLY STRANGE FILMS.** A functional guide to important territory neglected by the film-criticism establishment, spotlighting unhailed directors—Herschell Gordon Lewis, Russ Meyer, Larry Cohen, Ray Dennis Steckler, Ted V. Mikels and others—who have been critically consigned to the ghettos of gore and sexploitation films. 8½x11", 172 photos, 224 pages. **$17** ppd, **$18** sea mail (**$24** air overseas).

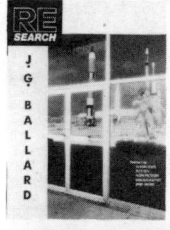

■ **RE/SEARCH #8/9: J.G. BALLARD.** A comprehensive special on this supremely relevant science fiction writer. Long interviews on many topics; key writings and rare short stories; a biography; bibliography; illustrations. 8½x11" with over 125 photos, 176 pages. **$12** ppd, **$13** sea mail (**$16** air overseas).

■ **RE/SEARCH #6/7: THE INDUSTRIAL CULTURE HANDBOOK.** Essential library reference guide to the deviant performance artists and musicians of the *Industrial Culture*: Throbbing Gristle, Cabaret Voltaire, SPK, Non, Monte Cazazza, Johanna Went, Mark Pauline, and others. Some topics discussed: new brain research, forbidden medical texts & films, creative crime & interesting criminals, modern warfare & weaponry, neglected gore films & their directors, psychotic lyrics in past pop songs, art brut, etc. Over 120 photos. 8½x11", 140 pages. **$12** ppd, **$13** sea mail (**$17** air overseas).

■ **RE/SEARCH #4/5: WILLIAM S. BURROUGHS, BRION GYSIN, THROBBING GRISTLE.** Interviews, scarce fiction, essays. Strikingly designed, with rare photos, bibliographies. 8½x11", 100 pp, **$12** ppd (**$16** air overseas).